THE TRAP

Chris Massarella

MINERVA PRESS
LONDON
MONTREUX LOS ANGELES SYDNEY

THE TRAP
Copyright © Chris Massarella 1997

All Rights Reserved

No part of this book may be reproduced in any form,
by photocopying or by any electronic or mechanical means,
including information storage or retrieval systems,
without permission in writing from both the copyright owner
and the publisher of this book.

ISBN 0 75410 013 8

First Published 1997 by
MINERVA PRESS
195 Knightsbridge
London SW7 1RE

Printed in Great Britain for Minerva Press

THE TRAP

For Jenny

Chapter One

He hated winter, a time of perpetual darkness. The insipid days indistinguishable from the nights, suspended immovably, both outside and inside the mind. It wasn't just the physical presence of the winter, but the hardship and the horrors that it brought with it. There was the persistent smell and sound of death and the dying within the community. It cruised the streets, seeping in through draughty keyholes or crawling relentlessly through unprotected letterboxes, searching out the corners of the rooms for its feckless victims. The old and the very young were its most common, vulnerable prey, those who had struggled on through the more benevolent summer and autumn, clinging to life when the air was clearer and cleaner and warmed by the sun's rays, keeping their resistance up. Then, when the winter came, the tell-tale signs appeared from inside the houses, beyond the flimsy wooden barriers to the harsh winter outside.

As he walked down the hill, towards the location of the winding gear, and his boots clattered on the shiny cobbles of the street, he could hear the intermittent coughing and wheezing and weeping and wailing of the sick and dying. It seemed to him that they were attempting to warn one another of the impending fate that was destined to befall them. Inevitably there would come a day when he trudged by just such a house and there would be no noise, no choking, nauseous gasps for breath. The silence would be noticeable only by the absence of the noise and only then would there be the realisation that another death had occurred. The noise, previously ignored because of its familiarity, suddenly became one of those things that you don't notice until after it's gone. Whilst the crying and coughing continued, the implications weren't acknowledged, but as soon as it stopped, the reality struck. Even then it wouldn't be until he returned home after his shift that he would hear, through the village grapevine, that another one or two or even more had succumbed to the inevitable. It was this that contributed to the general malaise and lethargy that seemed to hang in the cold black air.

Then there was the invisibility that the winter generated, the darkness isolated everyone. If you met a neighbour or friend in the street, you wouldn't see them before you could hear them. Sound became the sharpest sense and sight only served as a close-up confirmation that you had met someone you knew. Even the faint glow of candlelight which revealed itself at a few windows in the street offered only a limited interlude to the dim isolation of the darkness. On certain mornings, the winter mist embraced the village and lurked silently between the terraces, cascading down the hill towards the colliery yard. Its intensity would be enhanced by the belching smoke of new-laid fires rising from the soot-blackened chimneys and mingling with the hanging fog. The two merged into a vast diffuser which dissipated the insipid glow which emerged from behind the flimsy curtains of the occasional bedroom window.

It would be a further two hours before the sun rose to disperse the darkness and present in its place a feeble cold grey light hanging uncertainly in the equally cold grey sky. The smoke from the fires, by then well-ignited, would be reduced to barely noticeable wisps that blended well with the cold subdued daylight. By now he would be well into his day's shift, still in the clutches of perpetual night, with only the near and distant glow of Davy lamps to indicate the presence of his workmates. He would not see the transition from night to day, nor that from day to night – the only compensation offered by his situation was that of the heat transmitted by the black rock which so ruled his life. Nor would he bear witness to the waking of the community which had been created by courtesy of the blackness that he was obliged to endure for half a year at a time. The only respite came once a week on the Sabbath, a day of rest grudgingly granted to the workforce by the colliery owner.

He had occasion to daydream as a form of escape from his barely tolerable existence. The warmth transmitted through the coal-face often prompted him to consider that it was merely the residual heat of the fires of hell burning beyond the black barrier at which he so recklessly hacked away. He frequently thought that one day he would burst through the face and before him would stretch the vast expanse of Hades. A gang of horned devils would rise up from the cavernous depths and reach into the workings to take hold of his flailing arms.

They would drag him mercilessly through the gaping hole and into the flames which roared upwards from the bottomless pit below. He would be engulfed by the raging inferno which, he had been taught, lay beneath the earth's crust. Down, ever downwards, he would plunge until the sulphurous stench of burning flesh invaded his nostrils and the searing heat scorched his body. He would descend helplessly until he fell into the outstretched arms of Satan himself and, for his sins, he would struggle in vain to escape the eternal damnation which was to become his destiny.

The hardship of his work, and the concentration required to perform it, fortunately did not allow him to dwell for long on these disturbing thoughts and he was soon back in the fragile reality of his black world. He had only been underground himself for five years but he had noticed the gradual change of some of his workmates. He was aware, for instance, of Jim Gallagher's condition – he had begun wheezing and coughing a couple of years previously and his condition was worsening progressively. Nothing was ever said, it was like some mass conspiracy of denial – the men knew that their mates were becoming ill but nobody ever mentioned it. Needless to say, this particular November morning was just such a morning. Having had the luxury of the only day off allowed in the week, that of Sunday, he now had the unenviable task of preparing himself for the gruelling week ahead.

Much in keeping with any other workday morning, he had grudgingly hauled himself out of his relatively warm bed into the cold damp atmosphere of his room. In winter he made a point of sleeping with his underwear on under his nightgown, not so much to keep himself warm in bed but to soften the impact of the freezing air as it attacked his waking flesh. If he wasn't fully awake when he dragged his reluctant body from his bed, he soon would be when his feet touched the cold linoleum which covered the bedroom floor. This was not how it should have been – when he went to bed the previous night, there was a peg rug strategically placed on the floor next to his side of the bed, the idea being that his feet would land directly upon it the moment they touched the floor.

However, sharing a bedroom with a younger brother wasn't the most satisfactory of arrangements, especially when the person in question had retired at a later time and removed the rug to his side of the bed. So the ritual began, the elder brother, incensed by the younger's action, whilst recovering from the initial shock to his system, would creep to the foot of the bed and reach forward to grasp the blanket which protected his soundly slumbering sibling from the chilled air. A quick, sharp yank of the blanket ensured immediate exposure of the limp physique of his younger brother to the brutally cold air. The verbal exchange was short but emphatic.

"Bastard!"

"Piss off!"

Which expletive belonged to whom is irrelevant, the exchange was purely reactive and lasted just for the duration of the verbal gesticulations. The blanket was dragged back to its former resting-place and the elder brother, by this time reconciled to his early morning ablutions, continued to prepare himself for work. The younger brother, on the other hand, who hadn't yet started work, had a few minutes more to collect himself before emerging to get ready for school.

Of course, in this twilight zone, of the Baxters' early morning household, there existed two worlds, one of which had begun at least an hour earlier, the world of Mrs Baxter. Her defined role in life was to ensure that her eldest son was fit and ready for work each morning. It was a purely practical arrangement.

"You've got to look after the men folk," she used to say, "it's them that bring the money in, it's them that provide for us." In the Baxter household there was no resistance to this philosophy – in the absence of any female siblings, unanimous acceptance was automatic. However, 'looking after the men folk' was not as subservient a role as it might at first appear. The role in fact, was quite authoritative and dictatorial; the weekly pay-packet was dutifully handed over to Mrs Baxter who proceeded to 'dole' out the beer money. This was an amount set purely at her own discretion and calculated on the basis of the immediate financial and practical needs of the family. In other words, Clem received what was left, and this varied considerably from week to week, since his earnings were directly related to the amount of coal that he shifted.

Finances apart, there were other areas in which this matriarchal situation proved to be more authoritative than subservient. Just such an area was the organisation and control of the household. 'Looking after the men folk' also related to the task of dragging Clem out of bed, often literally, the morning after a night of heavy drinking. Ensuring continuity of income by fair means or foul was a priority in the households of the community, although it has to be said that the Baxter household was not typical of the rest of the village.

Clem's father had died at the age of thirty five and as with many cases of the death of younger men, the cause was not entirely clear. The death certificate cited consumption but that explanation was widely used and seemed to account for a great number of deaths, ranging from those of children to older folk. Clem was fourteen when his father died and had just started work on the pit-top in the screening sheds. He remembered vividly the months leading up to the event. He witnessed the physical deterioration of a man who had been a collier for twenty one years and whose death, Clem was sure, could only have been attributed to his life underground. Clem had sworn that he would never accept working down the pit permanently but he realised shortly after his father's death that any control he thought he had over his life was purely notional. Less than a year after he was apprenticed to work at the mine, he was underground where he had been ever since. In an existence where survival is a prerequisite of life, personal aspirations and desires are excluded.

There was no other work in the area – indeed, the emergence of the colliery had created the community. His flirtation with 'pit-top' duties was short-lived simply because those jobs were reserved, in the main, for older workers, who were no longer able to meet the production quotas as a result of physical deterioration. 'Pit-top' jobs provided the support services for the production below ground and were extremely poorly paid. The notion of 'subsistence wages' or 'living below the poverty line' had not yet been formulated. People worked for the wages on offer or they didn't receive an income, the influence of the Trade Unions being suspect to say the least. Within the coal industry, branches were isolated and dispersed and the resulting division diluted their power. Inevitably the negotiating base was quite fragile and the pay structure was almost always dictated by the colliery owners. It was true that the unions had been successful in some instances in improving working conditions and pay structures through taking industrial action. Clem could not help but think, however, that the gains were simply concessions that the colliery owners and companies could easily afford to concede. Having prematurely become the main wage-earner of the family, it was imperative that he went underground where he could earn a wage relative to the production of coal.

The way Clem lived was dictated purely and simply by the efficiency of the pit. If coal was in demand, he worked; if it wasn't he didn't work and the whole community was affected by this principle. Clem's desire to rid himself of this pathetic existence was not an isolated one but nor was it a universal longing. There were those who deferentially accepted the situation and claimed that it was their birthright. To question the hierarchy of society was tantamount to blasphemy and punishable by ridicule and ostracism. This blind deference was, for Clem, a major reason for the slow progress of the unions in making any gains or progress within the industry and society in general. He attended union meetings regularly but was constantly dismayed and angered by the low number of other men who presented themselves. It was as a result of this apathy that Clem sought refuge and solace in his daydreams and in his excursions into the local countryside which surrounded the village.

This was yet another reason why he hated the winter for his excursions to the surrounding hills were severely restricted during the winter months. Sundays offered the only respite and with the mornings taken up with chapel and recovering from the night before (finances permitting), he was limited to a few short daylight hours in the afternoon. He longed for the soft light of the summer evenings when he could make his escape into the hills and set his snares around the rabbit warrens which dotted the area. In particular, he derived a great deal of pleasure from sneaking onto his Lordship's land and dodging the gamekeeper to lay his traps.

He was constantly bemused by the irony of it all. On the one hand, rabbits were considered vermin and the landowners waged perpetual war against them, exterminating them by whatever means were available. On the other hand, if an outsider, such as a collier, offered assistance by infiltrating the estates he would be severely dealt with. Such were the idiosyncrasies of the 'upper classes' to prevent the intrusion of 'lesser mortals' even if it meant acting totally irrationally.

With one smooth rapid action Clem stepped down to the floor, grabbed his trousers and thrust one leg then another into the garment. Simultaneously, he shuffled over to his boots and persuaded his feet inside without having to undo and retie the laces. His chilled fingers struggled momentarily with the buttons on his flies and he sucked in sharply as his feet hit the inside of his shoes, an even colder environment than the floor. He grabbed his collarless shirt and made his way across the bedroom and down the stairs, through the door at the bottom and straight into the 'backroom'. The familiarity of his mother's presence went unnoticed – without even making visual contact he retorted; "Morning Mam." May Baxter responded with equal indifference, "Morning son."

With that innocuous exchange and without breaking his stride, Clem proceeded across the flagged floor and on into the scullery. He hadn't noticed the slight increase in temperature of the backroom, courtesy of the person within, who an hour earlier had managed to rekindle the dying embers in the grate. He did, however, notice the stark chill of the scullery as the cold air embraced the pale grey skin of his torso and caused an infinite number of minute goose-pimples which in turn generated a coarse rasping feeling on his skin. A verbal response to this shock was inevitable.

"Christ!"

His blasphemous exclamation initiated a response from within the backroom.

"Pardon?"

"Sorry. But it's damned cold in 'ere."

"Well, if you hurry up you won't feel it," responded May as she carried in an enamelled jug full of hot water and proceeded to empty it into the porcelain sink before which Clem was now standing. He turned on the cold water tap and intermittently tested the temperature of the water with his fingers as its level steadily rose. All the while he was struggling to hold back the drop of moisture which had formed on the end of his nose; he longed to be able to just wipe it away with a brush of his forearm, but dignity in the presence of his mother persuaded him otherwise.

"Towels ont' back o't chair," she informed him as she stepped purposefully back up into the backroom. With no small feeling of relief, Clem proceeded to remove the bead of moisture from the end of his nose with his forearm which he immediately immersed in the water within the sink.

"There's 'anky int' dresser drawer when you've done son."

Clem sighed dejectedly and with some little embarrassment as he leant momentarily with both hands resting on the edge of the sink. He looked out of the scullery window, over the half-net placed there to preserve modesty, into the dense blackness which obscured the waking day. Again he sighed before continuing with his ablutions.

One minor compensation for living in a 'modern' mining community such as Connington was that the housing was relatively new. Connington Main was established as the result of Britain's world domination of heavy industrial manufacturing. Vast quantities of the right quality of coal were required to fire the furnaces and stoke the boilers of the great iron and steel works in neighbouring Sheffield and Rotherham. Shafts had been sunk throughout South Yorkshire during the second half of the last century in order to satisfy the insatiable appetite of the local industry for quality coal. The oldest houses in Connington mining village were only thirty years old and a few of those early houses were built with earth toilets at the bottom of the yards. The more recent ones were blessed with a cold water supply and foul drainage which permitted the use of flush toilets. They had privies which were attached to the back of the scullery instead of being flung up at the bottom of the yard. Modern sanitation had seen to the demise of the old earth toilets which, for obvious reasons, had to be situated at the extremities of the property. The more recently constructed houses in Connington were connected to a common foul drainage system which meant that the Baxter household enjoyed the luxury of a lavatory with a high-flush cistern. This product of modern technology was to be Clem's next 'port of call' before re-entering the backroom and sitting down to his breakfast.

Although the housing was modern, it was also designed to meet certain specific requirements as stipulated by the colliery owners. For instance, there were no houses with gardens – all of the properties fronted directly onto the street and only boasted rear yards which were flagged with stone slabs. The dimensions of the rear yard were such that a washing line could be rigged and parking for a bicycle or two was possible. In the absence of bicycles or as a result of careful planning, some tenants had managed to install small but functional pigeon-keeps.

All of the houses were constructed to the same design: two up, two down with a scullery offshoot and an attached privy or detached earth toilet. They all formed part of the terraces which cascaded down the hillside to converge on the colliery gates. The reason for this, of course, was that the absence of gardens meant no wasted time and energy spent on gardening or potential tiredness or injuries resulting from same. Uniformity of living accommodation and arrangements maintained uniformity of lifestyle within the workforce and restricted competition and jealousy which might undermine the efficiency of the workforce.

The only concession to the colliery owners' control of the village development was granted to nature itself. It was nature which designed the contours and boundaries of the village, as if nature insisted on having the final say in the construction of these microcosms of existence and allowed mankind's progress to proceed only so far without being checked by an infinitely greater force. It was the contours of the hills, which had formed and shifted during the life of the planet, and the substrata of rock and invisible underground watercourses which denied the planners a free hand. As the village expanded, it grew into the hillsides around the colliery head. Some areas were inaccessible to the builders because the gradient was too steep or a probe into the rocks beneath the surface had exposed a previously uncharted watercourse.

Where the rock had resisted the puny efforts of the intruder to hack out a plateau suitable for house construction, the village had become infiltrated by areas of hillside which remained in its natural state, a constant reminder that the community survived only on sufferance and was but a temporary intrusion into the eternity which is nature. It would remind the villagers annually with the changing of the seasons: the wild winter winds which shook the houses and rattled at the windows and doors; the driving rain which seeped in through seemingly impenetrable defences; and the blazing sun which had everyone scurrying for shade. No other entity can create such muddle and confusion in the existence of mankind. When the climate is hot, we yearn for it to be cooler; when it is cold, we yearn for it to be hotter. When it rains, we yearn for the sun; when the days are hot and dry, we yearn for the rain. The mightiest example of nature's power over mankind was illustrated whenever a tragedy occurred underground.

Whether it was water, gas or a roof collapsing the reminder was vigorously emphasised. Clem Baxter had a healthy respect for nature and often debated with himself the conflicts of ideology between nature and religion and his belief in God.

On his return to the backroom Clem, this time, acknowledged the warmth radiating from the rekindled fire, its flames stretching up into the sooted blackness of the chimney-void from the burning nest of coal within the grate. Occasionally there would be a spit and a crackle or a gaseous flare which combined with the heat to create a comforting audible and visual welcome to the room. Attracted by this magnetic lure within the lead-black range, he strode purposefully over and took up position directly in front of the fire with his rump turned towards the heat. He felt the hair on his shoulders and back bristle as they parted and stood on end to allow the warmth through to his chilled skin.

"Ah, that's better!" he exclaimed. "You draw' best fire in't village, Mam."

"Yes and I'll draw you if you don't shift yourself sharpish, lad. No good mekin yourself comfortable. Get sat up now and eat your breakfast else you'll be pushed for time."

May's response was supported by a brisk shove against Clem's upper arm directing him towards the sparsely laid table as she simultaneously reached for an enamelled dish warming on the range. Clem reluctantly shuffled away from the range and over to the table, whilst his mother reached for the hem of her apron and brought it up to grasp the handle protruding from the top of the black iron pot hanging over the grate. "Get this inside you while it's good and hot," she ordered emphatically. "You know where the bread is and don't take it all, leave some for your brother."

Breakfast in the Baxter household was also a signifier of the changing of the seasons. The winter heralded in the 'tummy warming' introduction of oatmeal grog or porridge, thick and hot and accompanied by bread, usually left over from the day before and warmed through on the range in an effort to soften it up a little. The whole lot was washed down with a large pot full of strong hot tea. In the summer, on the other hand, breakfast would still consist of the bread but accompanied by whatever preserve had been available at the time, sometimes it might be fresh honey or jam or other fruit conserve. If supplies were available, often through dubious channels, there might be some local cheese or even a slice of cured ham.

Eating a reasonable diet in the village was more the result of ingenuity rather than procurement of the means to purchase the food. Even when coal was in great demand and shifts were long and frequent, the wages were barely sufficient to support a family. Conversely, when demand for coal fell, usually in the summer months, wages were low and many colliers spent their limited spare time hunting and snaring local game to supplement bought produce – hence Clem's desire to undertake his excursions into the local countryside during the long summer evenings. For the present, however, there was the prospect of long, cold, black winter ahead and all of the accompanying hardship that came with it.

His repast complete, Clem withdrew from the table and reached for his rough wool jacket which his mother had placed on the hearth to warm by the fire. He reached his hand into the right-hand pocket of his jacket and produced a compressed piece of cloth which, with a little manipulation, he miraculously transformed into a cap. Having pulled the cap onto his head and adjusted his hair-line, he reached into the other pocket and withdrew another piece of cloth. This in turn unfurled to reveal its true identity, a scarf, which he duly flung around his neck. Finally he pulled on his ageing jacket with the assistance of his mother who instinctively brushed the coal-dust laden shoulders, as if this act would improve the condition of the garment. She sighed and exited the room momentarily and reappeared carrying a discoloured sackcloth shoulder-bag. She handed it to Clem and met his enquiring gaze with an apologetic one of her own.

"It's not much, son, but I'll try to find something solid for your dinner tonight," she said with a not altogether convincing tone of reassurance in her voice. Clem smiled equally unconvincingly, leant forward and kissed his mother on the cheek.

"It'll be rate Mam. See you later."

He proceeded through the scullery, opened the back door and stepped out into the hostile air. As soon as he closed the door behind himself, he hunched the collar of his jacket up around his chin and pulled the peak of his cap down over his brow. By the time he reached the back gate, the cold had penetrated his flimsy defences and once again he felt a bead of moisture forming on the end of his nose. With a guilt-ridden glance over his shoulder towards the half-lit scullery window, he raised his forearm and removed the offending appendage with his sleeve. He had, of course, omitted to follow his mother's instructions regarding the handkerchief which remained neatly folded inside the dresser drawer.

He thrust his hands into his jacket pockets and hunched his shoulders up in an effort to cocoon himself against the persistent probing of the invading climate. As he stepped out into the back ginel, he slowly became aware of the noise made by other closing doors and the sound of the winter, crackling and crunching beneath the steel-tipped soles and heels of his fellow colliers' boots.

Clem's house stood in the middle of a terrace about halfway up what was once known as Bank Hill but, having been usurped by the intrusion of the houses, was now known as Bank Street. Constructed about ten years earlier due to the opening of a new coal-face and the need for more labour, the street was roughly in the midst of the Bank Hill estate. His walk to the colliery gates would take him approximately ten minutes on a route which would take him past Jim Gallagher's front door.

"Wait up Clem!" The instruction came from behind as he turned out of the back ginel into the street. He knew who the owner of the voice was even though he couldn't see him so he leant on the wall and waited.

"What's up, Josh?"

"Walk down wi' yu', mate. 'Ave you heard news about Jim, Jim Gallagher?" asked Josh urgently. Clem turned towards Josh as his shadowy outline emerged from the blackness beyond and perceived a look of great concern on his face. Immediately Clem's own facial expression altered to emulate that of Josh's.

"What's that then, Josh?" he enquired guardedly.

"Teken a turn fo't worst by sounds of it. Wern't at chapel yest'y mornin' nor wor his missus. Bairns were there wi't gran'ma but no sign o' Jim and his missus. By all accounts 'e's laid up in bed wi that there chest trouble 'e's had. Won't be in today. You were at t' chapel yesterday you must have noticed he wasn't there." Clem's immediate recollection of the previous morning was that of suffering a severe hangover, hence his failure to recollect virtually any of the morning's proceedings.

"Aye, now I come to think of it," was the best reply he could muster. "That's a bugger, this fuckin' weather. He seemed all right through summer, didn't miss a shift. So's doctor been round do you know?"

"Doubt it, 'e was only telling me t'other day, as how they're still trying to pay off t'doctor's bill from last winter when little Sheila took poorly and a fat lot of good that did poor little mite. Then whi't funeral an' all."

The distraction of the bad news had relegated the impact of the morning frost to one of total insignificance. Clem's shoulders had assumed their natural position and his hands, although still entrenched in his pockets, no longer ached from the pain of the cold. If we believe in relativity, we would observe that many of our own grievances pale into insignificance when we encounter the suffering of others, especially if it is life-threatening (unless, of course, our own experiences are of the same magnitude which is also relative). Clem and Josh resumed their journey to the colliery gates in silence, each consulting their own thoughts on the fate of their mate.

As they passed by the front door of Jim's house, they slowed down and surveyed the façade. Other than a dim glow barely penetrating the flimsy material which curtained the bedroom window, there was no sign of any early morning activity. The most disturbing thing was the distinct lack of any sound from behind the grey stone frontage. They simultaneously diverted their gaze towards one another, this time their faces bore no discernible expression. One of them broke the uneasy silence, it doesn't matter who.

"Think I'll pop round this evening, see how things are, check if they need anything or what's to be done."

"Me, too." The short verbal exchange seemed to alert them to the rest of the morning's activity. The prevailing silence had merely been louder than the surrounding noise emitted by the waking community and their disturbed thoughts had blocked out the stirrings around them. As they turned to continue their trek to the colliery, the sound of a sudden convulsive coughing fit burst out from behind the bedroom curtains. Clem raised his eyebrows as if to acknowledge this ironic symbol of life.

Chapter Two

During the shift, Clem managed to divert his thoughts away from the scenario of possible events that might have occurred at number 28. The shift had been a particularly hard one due to the fact that, when a man knocked off sick, his mates had to make-up for his quota. If the rest of the team couldn't do this, then the man would be sacked and replaced; when he became well again, he didn't start back unless a new place could be found for him. The man didn't receive any pay so he had to rely on his mates to make up his wages for him. If the illness was a prolonged one, he ran the risk of eviction from his home, even if he was able and willing to pay the rent. Since this terrible predicament could befall any of the men, it wasn't surprising that they all pulled together to help each other as much as possible.

It was only during his walk back home with Josh that they each reminded the other of the promise to visit and see if there was anything to be done. There was no possibility of calling in on the way, the foremost priority after the shift was to get home and wash the graft and grime of the day out of their skin. The only place a collier might divert himself to, straight from his shift, was the public bar at The Queen's Head.

Very occasionally after a particularly gruelling shift, such as the one they had just experienced, for instance, they might head for The Queens. These excursions were few and far between, during the week, because drinks usually had to be 'slated' and paid for at the weekend. A direct path home was the usual course of action, though there were those who, for various reasons, were frequent visitors to The Queens, regardless of their financial situation and the ensuing consequences. This night, anyway, there was a mission to fulfil, and Clem's priority was to return home, wash and eat his dinner, and call back to Jim's house.

As he entered the scullery and adjusted his vision to accommodate the brightness within, he could smell the greeting offered by his waiting dinner. His mother, as always, had managed to produce at least something substantial even if the contents of the meal were sometimes suspicious. Clem halted before entering the backroom and, with almost violent intent, discarded his jacket and yanked his shirt over his head, hurling the two garments to the floor. As at breakfast, his mother emerged from the backroom with a jug full of hot water. On this occasion, the cold did not interfere with his activities and he was soon drying himself off and pursuing the source of the odour that had so stimulated his sense of smell.

At this time of the year, May frequently made use of the disguising characteristics of a sauce known as Henderson's Relish. The not insubstantial effect of this addition to a meal was capable of changing what might otherwise have been a fairly innocuous presentation into one that immediately destroyed any residual taste of coal-dust. The hotpot of vegetables and a hardly discernible quantity of salted if somewhat fatty pork was eagerly and rapidly ingested by Clem. Any relish-laden sauce was moped up with copious quantities of freshly-baked bread. Unfortunately for Tom, who had to wait for his evening meal until after Clem had finished, there was always the possibility that Clem's raging appetite would ensure the emptying of the blackened cast-iron pot and reduce his expectations of a similar taste experience – to his abject dejection and disappointment. This unfortunate circumstance was a direct result of May's 'always look after the menfolk' policy. Since Tom was not yet a man (i.e. a wage earner), he could not be the recipient of the dubious benefits of the policy, and often finished up with some bread and whatever preserves or other remained in the larder. This was destined to be just such an occasion. Clem's particularly rigorous day's work had ensured a ferocious hunger and the expression of expectation on Tom's face was destined to slowly change to one of dismay and consternation.

There had been some conversation between the three of them during Clem's demolition of his dinner, mainly concerning the latest news regarding the affliction of Jim Gallagher. May recollected meeting Jim's eldest daughter Florence on her earlier excursion to the local general store. These premises were the centre of parochial knowledge within the village, and as with all the other facilities in the village, it belonged to the owner of the colliery. The staff of the shop were employed by the colliery management, and the price of goods available was set by the same authority. It was common practice for prices to increase quite considerably when earnings were up as a result of increased demand and production. On the other hand, when earnings were down due to adverse trading conditions, the prices came down but never by quite as much as they might have previously or subsequently gone up. The same trading conditions applied to the local public house which also belonged to the colliery owner.

All of the gossip, the whispers, secrets and general information converged on and subsequently emerged from, in some suitably edited form, this epicentre of the tremulous community. What were normally her mother's duties had fallen upon Florence to perform owing to the illness of her father. She had explained that her father had not slept well or eaten at all for three days and nights and that his weakened state was giving them a great deal of cause for concern. When May enquired whether or not the doctor had been sent for, Florence's response was to say sheepishly that they couldn't afford the doctor. However, she added somewhat more cheerfully, Mrs Cook had been attending to him and they hoped that there would soon be an improvement.

Mrs Cook was the local unofficial nurse and midwife who had taken it upon herself at an early age to study tried and tested natural and herbal remedies for ailments. Most of her knowledge had been imparted to her by her mother, who in turn had received the same tutoring from her mother. Since most of the members of the community were unable to afford anything other than very infrequent medical attention, Mrs Cook and her herbal remedies were in constant demand. Over the years, her reputation had grown and she enjoyed substantial acclaim for her ability to relieve the suffering of many people within the village. Clem informed his mother of his intention to call round at the Gallaghers' and see if there was anything to be done; she duly approved this course of action and asked that he pass on her regards.

After he had eaten, Clem went upstairs to change and, having considered his reflection in the mirror on the bedroom table, decided that it might be prudent to have a shave. It has to be added at this stage that there was an ulterior motive behind Clem's proposed visit to Jim Gallagher's house. He had in the recent past noticed the development of Florence whom he had previously considered a young girl – she was now at the blossoming age of sixteen, and was inexplicably attracting his attention. This had caused Clem some cause for concern because Florence was obviously not the only female in the village. He had begun to wonder why a glance in her direction during a chance passing in the street frequently turned into what might be considered a prolonged stare. In fact it had got to the stage just lately where he was making a point of looking out for her, mainly at chapel, but more disturbingly at places where he was fairly sure she wouldn't be. The most perplexing thing regarding this phenomenon was that his actions, responses, and feelings were totally involuntary. Certainly, it was a force that he had never before experienced but not, he felt, at all distasteful, though certainly at times somewhat troublesome. It was with some trepidation and a certain amount of guilt regarding this ulterior motive within the more serious context of Jim Gallagher's condition that he ventured forth on his evening's errand.

During the short walk between his home and number 28, Clem's thoughts flitted uncontrollably between his concern for Jim and the nervous excitement he was experiencing regarding this chance, contrived meeting with Florence. On the earlier visual encounters that had occurred between himself and the cause of these new emotional and physical experiences, Clem's reaction had been a kind of self-denial. Once the visual encounter had passed, he diverted his thoughts to other matters and although he had given some consideration to the possibility of a liaison, he had not pursued the matter further. This time, however, fate had intervened, as though giving him the impetus that he had previously lacked either through design or circumstance. Visual encounter, he felt sure, was about to make way for a personal encounter and Clem quietly congratulated himself on the way in which he had engineered this opportunity. So intense and distracting were his thoughts that he omitted in his oblivion to notice the passing of number 28 until he was nearly at the end of the street. It was only the sight of the street corner, suddenly appearing through the blackness, which brought him to an abrupt halt.

His guilt returned like a crashing wave and totally engulfed him to the extent that he had to wait a moment to recover his composure before turning back towards the house. He had in fact to go past the house again until he reached the passageway that would lead him to the back ginel. By the time he had completed this manoeuvre, he had regained his composure and set his mind firmly to the task at hand. He stood before the back door and raised his hand before, inexplicably, hesitating momentarily and then knocked purposefully. A dim light from within illuminated the scullery and, again inexplicably, he experienced a surge of rapid palpitations inside his chest. The next few seconds seemed to span a chasm of time that stretched into eternity and beyond. He stared straight ahead at the door and didn't adjust his gaze even when he heard the turning of the door handle. The palpitations inside his chest came to a sudden halt as the door opened to reveal the person within.

"'Ey up! It's Clem Baxter," squealed the youngster on the other side of the threshold. "It's Clem Baxter Mam," he shouted as he turned his head towards the opening to the backroom. The response to this enthusiastic greeting was more subdued.

"Well, ask Clem to come in," whispered the lad's mother. "And keep your voice down, James. I won't tell you again."

Clem's disappointment was immeasurable, though had he considered the scenario beforehand, before his mind had become so befuddled, he might have calculated that here was a household of five children, four of whom were capable of answering the door, and the chances of one person in particular fulfilling that duty were less than certain.

"Mam says to come in," instructed a barely discernible voice. In fact the visitor was already aware of the invitation to enter since he had been privy to the original direction. Had it not been for his acute disappointment which held his feet firmly rooted to the flagstones, he would have entered upon hearing the original request. "Mam says you've to come in!" repeated the child at the top of his whisper as he crossed one leg over the other in an effort to prevent the cold air from surging up his nightshirt. He clung to the door handle as though, if he were to release it, he would be sucked out into the clutches of winter beyond, never to return. He was becoming increasingly agitated as he rolled his eyes up to the top of their sockets and fixed his gaze on the ceiling above. His expletive was curse and succinct. "Tut!" This was followed by a deep and exaggerated sigh which amply illustrated his disdain.

Clem's dismay was apparent to no one but himself as he surveyed those present in the backroom at the Gallaghers'.

"Hello, Clem. Come to see our Jim have you?" Mrs Gallagher's quiet words sailed through the air and entered in a neat and orderly fashion into Clem's ear but they registered nothing once inside his head. They simply drifted around within his mind looking for somewhere receptive to convey their message. Eventually they succeeded and Clem responded politely.

"Hello, Mrs Gallagher, Aye I've come to see how he is and if there's owt to be done."

"He's resting at present, Clem. You've just missed Josh – he said you might be calling. It's good o' you both to be so concerned but I'd sooner he wasn't disturbed if you don't mind. I'll tell him that you called and thank you for the offer of help, but we're managing just now thanks." Clem's guilt by this time was overwhelming, indeed, he was now beginning to feel acute shame for his selfishness. This culminated in a moment's self-admonishment. 'Serves you right, selfish bastard,' he thought to himself as he realised that Florence was only noticeable by her absence.

"Cup o' tea?" enquired Mrs Gallagher.

"Aye thanks very much, if it's not too much bother."

"No bother lad, sit thi sen down." Mrs Gallagher raised herself up from the chair and walked over to the range. "Fetch a cup for Clem then James," she insisted. Jimmy's (as he preferred to be known) eyeballs rolled up to the top of their sockets once again, and he repeated the expletive and gesture that he had performed earlier.

Clem sat himself down on the dining-chair, thankful for the excuse to prolong his visit for a few minutes more and hopeful that his patience would be rewarded. With this tenuous security in mind, he was able to relax and enquire further as to the well-being of Jim. Mrs Gallagher informed him that Jim seemed to be over the worst and had managed to eat something that day. The fact that he was now resting was acknowledged by all present as further evidence of tentative recovery. This positive news was greeted with enthusiasm by Clem whose feeling of guilt was now beginning to subside.

"Tell him we'll cover his shift till 'e gets better and not to worry himself wi' it," he said reassuringly as he struggled within himself to find a way of enquiring about the whereabouts of Florence, without revealing his intentions.

"I'll tell him Clem, it'll set his mind at rest. He's been mithering on about the job a bit just lately." There was a pause in the conversation. Clem's gaze had been diverted to the fire in the hearth, its bright, warm, hypnotic, flickering glow dominated the room's otherwise gloomy atmosphere. He was not aware that the scenario, which he had just placed to the back of his mind, was slowly creeping to the forefront of his attention.

Abruptly, and without thinking, he turned to Mrs Gallagher.

"Florence not home then?" His stomach muscles immediately contracted, he couldn't believe what he had just said. He wished desperately that he could reach out with his hand, and clutch the words out of the air, and thrust them deep into his jacket pocket. Or that he could alter their linguistic formation in mid-flight so that, by the time they reached the ears of the assembled group, they would say, "Gosh, is that the time already?" or "That's a lovely dress you're wearing, Mrs Gallagher." Anything, but the statement that had just manifested his interest in Mrs Gallagher's eldest daughter.

The ensuing pause persisted for what seemed to be some immeasurable length of time. His glance towards Mrs Gallagher had facilitated eye contact which remained immovably transfixed between the two of them. Her facial expression gave no indication as to the contents of her thoughts at that moment, which only served to magnify Clem's embarrassment. A voice from the floor broke the impasse.

"Clem Baxter fancies our Flori!" exclaimed Jimmy, his voice straining at the leash, desperately trying to break free from the constraints of the enforced whisper. A wry smile formed on his face. For the third time his eyeballs rolled up to the top of his sockets but this time the verbal accompaniment was a shrill though subdued whistle of the type normally associated with the male's admiration of the female's figure. Clem's defensive reply was to say the least blustered.

"Dun't tha be daft, young Jimmy," he glanced nervously at Mrs Gallagher and qualified the pronoun. "James, Florence's nowt but a bairn, I'm just enquiring of your mother as to her whereabouts."

"Aye but she's turned sixteen now," insisted Jimmy, "and she's got bussoms an' all." Prior to Jimmy's last statement, the leash had broken and the revelation cascaded from his mouth with gleeful, authoritative clarity. His mother's admonishment was swift and equally clear. He was sent scurrying up the stairs to the bedroom with a sharp pain at the back of his head.

Jimmy's comments had inadvertently worked in Clem's favour, the disruptive aftermath had created a much needed breathing-space for him. Mrs Gallagher had vacated the room in hot pursuit of her wayward child and did not return for some minutes. When she finally emerged through the door at the foot of the stairs, it was she who started to apologise to Clem for the unforgivable behaviour of her offspring.

"He's too cheeky for his own good," she said in a tone which indicated that she had used this particular statement before. "He wants to mind his tongue or he'll get it chopped off one o' these days."

"Aye, 'e's a rare one, right enough. Dare say he meant no harm though. Any rate I take no offence, Mrs Gallagher." He felt smug in his reassurance. 'No harm meant, no harm done,' he thought to himself.

"Anyway Clem, to answer your question, our Florence is round at Mrs Cook's, collecting some of her home remedy for Jim. Done 'im a world o' good it has. She'll be back shortly if you'd care to hang on a bit."

Clem frowned, this was a dilemma he wasn't prepared for. A 'chance' meeting was one thing, but to stay put under the present circumstances would surely reveal his true intentions. He gulped down the remainder of his tea and offered his apologies and excuses to Mrs Gallagher.

"If it's all the same to you, I think I'll be getting off thanks. I was only enquiring anyway." His sentence withered up and petered out into a pathetic silence as he made his way towards the scullery. "Goodnight Mrs Gallagher," he blurted as he entered the neutrality of the cold black air and closed the backdoor behind himself.

His mind continued to wrestle with a mixed array of thoughts and emotions. How could he feel so confused and disappointed after being reassured of the recovery of Jim? He should have emerged from his visit relieved and gratified that his workmate's condition was improving, even though the death of an acquaintance was not an uncommon occurrence in the community. It did not affect those associated with the party as it might do, for instance, in contemporary society, which might have accounted in part for the way in which he was so easily distracted. He had, after all, within his own immediate family, borne witness to the death of his father and two siblings during the past fifteen years. Although one of the siblings, a sister, was in fact stillborn and therefore, could not readily be classified as ever having actually lived. On the other hand, he had lost a brother at the age of two and a half to the ravages of pneumonia. Such was the level of infant mortality in those days.

It would be a relatively simple task to count on the fingers of both hands, the number of families in the village which hadn't fallen victim of the angel of death, taking a child or two from their midst. Occurrences such as these served to reinforce the hold of the church and religious belief upon small communities. The notion that God had seen fit to take away small children and invest upon them the eternal benefits of the Kingdom of Heaven had given the Church a kind of ecclesiastical hegemony. If the community didn't cling to the belief that these children had been snatched from the evil and suffering of this life to enjoy eternal happiness in the hereafter, then there might be reason to question the cause of these premature deaths. These causes might have been confirmed as being the result of the abject poverty and substandard living and working conditions which prevailed amongst the lower classes. Certainly, from what those in service as domestics had communicated regarding the upper classes for whom they worked, the instances of premature deaths seemed to be much less than within the community. These deliberations apart, Clem had still not reconciled the perplexity of his predicament. He was still unable to escape the disappointment of not fulfilling his desire to make personal contact with Florence. Had he, however, lived in the opposite direction to his present course then it is likely that he would have accomplished his mission.

Unknown to Clem, as he was walking home, Florence was returning with a batch of herbal remedies for her father. If his house had been located in the direction of Mrs Cook's house, then he would no doubt have encountered Florence on her return journey. He could have used the privacy and intimacy of the night to pass the time of day with her. Their chance meeting might have aroused the chemistry between them as they stared into each other's eyes in knowing silence. She would naturally have averted her eyes in a shy, innocent, gesture of embarrassment and he in return would have reached out his forefinger, lifted her chin and she would have melted under his gaze.

He might have offered to escort her home, providing his protection from anything unpleasant that may have befallen her as she proceeded on her walk through the chilled air. Possibly even offered her his jacket as a wrap to place around her shoulders. A gallant gesture which would surely have won over the heart of this impressionable young woman. She might have warmed to the attention of this gracious young man and succumbed to the spell of his charming demeanour. They might have seized the moment and fallen blissfully in love, got married and had two babies, one boy and one girl. He might have been left a great inheritance from some long-lost relative, thereby ensuring their future life as one of comfortable marital bliss.

Had they been characters in a romantic Victorian novel, these things might have come to pass but they were simply working class folk in a South Yorkshire mining community. They were subject to the same frustrations and turns of fate as anyone else living in the real world and not subject to the whims and fancies of some writer of fictitious novels. The simple fact of the matter was that Clem had missed his chance to establish an acquaintance with Florence and Florence in return was aware of Clem only as a neighbour from down the street who worked with her Dad. That is until she arrived in the warmth of the backroom at home where she drank a cup of tea and conversed with her mother, who failed to mention Clem's interest in her whereabouts, because Florence was still her little girl. Mrs Gallagher was unable, just yet, to contemplate the notion of any sexuality manifesting itself within the slight frame of her daughter's being. This scenario was not the case, as we have discovered, with another member of the Gallagher household.

After about an hour, Florence offered to assist her mother with getting the rest of the children ready for bed and informed her of her own intention to retire. The past few days had been difficult for both Florence and her mother, each of them being kept busy through the night by the disturbances caused by her ailing father. They were both keen to take advantage of the recent improvement in Jim's condition. The children were duly put to bed and Florence put her head around the door of the bedroom, where her father was, to reassure herself of his condition. She kissed her mother goodnight and retired herself to her room. The term 'her room' was actually a theoretical one. It was her room in so far as she slept in it but it was also Jimmy's room, Clare's room, and Mary's room, the baby slept in their parent's room. The only dispensation made to accommodate Florence's transformation into maturity was the provision recently of her own bed. Even this was the result of the death of her grandmother and the availability of her vacated single bed. Prior to this, all four children had slept in a large double bed purchased some years earlier at one of the frequent auctions of household goods seized for non-payment of rent. Partly to accommodate Florence's need for some privacy and also because the other bed seemed to be diminishing in size, it had proved expedient to provide her with this facility. It was no surprise to Florence as she prepared for her bed to find that Jimmy was still awake. She knew he'd been sent to bed early but hadn't enquired why of her mother. She was about to find out.

Jimmy lurched himself up onto his elbow with his head propped up by his hand and faced the shadowy form of his sister as she pulled her nightgown over her head before removing her undergarments from beneath. She had recently taken to this method of undressing seemingly by an instinct she had newly acquired to preserve her modesty. She hadn't consciously come to the decision to prepare for bed in this way and probably didn't even realise that she was doing it. Jimmy, for his part, had been totally unaware of any change in routine regarding Florence's personal disposition. He preferred to analyse any snippets of conversation regarding human relationships which he may have overheard, especially those relating to his older sister.

It was for this reason that Jimmy had purposely remained awake, so that he could inform her of the evening's events; well not quite all of the evening's events.

"Sis," he hissed in an effort to attract his sister's attention. She turned towards him with her index finger pressed firmly against her lips.

"Keep the noise down," she instructed in a loud whisper.

"I know sumat you don't know." His voice was once again straining at the leash. Florence had played this game before. She shrugged her shoulders.

"Not interested," she explained as she climbed under the blanket and pulled her nightgown down in an effort to minimise the impact of the cold on her skin.

"Right then," the game continued. He remained fixed, in the propped position he had adopted, and waited. There was a short pause in the conversation.

"Two minutes and I'm putting the candle out." Jimmy considered the extent of further satisfaction that he might achieve by delaying the proceedings, but had detected a tone of irritation in Florence's voice.

"We 'ad visitors tonight."

"I know."

"But do you know who?"

"Does it matter? Some workmates o' mi dad's."

"One on 'em fancies thee."

"Don't be stupid."

Florence slipped her tongue between her thumb and forefinger before reaching over and nipping the flickering wick of the candle. The flame was immediately extinguished and replaced by an invisible wisp of smoke. Florence rolled over, turning her back towards Jimmy, in embarrassed disbelief. From that moment, for the short time during which she remained awake, Florence's thoughts were her own. Jimmy relieved the weight of his upper body from his elbow and planted his head firmly on the pillow. He was well satisfied with the outcome of his exchange with Florence knowing that there was further mileage to be extracted from his little game. After some deliberation, he decided to wait until Florence broached the subject again in the meantime; he would prepare his strategy for producing maximum impact. The tranquil blackness of the room slowly fused with his tiredness and was soon transformed into the tranquil blackness of sleep.

Unaware of the intrigue and speculation being generated within the confines of the back bedroom at number 28, Clem, who was wrestling with his own deliberations, had, for the second time that night, passed by his intended destination. He had failed to notice his own house and had continued strolling absentmindedly up the hill. He only realised his mistake when he reached the end of the cobbles which was an inevitable eventuality, since Bank Street terminated on the edge of the fields. He cursed himself for being so distracted and spun round to retrace his steps back down the hill. He couldn't rid his mind of the major non-event which had spoiled his evening.

He considered the implications of his incompetent babbling – even now as he wrestled with his thoughts, he shuddered at the recollection of his incriminating statement. It was as though he felt he could erase it from the conversation by reforming it in his mind to say something else but he constantly returned to the same statement. His only course of action, he eventually conceded, was one of damage limitation. How could he retrieve the initiative? Or more importantly, how could he find out whether Florence had been made aware of his interest? Jimmy was the problem – he had correctly assumed that Mrs Gallagher would have dismissed the incident as being insignificant – but Jimmy, he felt sure, would capitalise on the situation. He assumed that Jimmy would have told Florence of his interest and that she would now be aware that Clem Baxter 'fancied' her. How had she reacted? Would she have shrugged it off as the demented ramblings of a ten year old child or would she have accepted the information as true and considered the implications?

He considered the first scenario. If she had shrugged it off, then he could proceed with caution and try to initiate a 'chance' encounter. On the other hand, if she was aware of his interest, how could he face her? He couldn't know whether the prospect pleased her or offended her or if it simply left her unmoved. Then, what of gossip? If the little brat were to make his intentions known to all and sundry through the village grapevine, the repercussions could be horrendous. "But not as horrendous as they would be for you, you little brat," he found himself saying out loud. He looked around nervously and again cursed himself, his vocal outburst had brought him back to his senses. "Sod it," he muttered to himself as he turned down the passage to the rear of the house. "It'll be rate."

Chapter Three

When Jim Gallagher died, it was a cause of distress but not surprise to the community of Connington Village. It was only three weeks since Clem's visit to number 28, and he hadn't been back since, because Jim had managed to get into work. Stricken by constant convulsive coughing and obviously acute pains in his chest, he had nevertheless been able to do his job, though at a somewhat reduced rate. The resulting shortfall in production was made up by the remainder of the gang, that way at least Jim received his wages. The threats of the overman to replace him were successfully parried by various means of persuasion, some of which were not so subtle.

One member of the gang was a particularly nasty piece of work who, although usually loyal to his workmates, was solidly built and well known for having a quick temper. The shift overman was no match for Sam Jackson. There was also, as in many such cases, an unspoken opinion that Jim's time was imminent and that the accepted way of coping with the issue was to avoid mentioning it.

Eventually, his condition deteriorated to the extent that he was obliged to absent himself from work again. Within forty eight hours, his life had expired. The doctor had been sent for as a last resort, but it was by that time, of course, too little, too late. The only relief that the doctor could administer came from laudanum. Jim had already been taking opium but the morphine in laudanum offered the relief of a painkiller along with the mind-numbing effect of opium. The one single dose, which was all that the Gallaghers could afford, was administered to make the last few hours of Jim's life more comfortable.

During the previous three weeks, little had transpired from Clem's quest to make contact with Florence. Up to her father's death she had continued to be preoccupied with his welfare, since the family were also aware of the pending finality of the situation. Every time Jimmy tried to broach the subject of the mystery admirer, Florence reprimanded him, telling him not to be so stupid. After a couple of days, he just gave up the ghost, totally dejected by his sister's refusal to take any bait which he might offer. Now there was the funeral to arrange. Such an event had for many years been a community effort.

There were those who were fortunate enough to have paid into a Friendly Society to ensure avoidance of the indignity of burial in a common grave but the Gallagher family, like many others, could not afford the financial burden. The community then, tied by a mutual interest, 'It might be us next time,' was always ready and willing to assist by having 'whip rounds' in the local and amongst fellow-colliers. The women offered their services regarding the laying out of the body and the provision of a wreath composed of whatever flora, cultivated or wild, might have been available at the time. Mrs Cook generally took charge of these proceedings and organised the volunteers.

Ironically, it was the frequency of these occasions which helped to secure a strong bonding within the community and it was also that same frequency which generated something of a social occasion as opposed to one of deep grief and mourning. Not surprisingly, Clem took it upon himself to organise the fund raising, once again seizing the opportunity to manipulate the situation in his favour.

The Queens was never the easiest place to procure contributions for events such as funerals. The secret was to get in there early. Not too early though, otherwise the opportunity might be missed of encountering all possible contributors. Of course, there were always those for whom early was never early enough. Clem arrived at around eight o'clock on the Saturday night after Jim's death.

If the village shop was the communication centre of the village, then the pub was the focus of emotional release. As with the shop, the pub was owned by the mining company, which in turn was owned, lock stock and barrel, by Lord Hase-Lore. The opening hours of the premises and the prices charged were set by the company and altered according to the efficiency of the pit and the income of the miners. The landlord was appointed by the company and, as a result, was as vulnerable to the control of the bosses as the miners were. In some mining villages, the local branch of the Trade Union might have been able to procure the use of a room in the pub to hold their periodical meetings. This facility was, not surprisingly, denied to the members of the Connington Main branch of the Yorkshire Miners' Union who usually held their meetings at various members houses.

The Queens was a facility provided primarily for the patronage of the colliers since they comprised some ninety five per cent of the clientele. It was, in one respect, a haven where the miners were able to dissolve their frustrations and anxieties in the therapeutic powers of alcoholic beverages. In another respect, it was a useful tool of the employers to divert attention away from the realities of the living and working conditions which the colliers were obliged to endure. Whatever grievances might have been discussed during the evening's excursion into the hazy world of intoxication were easily forgotten during the period of regret and self-pity the following morning.

Even the physiological structure of the establishment generated an environment conducive to a diversion from the burdens of the world. When the atmosphere became intimidating, as it often did, depending on the subject of discussion and the assertion of those participating, the pub was fulfilling its role. The release of aggression, sometimes physical, and usually due to a breakdown of communication and too much beer, was facilitated, though not encouraged. This helped to eliminate just such a release in the workplace which served both the employers and colliers. The employers were able to exert easier control over a more amiable workforce and the colliers weren't faced with the dangers that aggression underground might bring.

When Clem entered the pub he proceeded directly to the bar and procured for himself a pint of bitter before 'doing the rounds'. The smoke hung aimlessly in the dim gaslight of the pub which helped to establish the ambience for these emotional outpourings. Coal-fires smouldering and spitting in the fireplaces served as focal points for the gathering of thoughts during any lull in the conversation. The public bar was the undisputed domain of the men, some of whom sat around in groups forming mini-debating societies. Others sat alone, contemplating their lot and debating the issues with themselves in an equally vociferous manner. The occasional twitch or audible curse would signify the depth of soul searching being pursued by the individual.

Most men gave willingly a couple of pennies each until he eventually encountered Sam Jackson. Sam had been ensconced in his chair for a couple of hours after calling in straight from work, as was his usual course of action. As Clem approached him, he sensed an air of uneasiness. He shook the tin gently and alerted the man of his presence.

"Sam."

"What's up wi' thee Baxter?" Sam's response immediately signified to Clem the fact that he was 'a bit worse for wear'. He proceeded with caution.

"Gi' a bit o' sumat for Jim's funeral, Sam?" Clem tried to cloak his appeal in a deep, solid, tone of voice, in the hope that a certain degree of assertion would disguise his trepidation.

"Piss off, Baxter, I gid mi sweat for that prat, for three week." He paused and emitted a ferocious belch from deep inside his gut. "'E's not gerrin mi brass an' all."

Clem had seen Sam in this mood before and he had witnessed the outcome for anyone who had persisted in invading his privacy. For some inexplicable reason, he ignored the signs, possibly because he was determined to raise funds sufficient enough to create the right impression with Florence. He maintained the same assertive tone.

"Just a couple o' coppers, Sam." Unfortunately this tenacity didn't create the right impression with Sam. It was doubtful that he would have seen the expanding size of Sam's fist as it hurled its way towards his face. What was not in doubt was that he felt the full impact of his knuckles smash against his nose.

Clem's reaction was totally predictable. Since the top half of his body was suddenly being propelled backwards at much greater velocity than the bottom half of his body, the only way to go was down. His centre of gravity shifted irretrievably to a location some distance to the rear of where his feet were placed and he collapsed onto his back, virtually flat out on the floor. The blow triggered a variety of other events. The half-filled pint-pot remained firmly in Clem's grasp but unfortunately the contents didn't remain in the pot. As he headed for the floor encountering various ineffective obstacles on the way, including one table and at least two chairs, he was followed by a shower of foaming beer which cascaded down on top of him. His makeshift collection tin followed much the same route. As he fell, he could hear a stream of words desperately trying to catch up with him.

"You deaf, Baxter? I told... you... to... pi..." Whether the statement failed in its pursuit or Clem's hearing had been impaired by semi-consciousness is not important, he understood with great clarity the significance of every syllable uttered.

There was an immediate hush in the room as everyone turned towards the disturbance – it was as though people were waiting to witness that which had already happened. Sam regained his own balance which had momentarily deserted him during his lunge at Clem and calmly resumed his seat. He surveyed the onlookers defiantly before breaking the spell which had them transfixed like some sort of rehearsal for Sleeping Beauty. He spoke.

"There's just no tellin' some folk, is there?"

It was as though Sam had given his permission for the onlookers to react to the incident. Two or three moved forward cautiously to attend to Clem who by this time had propped himself up on one elbow. Admonishment of Sam's aggression was noticeable only by its absence, the prime concern being to assist Clem, whose prime concern in turn was his empty pot. In his confused state, he raised the pot to his lips but encountered only the taste of his own blood streaming from the end of his nose. His response was directed to the lack of refreshment as opposed to the state of his face.

"Shit!" he peered ponderously into his empty pot. "Spilt it!"

Sam looked on and spoke again. "On second thoughts..." He reached for some change on the table and after sifting through it, tossed a couple of coins in the direction of Clem's still prostrate form. "Weren't such a bad un wor 'e?" His face twitched and contorted before reforming into a condescending smile.

Clem, still clutching his pint pot, instinctively made a gesture to wipe his jacket cuff across his face as he felt the warm blood trickling from his nose and over his upper lip. Whimsically, he paused as if he had received a direction from somewhere not to do it. Instead he released the pot and pushed his hand into his pocket to obtain what he knew wasn't there, it was in the dresser drawer at home. As he tilted his head back and sniffed in an attempt to hold back the blood, he felt a sodden cloth slapped indelicately onto his face. As he screamed with excruciating pain, he could detect the odour of stale beer on the cloth. He immediately passed out.

A jumbled procession of sounds cascaded onto his head as he slowly regained consciousness. He had been senseless for only a few minutes. As he opened his eyes he could decipher the words, "'E's all rate, 'e's comin' round." The remark sparked off a chorus of sarcastic comments.

"'Ad a nice kip, Clem?"

"Come on Clem, your round."

"Ne' mind, Clem, Sam's improved yer looks no end."

"Tha's in for t' regional title next week, Clem." He looked around and smiled, then grimaced, the latter expression being the direct consequence of the former, but both unfortunately caused renewed pain and discomfort. The rancid smelling cloth had been removed leaving a splattering of dried blood around Clem's face and mouth.

"Have you gor 'anky, Clem?" enquired one of his attendants. This time his facial expression remained firmly within the parameters of his mind as he just shook his head slowly and listened attentively for his mother's voice.

"Pity," retorted the voice with an air of sarcastic admonishment.

"'Ere y' are," instructed another as a hand appeared in front of his face holding a water-soaked handkerchief. He took it gratefully and proceeded, carefully, to wipe the area around his injury. "Give it 'ere lad," instructed the same voice, "thas only mekin it worse." A rough grey hand relieved him of the cloth and took over the mopping up operation with all of the caution of a six-pounder driving a split wedge into a coal-face.

Clem couldn't believe that a mere voice could create such agony as it concluded the exercise with the reassuring comment, "Looks brock to me, what's tha reckon." His field of view was suddenly invaded by a cluster of faces, the eyes of which began scrutinising and surveying the damaged area with the same concern as they might have for a lump of coal.

"Hard to tell, wouldn't blow it for a while though if I were you." Needless to say, Clem was well-impressed by this impromptu, anonymous diagnosis and subsequent prognosis. He leant back in the chair they had placed him on, being as reassured as he might have been at the sight of a prostrate canary laying on the floor of its cage. The next gesture, however, totally vindicated the well-meaning but decidedly annoying throng.

A pint pot full of beer appeared in front of his rearranged face and as his eyes focused on it, he could hear it say sympathetically, "'Ere y'are lad, get this down yer neck." He reached out his hand and accepted it gratefully.

The fact that there had been a minor fracas in the pub was not an uncommon one. A combination of alcohol and depression regarding the inescapable circumstances of work and life in the village often resulted in acts of aggression. The more usual scenario was that of a slanging match which was invariably calmed down by the intercession of workmates. Physical violence generally erupted as sudden impromptu acts which didn't usually become prolonged or particularly vicious, and invariably depended on the role of the protagonists (victor or vanquished). They usually consisted of a short exchange of punches which often terminated in the sharing of drink between the adversaries. In this particular instance, the exchange of punches was limited to one, since Clem was rendered incapable of responding to Sam's knuckle missile.

The evening passed without further disturbance. Whilst Clem took to treating his condition with various well-recommended liquid remedies, his collection tin was passed around and returned to him. He had intended to present the collection to Mrs Gallagher after chapel on the following Sunday morning, and at the same time present himself to Florence.

Once each week, Clem woke to the grey glow of winter daylight which filled the bedroom. Ironically, it was usually the one day that he would sooner wake up to a room in darkness. This preference was even more desirable on this particular Sunday morning. He wasn't sure which was the more painful, his head or his nose, although the pain did seem to merge into one solid ache all over his face.

"Shine on, wor a mess," Clem's younger brother had a special way with words. The semantic economy with which he constructed his sentences was always impressive. The enormous implications of such a short precise utterance were immediately apparent to Clem. He emerged from his bed with all the haste of a one-legged tortoise at a pace marginally faster than stop, and headed for the table.

He held his head, cradled in his hands, at somewhere around waist height until he reached the table. After replacing his head on his shoulders, he focused his vision and searched for the mirror. Had his head been capable of withstanding the shock, he would have jerked back in horror at the image that confronted him. Instead, he just stared in disbelief, and groaned. Slowly and tentatively, he reached up his hand and started to touch his face. He carefully and gently started to prod at it, as if he could somehow rework or rearrange it into something that he recognised. Unfortunately all he succeeded in doing was increasing the level of pain.

On the positive side, the usually grey pallor of his skin had turned into a deep indigo blue which glowed eminently around his swollen nose. After some minutes' contemplation and checking and rechecking that the image was his and not a figment of his imagination, a voice from the bed scoffed.

"If you turn the mirror round, our Clem, it'll go away." Tom's words merged with his laughter. He knew he could capitalise on this opportunity to ridicule his elder brother who was in no fit state to react either physically or verbally to his gloating. "Tell thee what," he continued, "if tha puts my balaclava on, rest o' t' 'ed'll match your face." His laughter increased, fuelled by his recognition of the depth and ingenuity of his own wit (in case the point's been missed, his balaclava was blue.)

"Idiot," was the only response Clem could mutter as he continued to gaze into the mirror, trying in vain to ignore his younger brother's ridicule. All the same, he wasn't entirely sure whether his remark was directed at his rambling sibling in the bed or his own image in the mirror.

The initial shock subsided and Clem turned his thoughts to the problem which now arose as a result of his previous encounter with Sam's fist. He had to decide whether or not to proceed with the original plan, or pass the collected cash on to someone else to deliver and not bother going to chapel.

If he were to follow the latter course, and Florence or her mother were to enquire as to his whereabouts, some bright spark might drop him in it. They might be informed that Clem had got into a fight, and had been incapacitated as a result. This could produce one of two reactions. Firstly, Florence might think that he was a brawler and be appalled at the thought of being associated with such a thug. Conversely, she might respond sympathetically and enquire with some concern as to his well-being. This second scenario would then endear Clem to her and she might also ask if she could visit in order to comfort him.

Clem's mental wanderings came to an abrupt halt.

"Fat chance," he thought to himself as he once again considered the reality of the situation. The first proposition was the most likely, and the probability of the truth being distorted was also extremely high. The most sensible course of action was to attend himself and explain, should the necessity arise, the circumstances of his injury. At least that way, Florence would know the truth, that he was a victim and not the aggressor.

After having parried his mother's interrogation regarding the nature and reason for his injury, Clem finished his breakfast and emerged from the house into the cold crisp December air. He was followed almost immediately by the remainder of the Baxter household, a family group which rarely appeared in public at times other than Sunday mornings. He raised his head and glared at the heavy grey sky above. Had his nostrils been able to function efficiently, he would have taken a deep breath in an effort to absorb some of the fresh daylight air into his system. The impact of the chilled morning air on his face actually relieved the pain somewhat and as he proceeded with his mother and brother towards the church, he was able to generate a cautious smile of expectation.

Winter Sundays constantly reminded Clem of the lighter days to come, of the spring and the summer. Despite the cold and the greyness of the light, the prospect of the spring and summer seemed to offer partial escape from the life which fate had thrust upon him. He stared at the surrounding hills, which were actually more like rolling folds or waves of land in the natural terrain, and longed to be up there setting his snares and enjoying the mental, emotional and physical freedom which his excursions allowed. The village chapel was situated on the far side of the valley offering easy access to the local gentry of the area and the estate and colliery managers. That side of the valley was south-facing so that in the summer, it was bathed in sunshine all day long. The village proper, on the other hand, was crammed into terraces on the opposite side. The pit-top lay between the two areas in the valley bottom with the slag heaps flanking it on the village side.

The colliery owner, who also owned all of the land in the surrounding area, had built a new house during the early years of production. It was located on the upper reaches of the hillside, higher than any other houses in the area, and was visible from any aspect of the valley. From this prominent location, Lord Hase-Lore commanded a panoramic view of all that he owned including the village and its inhabitants. For the Baxter family, the walk to chapel took about forty minutes and was mostly uphill. The church was perched just below the owner's house and was linked to the latter by a winding track along which the horse-drawn carriages of the owner's family travelled. There were several other properties of distinction on the south-facing hillside. The vicarage was located adjacent to the chapel, the colliery manager's and deputy manager's houses were lower down, offering easy access to the pit. These two properties were considerably more substantial than the terraced houses of the colliers. They composed a pair of four-bedroomed semi-detached houses with front and rear gardens and the provision of a gas supply. They had internal bathrooms, which contained a washbasin and a cast-iron enamelled bath, located on the first floor and a downstairs inside, flush toilet. Hot water was piped to the bathroom and kitchen from a boiler at the back of the kitchen range. Both families enjoyed the services of daily help supplied from within the village population and consisting of one general maid and a cook.

About halfway up, just below the chapel, was the estate manager's house. He enjoyed the same facilities as the colliery management, although his house was a detached one and he had the services of a live in housekeeper. Behind the slag heaps, at the very bottom of the slope, there stood a row of six farm labourer's cottages.

The farm labourers enjoyed an even lower status than the colliers and since the construction of the slag-heaps, the cottages had become engulfed in their gigantic shadow. Even through the summer months the sunlight was severely restricted and because of the constant and ever-increasing presence of coal-dust, the stonework had become encrusted in a dingy, dark grey shroud. Where once there lay small but essential kitchen gardens and chicken-runs now lay a blanket of creeping blackness. The colliers at least were assured of long-term employment, even though the remuneration was subject to market-forces, health and life-span. On the other hand, the farm labourers' cottages were constantly being vacated and then re-inhabited.

Work on the land was at the mercy of the elements which were beyond the control even of the landowners, not that their lifestyle was subject to the same extremes as their employees. Their income varied marginally between excellent and obscene, much of their income from the land being derived through rents from tenant farmers in the area. They demanded the same rent whatever the climate's influence and blamed many poor harvests and stock depletions from disease on bad land-management. The tenants of 'slag row' as the terrace came to be known, were employed directly by the landowner and so were subject to his unpredictable whims as well as the climate.

As they climbed the path and approached the chapel, Clem began to scan the vicinity hoping to catch sight of Florence. This was an unnecessary exercise since he knew precisely where she would be sitting in chapel and would be able to confirm her presence in the next few minutes. It was yet another example of an involuntary action associated with the complexities of human emotions and relationships. He didn't locate Florence, but after passing the time of day with sundry acquaintances as they entered the chapel, he experienced a wave of relief on observing that her usual place was occupied. He was able to confirm his initial assumption that the person *in situ* was Florence by recognition of the apparel which adorned her slight frame. He also recognised the rear-view of her mother and the other siblings.

As if by some sonar or radar detection system there were at least two other members of the congregation who recognised Clem's urgency. One was standing next to him. He felt a nudge on his right hip which prompted him to react. He peered over and down, a look of disdain was already forming (though barely discernible amidst the bruising) as he made eye contact with the smirking grin that was Tom's face.

"Is she 'ere?" asked a subdued voice from within the grin. It became apparent to Clem that Jimmy had at the least confided in Tom his interpretation of the interaction which took place those three weeks earlier. Tom's diminutive stature, (he was not yet five foot tall) denied him vision beyond his immediate vicinity. He didn't receive a reply, but answered his own question a few seconds later when those in front of them took their seats.

As Clem turned his stare away from Tom, he made eye contact with another Cheshire cat, this one perched next to the subject of his affections. He felt for a second that there was a conspiracy against him. He generated an image of pews occupied by an abundance of diminutive people all staring at him from different angles and sporting the heads of Cheshire cats on their shoulders. A hand suddenly reached out to the top of the head of this particular one and spun it round to face the pulpit at the front of the chapel. To Clem's dismay or relief, he couldn't tell which, the head of the perpetrator of the act didn't bother to investigate the source of her younger brother's distraction.

The service was the same usual droll message of hellfire and damnation accompanied by a sermon which Clem found somewhat amusing – something to do with turning the other cheek when faced with aggression. The vicar admonished the members of the congregation for their evil actions and blasphemous thoughts and warned them of the consequences of having aspirations above their station. He then commenced to reaffirm the adage that the meek would inherit the earth, whilst constantly checking the facial expression of Lord Hase-Lore for signs of approval or disapproval. Whenever the sermon concentrated on the spiritual virtues of humility and blind deference, the expression remained one of approval. After all, religion had, through the ages, been a useful tool for ensuring subjugation of the masses. The premise that however harsh the realities of life, one's reward and redemption was waiting in the afterlife for those who accepted their lot, had long been effective in suppressing dissent.

Throughout the service, Clem's injury had been the cause of some discomfort. He constantly reached up to prod the injured area to see if the throbbing pain that he felt was actually causing his face to pulse in and out in unison with it. He eventually walked out of the church after shaking hands with the vicar, evading his disparaging stare, and stood in the churchyard to wait for Mrs Gallagher and family. When she eventually emerged from the church she was intercepted by the deputy manager of the colliery who was going through the usual well-rehearsed rhetoric of condolences relating to the death of her husband. The same man would later in the week put his signature to a letter demanding that Mrs Gallagher vacate her house by the end of the month with no regard for the welfare of her or her family. Within a week of vacating, the house would be re-inhabited by another collier tenant.

During this short interlude, Clem began to experience the same palpitations in his chest as he had experienced three weeks earlier. Mrs Gallagher proceeded along the path accepting the various gestures of sympathy from the remainder of the congregation whilst, to Clem's relief, the younger members of her brood, bored with the proceedings, peeled off to join sundry friends. By the time Mrs Gallagher had reached Clem, she was accompanied only by her oldest daughter,

Florence. As they approached, the spell was shattered for he could see a broad smile forming on Florence's face. This was not a smile of acknowledgement, but a smile of ridicule initiated by the state of Clem's complexion. Mrs Gallagher's reaction to the scene was more considerate, though equally unnerving.

"Oh dear! Clem, that looks nasty," she paused. "How on earth did that happen lad?"

Clem was taken completely by surprise by the mocking smile of Florence and the enquiring remark of Mrs Gallagher's. He had presupposed that any conversation would focus on Jim Gallagher's death and that he would not only initiate the conversation but would be in full control of the interaction. He had arranged his discourse accordingly. He had meant to tender his condolences and offer the money which he had collected. This in turn would put both Mrs Gallagher and Florence in a position of humility and generate an expression of gratitude. Clem would respond in a modest manner and win the affection of Florence and the appreciation of Mrs Gallagher.

Instead, he was completely bewildered, his mind struggled to assimilate a coherent response to Mrs Gallagher's remark and subsequent question. He wished that he could return the words to her and substitute them for something else, something that he could cope with or nothing at all, so that he could control the situation, but he couldn't. He couldn't formulate an immediate response and the ensuing lull in the conversation only served to focus even more the subject of her remarks.

Florence detected Clem's embarrassment and her impish smile slowly gave way to a more obvious snigger which she tried to stifle by putting her hand up to cover her mouth. The domino effect had been brought into play and Clem responded by instinctively raising his hand to his face in an attempt to hide his injury. He wanted to pull a hanky out of his pocket and wipe away his humiliation. Florence immediately turned her head away. He could say nothing, he just thrust out his other hand, which held the collection tin, towards Mrs Gallagher and muttered from behind his hand. "This is for you."

"Sorry Clem?" She hadn't heard a word he'd said and left the tin hanging in mid air at the end of Clem's arm.

"He said, it's for you Mam." Florence's controlled intervention took him totally by surprise.

The tin slipped from his grasp and crashed irretrievably to the ground. What had up until then been a private and personal embarrassment was now being shared with other church-goers who had remained in the immediate vicinity. It would be easy for the scene to develop into one of farcical proportions. Clem and Florence would stoop simultaneously in an attempt to retrieve the tin and its dispersed contents. This action would produce the inevitable – a clash of heads which would rock the two of them back on their heels and leave the onlookers in uproar. Clem's desire for personal contact with Florence would be, finally, fulfilled.

In reality, the situation developed somewhat differently. Clem froze, he stood gawping at Florence whose giggle had evolved into full-blown laughter. For the first time they made full eye contact, but this was not what Clem had planned and his thoughts were in total disarray. He stooped, in a solitary gesture of humility, in an effort to retrieve his abandoned charge and as he did so, the blood surged to the injured area of his face, causing a sudden rush of pain.

"Jesus Christ!" The exclamation signified his ultimate degradation, with any modicum of control being completely surrendered to the hand of fate or considering the location of the commotion, the hand of God. He resigned himself to his humiliation as he recovered the cash and almost immediately felt a wave of relief flow through his mind. Having finally ceased his attempts to retrieve the situation, he strangely felt more relaxed.

"I'm really sorry, Mrs Gallagher," he apologised as he regained his feet.

"Eh lad, don't be daft, tha's give me a bit o' light relief, what wi' all that's happened just lately. Any rate our Florence seems to have appreciated it. Cheered her up no end you have."

In one simple statement Mrs Gallagher had rescued the situation. If Clem's expression had been discernible behind his throbbing disguise, it would have displayed great relief, as though he were inwardly contemplating the wondrous power of the spoken word. The looks of indignation from those around them had changed to ones of guarded acceptance and the whole atmosphere softened in an audible kaleidoscope of peripheral conversations.

More surprisingly, Clem's resignation to the situation had released his mind and, without the restrictions of trying to plan his conversation, he found that his words had begun to form sentences of their own construction.

"Well, that's something at least." As he spoke he turned towards Florence whose laughter had diminished into a glowing smile of understanding tinged with just a touch of concern.

"Anyway, to answer your question Mrs Gallagher," his gaze remained fixed on Florence's smile. "I'm afraid I had a bit of a run in with Sam Jackson last night while I was making the collection and..."

Mrs Gallagher interrupted. "Say no more, lad. Everyone knows the temper of that one. Blows up regular for no reason at all, I know. I've seen the state of Mrs Jackson at times." As the statement progressed, the volume of her voice reduced to a whisper. "As it happens I was lucky, really. He only hit me the once." It paid in the community to develop a knack of turning a negative situation into a positive one and most people were capable of developing this talent.

"Thanks for the contribution Mr Baxter, we really appreciate it." Clem's ears welcomed Florence's interruption with open arms. The remark plunged in and floated gracefully around inside his head. He embraced it enthusiastically.

"It's Clem," he insisted, "and it's not just me you've to thank it's all t' village, everybody gave somat. Even Sam Jackson as it happens!" Florence didn't reply for her thoughts were suddenly elsewhere in time, drifting around a bedroom about three weeks previously and recollecting a certain conversation at bed time between a young boy and his older sister.

In the meantime Clem's free-flowing vocabulary continued to control his ability to formulate a coherent sentence.

"Talking about distractions," he enthused, this time directing his remarks to Mrs Gallagher's previous observation. "With your permission," he was looking at Mrs Gallagher, "and if your Florence is in agreement, I wondered if she might care to take a walk with me this afternoon as a bit of a distraction like?" There was only a short pause between his request and the response but he somehow managed a quick analysis of the statement that had just tumbled from his lips. Inside his head he felt complete astonishment at what had emerged from his mouth. He couldn't believe that he had just asked Florence to walk out with him. On the one hand he applauded his frankness and directness and on the other hand he felt a wave of mild terror overwhelming him. One question repeated itself constantly. 'What if she declined? At least up until now he had enjoyed the dubious comfort of uncertainty, the adrenalin-stimulating power of hope. Rejection would render him inconsolable, he would be utterly gutted. His thoughts were interrupted.

"Well, I'm sure I don't mind, Clem, but I'm not so sure our Florence is with us just now." They both looked over at her and perceived an air of meditation in her manner. "Florence! Clem's just asked you a question."

"Sorry Mam." She looked over obligingly at Clem. The palpitations returned, surely he didn't have to repeat the question, he hadn't yet recovered from the shock of his first effort. He could feel his word-power deserting him as he desperately, tried to arrange the sentence in the back of his throat again. All he seemed to be able to muster was a disorganised array of utterances, all jostling for position to create an intelligible structure, none of which where prepared to leave his voice-box until they had. He was saved, Mrs Gallagher intervened.

"Clem wants to know if you'd care to take a walk with him this afternoon?" He stood transfixed. If his disguise could have been removed, it would have revealed the kind of stupid smile that is associated with an imbecile.

"That would be very nice, thank you," she hesitated, "Clem."

Chapter Four

Mrs Gallagher gathered her children around her, after again thanking Clem for his efforts regarding the collection, and proceeded down the hill towards her home. She had left the youngest with a neighbour who herself was too arthritic to undertake the arduous walk to chapel. Florence's other brothers and sister, as always, meandered to and fro exploring gaps between the hedgerow and in the shrubbery looking for rabbit-runs and other signs of wildlife. Jimmy had already assured his mother that, since he was now the eldest male in the family, he would make sure that they were provided for.

He would set traps and catch wild beasts to serve up for supper. He would ask Clem Baxter to show him how to set the snares on the hillsides and he would supply them with more rabbit than they could eat. His mother thanked him but suggested that they might tire of eating rabbit everyday for the rest of their lives. Only a few years earlier she might have managed to get him work in the colliery by lying about his age, as people had previously done when times were hard. It was said that there had been a great deal of opposition to the Coal Mines Act passed some years earlier which prevented women and children from working underground. A child's or a woman's wages had often made the difference in income which kept people from the workhouse. Many parents, especially single mothers, would lie about the age of their sons to get them into work. Since the Compulsory Education Act, it had become more difficult to practice this feat of subterfuge because records were more accurate and parishes were able to monitor the whereabouts of children.

More recently, the Miners Eight Hours Act restricting underground work to just such a minimum had taken its toll on earnings. The only way to support these benevolent acts was to provide the resources to replenish lost income. The political agenda did not, however, accommodate such contingencies – it was more geared to supporting and promoting the moral fortitude of the upper classes. The best that the lower classes could hope for from the employers were concessions, which were only offered if they could be easily afforded or, at worst, total intransigence. Even then, the unions had to fight hard for any improvement in working conditions and usually had to settle for a compromise solution, which invariably favoured the employers more than the workers.

As Jimmy and his two younger sisters scoured the area, searching out new hunting-grounds, Florence and her mother returned to their own thoughts and deliberations. She had made the link between Clem and the conversation she had held, three weeks earlier, with her brother, and then discarded it simply because she didn't possess the knowledge to deal with it. The prospect of a relationship with anyone was not an immediate consideration. She had agreed to take a walk with Clem because she felt that a short separation from her siblings would do her good. For obvious reasons, she also found Clem Baxter quite amusing, and when the opportunity to be in the company of such a person arose, it wasn't something that was rejected lightly. Other than that, she was far too preoccupied with current family affairs to allow herself the luxury of a personal distraction.

There was little doubt that Florence would have to find work and contribute to the household income. The sight of tenants being evicted from colliery houses was a frequent occurrence in the community and, in the Gallagher's case, an inevitable one. Without a wage being earned from the colliery, the house would have to be vacated. They would be given time only to lay Jim Gallagher to rest, and then they would have to leave.

Not surprisingly, Florence's family history was one of hardship and fragmentation. Her great-grandfather, as implied by the family surname, was of Irish stock and had been driven from his homeland by The Great Famine, half a century earlier. He and his brother had taken leave of their family in county Cork and set sail on a Liverpool-bound clipper. They had heard about the work that was to be had, as a result of the great railways expansion, in England. The brothers remained in the north of England because that was where they had been offered work.

The trans-Pennine route stretched the design and engineering ingenuity of the day to its limits. Viaducts spanned vast pastoral voids across the High Peaks and North Yorkshire Moors. Track was routed into the bowels of the earth through long dark tunnels which snaked their way from one side of the peaks to the other. Men used as guinea pigs to test the effectiveness of new construction techniques fell to their deaths from unstable structures in the sky. Some were crushed and buried alive by angry rock formations which repelled their puny efforts to invade their subterranean domain. Her great-grandfather's brother met his death in just such an incident, or was it an accident?

Some would maintain that these massive engineering feats were monuments to the ingenuity of mankind, others that they defiled the natural landscape of the country. Either way, it was abundantly clear that there had been a price levied on mankind's intrusion into nature's domain. A pity that it was those who stood to gain the least who had to pay the highest price.

During the railway's progress through South Yorkshire, on route from Sheffield to Doncaster, Florence's great-grandfather met up with a young woman who was later to become her great-grandmother. He gave up his transient lifestyle on the railway construction as it thrust its way remorselessly towards the east coast, leaving a sinister scar in its wake. After taking up casual work in the area, he became one of the first men to be recruited to work at the, then newly-opened, Connington Main colliery.

Florence's physical appearance must, in some way, have been attributed to her Irish roots. Her most distinctive feature was her sapphire-blue eyes set against the backdrop of her soft, swarthy complexion which in turn was framed by an abundance of dark brown wavy hair. When the light caught it in a certain way, her hair displayed glowing highlights of dark red streaks. She was slightly built and looked as though she should have been a sickly child when she was younger but, on the contrary, her physical constitution was solid and evenly matched by her stalwart and tenacious temperament.

Had Florence not been the victim of social conditioning, and had she been better educated, she might well have had aspirations beyond those which she had been encouraged to embrace. The prospect of marriage, and the raising and nurturing of a family, was firmly entrenched in the notional expectations of young women of her class, status and era. Sometimes she found it difficult to reconcile her innermost desires with those objectives towards which she was constantly directed by the environment and community in which she lived.

As she strolled along with her mother, Florence contemplated her future. There had already been talk of her entering into domestic service which was the usual route for unmarried women in the community until marriage was undertaken. There were a limited number of jobs available to women on the pit-top at the colliery, but they had been slowly disappearing as a result of 'benevolent' acts by the employers. The jobs that remained were usually in the screening sheds and were not sought after except in the most desperate circumstances.

All of the village shops and businesses, though owned by the company, were family run and obviously any jobs in those areas were reserved for relatives and friends. The domestic servants, attending the houses on the other side of the hill, originated from the village but positions were in short supply. These properties were always the first choice and generally required a word from someone already working there; again, it benefited friends and relatives first. Although Mrs Gallagher had acquaintances whose daughters had obtained posts within these properties, the immediate opinion was that there was nothing to be had at present.

The only possibility was that a position might be found at a friend of Lord Hase-Lore's who lived in the next valley on the way to Rotherham. Since it was likely that the Gallagher family would finish up, at least in the short term, at Mrs Gallagher's sister's in Rotherham, then any position around there would meet with approval. The wheels had already been set in motion and grapevines rustled in order to secure a position for Florence.

Clem's arrival at number 28 was met with subdued greetings. Jim's body was still laid out in the parlour awaiting burial which had been arranged for the following Tuesday. In the meantime, it was customary for relatives and acquaintances to pay their last respects as and when it suited. Clem had already undertaken these duties and was not disposed to linger any longer than was necessary to exchange the time of day with Mrs Gallagher. He was naturally keen to spend as much time as he could in the solitary company of Florence.

It is funny how certain plans can be detected and waylaid by those around who wish to milk a situation to its full, especially younger siblings. They seem to have an uncanny knack of creating an embarrassing situation or predicament for their elders especially in the area of human relationships.

"Aren't you going to ask Clem if he wants a cup of tea, our Flori?" The suggestion was embraced by Florence since she saw the liaison as no more than a break from family commitments.

"Sorry Clem, I wasn't thinking. Sit yourself down and I'll mash a pot of tea." Clem responded quickly, irritated by the mischief behind Jimmy's suggestion. If Jimmy could see beyond the swollen indigo, which was Clem's face, he would have perceived a threatening glare.

"No!" The urgent tone in his voice made way for one of pleading resignation, "don't bother yourself Florence, I had one before I came out." A desperate lie. Jimmy sniggered.

"Don't be daft. It's no bother Clem. Dare say Mam could do with one anyway. That right Mam?"

"Thanks love. A cup of tea would be very nice." Clem sighed and sat down, Jimmy smiled and stared smugly. The conversation continued with Clem simply making up the numbers and scalding his tongue on the hot tea as a result of trying to speed up the proceedings. Jimmy didn't miss the opportunity.

"Careful Clem, you'll burn your tongue," he interjected, after the deed was done.

After what seemed to be an interminable length of time, Clem and Florence took their leave and ventured out into the dull grey daylight. Florence wore the same clothes as she did to chapel that morning with the exception that the black headscarf had been substituted for a brown one matching her skirt and shawl. They turned onto Bank Street front and strolled up the hill to where the cobbles terminated and made way for the open countryside. The air was chilled but they were able to combat its effects by maintaining a brisk pace.

Clem found it difficult to strike up a conversation – he didn't want to concentrate on her father's death and at the same time he didn't want to seem irreverent. Luckily, his words took charge again.

"It's smashing up 'ere, can't wait for Spring and the light nights to come."

"No idea where we'll be by next Spring," Florence's remark took him by surprise, he hadn't given any thought to the practical consequences of Jim's death, he just replied, "Oh! Right." He knew the response was pathetic but his mind had become confused again. While he tried to regain his mental composure, Florence continued the conversation.

"Looks like I'll be going into service. Mam and the kids are off to Rotherham to stay with Aunty Nell. Can't see that working though, she's little enough room for her lot, let alone ours. Jimmy doesn't want to go. I know that much. Says he'll run away if he has to move from here. Keeps telling Mam that he'll go hunting to get us food so we won't have to move." As she spoke, her gaze remained fixed on the frozen soil path which shifted along under their feet.

This was not what Clem had envisaged, just lately nothing much that Clem had envisaged had actually happened. He wanted to retrieve the situation as he looked across at her downturned head.

"Well, Rotherham's not that far away, you could take a post at one of the houses on t' other side and visit over to Rotherham regular like," he suggested, far too enthusiastically. She lifted her head and glanced back at Clem. He plunged, headlong, straight into the deep lagoon blue of her eyes and he just wanted to float around in there for ever. For the first time, Florence realised that, for Clem at least, there was something significant happening. She smiled, more as a gesture of sympathy than endearment, which was ironic under the circumstances. He reluctantly withdrew himself from within her gaze and tried to reshape his remark. "I mean you would still be able to see your friends here, if you worked nearby." His attempt was completely unconvincing.

"Well, that's true enough." Florence played along with him, seeking to relieve the tension which she sensed was building up inside his mind. She turned away from Clem and looked straight ahead as they approached the brow of the hill. They walked in silence for the next few minutes, during which time Clem tried to unravel his emotions.

He couldn't understand why an attempt at courtship should prove to be so evasive. After all, he had no trouble talking to his workmates about anything. He wasn't particularly shy by nature. He considered the stories in the limited number of books he had read. They were supposed to show real life but the hero never seemed to have any trouble striking up a relationship with his woman. He was supposed to sweep Florence off her feet, she was supposed to melt in his arms. So far there was absolutely no indication that this scenario was about to come to fruition.

Momentarily he contemplated writing a book himself and telling it like it really was. Suddenly, without engaging his brain, his mouth opened and a cluster of words cascaded out:

"He could come and stay with us." The renewed enthusiasm was unmistakable, but he couldn't tell if he had directed the proposition to Florence, himself or, for that matter, the world at large.

"Sorry!" The response denoted an apology, but sounded like a question. Florence turned towards him again, looking totally bemused. He found himself swimming around again in the warmth of the deep blue water.

"Jimmy," he paused, "he can come and stay with us, Florence." He jumped out of the water and looked away as if searching for the instigator of such a preposterous suggestion.

"Jimmy?" She almost found herself saying, "Jimmy who?"

"Yes." He was on a roll. His mind couldn't keep up with the urgency and euphoria that emerged from his mouth. "He can stay at our house with us. Your Mam can go to Rotherham to stay with your aunty, and you will get a job on t' other side," the grin on his face said the rest until Florence responded:

"Don't be so daft Clem. What would Mrs Baxter say? I mean you 'avn't even asked her about it."

Clem thought for a second – his commitment was total. "It wouldn't be a problem as long he fetched a bed." The look of amazement was far too enormous to fit into the petite area of her face. She couldn't believe that such a major event could hinge merely on the provision of something as simple as a bed. Nor could she help responding to Clem's grin and her expression soon gave way to a smile, this time tinged with just the slightest hint of endearment. "That's settled then." The announcement was triumphant. "I'll tell Mam when I get back and we'll get things sorted out." He immediately turned around and beckoned Florence to join him. "Come on then."

Florence was speechless – all she could do was listen to Clem raving about how Jimmy would keep Tom out of his hair and how good they'd be for each other. When they arrived back at the yard of number 28, Florence had regained her composure but she was unable to restrain Clem's gushing waterfall of confidence.

"Do you think we could go out for another walk, Florence, what about next Sunday?" It was more an insistence than a request.

"Yes. I think so Clem. Oh! and call me Flori will you?" She pulled the backdoor shut behind herself as she disappeared into the house. Suddenly he was floating in the lagoon again. "Call me Flori," he repeated to himself. He felt as though she had just offered herself – heart, mind, body and soul – to him.

The act of different families taking in the children of others after the death of a parent was not an unusual one within the community. Relatives were often the first to offer or be approached, but due to the cramped living conditions, families were often split up to avoid the parish taking control of them. It remained commonplace that the workhouse had been a real and obvious option for destitute and homeless families although imprisonment for vagrancy was still rigorously imposed in many cases. It was with this situation in mind that Clem considered the method by which he would persuade his mother to take in young Jimmy Gallagher.

Room wasn't a problem, he knew that three males sharing a bedroom would not give rise to concern. It was the extra mouth to feed and body to clothe that would present the greatest stumbling-block. At first he considered offering to give up his beer money and deliberated on that option for at least thirty seconds before rejecting it. Finally he settled on appealing to his mother's good nature and using his powers of persuasion on her. All of this benevolence was spurred on by an ulterior motive, of course. He knew that if Jimmy were to live with them Florence would take it upon herself to visit regularly which would ensure close contact with her.

"So what do you think Mam?" Clem asked after explaining the spiritual virtues and rewards of performing such an act of charity. Clem's mother was more concerned with his interest in Florence and the implied ulterior motive.

"Can't help thinking that there's more to this than meets the eye. You're a good lad Clem but can't some how see you sharing your bedroom, with another lad, by choice." She thought for a few seconds. "Specially not wi' them two young scallywags, you know what they're like when they get together. If they're not wreaking 'avock with the rest o' the world, they're at each other's throats." Naturally Tom and Jimmy were the best of pals. "'Course wi' that there Jimmy staying here it would mean that young Florence Gallagher would come visiting to keep an eye on him wouldn't it?"

Clem might as well have opened up his head and exposed the pages of his mind for his mother to read the very strategy which she had just described. "You say there'll be a bed then, and I suppose you'll be wanting that on your own leaving them two to share t'other." She wasn't just reading Clem's 'mind-book', she was writing it now. He tried to respond in surprised approval at his mother's observation.

"Well, come to mention it..." Her astute stare interrupted his statement in midflow. "That's not a bad idea in't that Mam," his tone was indicative of one who had achieved nothing and gained everything.

"Suppose you want me to have a word with Martha then and see what she's got to say about it. I'll talk to her after the funeral on Tuesday and see what can be done but it's going to mean a tightening o' belts round here."

"Aye rate, Mam."

Clem tried to make his response as serious as possible but couldn't help offering a wry smile.

It was commonplace in the village for funerals to be attended by a predominately female congregation. There was neither the financial possibility nor the working practice to enable men to forego even part of a shift in order to attend the funeral of a workmate. The only concession to this was during the aftermath of a fatal colliery disaster. It was the pit-owner's token gesture of humanity and compassion to allow a day off without pay for all the miners to attend any funerals – a somewhat empty gesture since most accidents, at least underground, usually took several days to clear up and get the pit reopened for production. In that instance, a day off fitted very nicely into the scheme of things. So Jim Gallagher's funeral was no exception and, whilst his body was being solemnly laid to rest in a hole in the ground, his workmates were busy subjecting themselves to the very elements which caused Jim's death, in another hole in the ground.

Even the union representative could only attend because his workmates covered his quota and he had his money made up from union funds. After the short predictable service, a small entourage of mourners returned to number 28 Bank Street, not to continue paying their respects but to set about reorganising the life of the Gallagher family. Martha's sister Nell from Rotherham was there, also

Mrs Winston, the housekeeper at the Hall and May Baxter completed the matriarchal quorum.

The meeting was an informal affair but the agenda was strictly adhered to. Many a union committee meeting would have benefited from the gentle efficiency with which these gatherings were conducted. The first item on the agenda was the imminent vacating of the pit-house. The letter of eviction had not yet arrived but it was expected by the end of the week so it was prudent to make arrangements immediately. Nell agreed to take Martha and her three youngest on a temporary basis until she could find work and take a room of her own. I use the word 'room' advisedly since that was the only prospect of accommodation available to Martha.

Even a 'good woman's' wage was, at that time, no more than half that of a working class man, making the acquisition of anything more palatial than one room pure fantasy. The next item on the agenda was the plight of Jimmy. Florence had already mentioned Clem's proposal to her mother who did not allow her emotions to overcome the practicalities of the arrangement and indicated that if May was in agreement, then the solution would be initiated. The only cause for concern was the provision of a bed. This was solved as a result of Florence's arrangements – her bed was to be made available, since she would not be needing it.

Finally, Florence's future was discussed. Mrs Winston had already put into motion the highly effective mechanism of the 'domestic's grapevine'. She confirmed what had been surmised, that there was a vacancy at the Manor in the next valley for a scullery-maid and she had already arranged for Florence to attend a meeting to discuss her possible appointment at the Hall. The usual procedure was for the housekeeper to grill all prospective servants and, subject to her approval, candidates would then be allowed an interview with the lady of the house. This was usually a formality, although it would be the Brigadier who would make the final decision, since his wife had died some years earlier.

Within the space of an hour and two cups of tea, the agenda had been fulfilled and arrangements completed. The only remaining thing was to await the arrival of the eviction notice.

Chapter Five

Clem reclined on the young shoots of a grassy bank, his head thrown back and his eyes squinting at the bright, early summer sky. He lay on his back, sprawled out, full-length, with his forearms raised above his shoulders and his hands tucked under the rear of his neck. From his lips there protruded a pale green, fledgling stem of wild grass and its top circled and twitched in the warm air as his tongue fondled and tantalised the moist lower end nestling in his mouth. His forearms were exposed to the sun's probing rays as they sought to apply some colour to his pale grey skin, through the soft layer of bristling hairs which adorned them. Very occasionally, the intense warmth would be dissipated by velvety white wisps as they floated between his thoughts and the ancient brilliance of the sunlight.

In a terrible, harsh existence it was interludes such as this into which Clem could make his escape – he could soar amongst the clouds beyond the clutches of reality and share his euphoria with the birds. He wallowed in the luxurious texture of the clear fresh air as it gently caressed the film of skin which overlaid his being. On such occasions, his thoughts were diverted away from the colliery and the village to a liberation which was only attainable from within the confines of his own imagination, delicately exposed by the heady environment into which be immersed himself. Normally these excursions would be solitary experiences but just lately he had been sharing occasional ones with another.

It was as though this other entity had completed a whole being previously divided and waiting, without the realisation that the fragmentation was there. He contemplated the imminent coming-together of the two halves, to realise the fusion into one, whilst flowing adrenalin fuelled his expectations. He wasn't yet aware of what the new-found emotions and physical responses were that he had encountered recently. All he knew was that they were uncontrollable and fraught with uncertainty and misgivings. The sexuality within his body had been summoned and he must obey – love it may have been, lust it certainly was, and if there was a difference between the two, he had yet to recognise it. Clem never dwelt on these emotional and physical experiences for long. All he knew was that when Florence was around, he was happy, though it was a feeling of happiness that seemed to thrive on the torment of trepidation and even frustration which accompanied it. All the while the stem of the young grass shoot writhed and twitched under the gentle caress of his flickering tongue.

As he lay musing and wondering at the forming and reforming of the sky's structure, he recalled his introduction to Florence. He considered the peculiar irony of the death of Jim Gallagher, that out of tragedy there emerges a positive situation. The death had facilitated his meeting with Florence and had led to their growing relationship. He addressed the proposition of an afterlife, of the sort in which he had been taught to believe.

His deliberations on the subject were really quite simplistic. Since religion posed so many unanswerable questions, he had decided that, for those people who accepted its teachings, it should serve a purpose for those who didn't, then so be it. For those believers who wished a man well in his afterlife, they would wish him to heaven; for those believers who wished a man ill in his after life, they would wish him to hell; for those non-believers, they would simply wish the worms a hearty meal. It seemed to Clem that the more he had been taught about religion, the more difficult it was to understand and accept. Far better, he thought, to be subjected to the uncompromising ranting of the hell, fire and damnation lot whose purpose it was to instil such a fear of God Almighty into people that they would not dare to question the status of religion in society. He suddenly realised that he had diverted his thoughts away from the more appealing focus of his attention.

The friendship between Florence and Clem had developed during the previous six months and it was now common knowledge in the village that they were walking out. Clem had reached the stage where he yearned to be with her all the time, he felt complete in her presence and was convinced that marriage would be the natural outcome of their relationship. The only decision which remained was, for him, when to ask Florence to be his wife.

When he first contemplated proposing, he had supposed that the right time would present itself as a matter of course but there was one nagging question on his mind. "What if she declined?" He would be devastated. Admittedly she hadn't told him that she felt anything deeper than friendship towards him, but there again, neither had he revealed his innermost feelings to Florence. During his recent deliberations on the subject, he had thought that someone should have produced a set of rules to apply to such a situation. He hadn't realised that the only thing holding him back was his own vanity entrenched in his fear of rejection. Such are the myriad emotions which compose the complexities surrounding human relationships. In order to resolve this dilemma, he had established for himself a schedule of sorts. In four weeks it would be Florence's seventeenth birthday so during the preceding time he would reveal his deepest feelings to her and he would make his proposal of marriage on the date of her birthday. Or sooner, if he could pluck up the courage.

Whilst Clem continued his meditations a distant figure was making its way up the other side of the bank towards the spot where he lay. It was the figure of a female, barely a child and hardly a woman, at a stage in her life when physical, emotional and mental influences were shaping her transition into maturity. On some occasions she would retain her childhood with girlish responses to given situations, on others she would tread tentatively into womanhood with the realisation that feelings and desires were not confined to the annals of fairy tales.

She had been at the Cropton household for over six months now and, during that time, had worked as the lowest denomination in the staff hierarchy. As the youngest and the scullery-maid, her duties had consisted, fundamentally, of serving the other servants, duties which carried the most menial though often quite physically demanding tasks. Her domain was the kitchen, and as her job title suggests, the scullery.

She had to scrub the flagged floors and wash the household dishes and linen of both employers and staff. Direct contact with the owners of the house was a rare occurrence although just lately she had been performing certain special duties which gave her more access to the main part of the house. Even from her lowly view point, she could not help but marvel at the grandeur and splendour which surrounded the privileged occupants of the house. One person in particular was the subject of many of her more 'maturing' thoughts.

The Brigadier's son, Harry Cropton, had recently returned from a year's sabbatical (the word sabbatical, in this case, being something of a euphemism) to Europe, Paris no less. This sojourn was carried out in the guise of requiring time and space to decide which life of privilege he would select now that he had completed his education. In reality, of course, his education had been continued, though not in any manner resembling one of academia.

The choices laid open to him were fairly predictable for a young man in his position. They consisted of three main options: the diplomatic corps, a commission in the armed forces or a position in the family business running the estate. It was common practice for young men of his status to travel to Europe and spend some time in one of the more fashionable cities such as Paris or Rome and develop their 'cultural' appreciation of life. Harry embraced the quasi-bohemian environment with great enthusiasm and became well acquainted with the more colourful aspects of society. He also became well acquainted with a little parasite known as 'crabs'. Even by his own admission, though, he had often felt that he had encountered a more intellectual species than many of his other companions. However, Florence was not aware of these life experiences and acknowledged only the well-spoken, and it has to be admitted, courteous disposition, of this extensively travelled young man, a disposition which was neatly framed within the attributions of good looks and good dress sense.

On the not so infrequent occasions which she and young master Cropton, as he was known amongst the staff, had encountered one another, she had felt an undeniable attraction towards him. For his part, he had not been backward at coming forwards as it were, and had offered what she had interpreted as being endearing compliments. Not surprisingly, her attitude towards Clem had not developed beyond one of close friendship and, unlike him, she had not at any time contemplated the notion of marriage. Not to Clem anyway. On the contrary, she had become quite adamant that she would not become the wife of a miner – her aspirations for herself and any potential issue which she might produce were to transcend the existence which she had been forced to endure until that time. Her two weekly meetings with Clem were necessary rather than desirable. She was naturally concerned with the well-being of her younger brother which required her to spend time in the company of Clem and his family.

In these close-knit mining communities, it was the rule rather than the exception that marriages would be generated from within. Friends, neighbours and sometimes relatives were all potential suitors and suitable. The structure of the community promoted and encouraged this tradition. Extended families were commonplace, often under the same roof. This meant that although company-owned, pit-houses were generally quite modern, they remained extremely cramped, often providing shelter for three generations under one roof. This is not to say that all households had within their confines a pair of infirmed and elderly residents. Indeed, very few housed people older than fifty and most of these were women who proved invaluable as aids to the rearing of children.

As usual, the main beneficiaries of this situation were the colliery owners. In an age when geographical mobility was actively discouraged for the sake of a stable work force, local marriages and extended families served to reinforce the situation. It was not surprising therefore that many couples underwent two marriages in their relationship, the first being ordained by community consensus, via the village shopping centre, and the second by the vicar at the local chapel. The result was that many marriages took place due to the culmination of persuasion and expectation from family and friends. The concept of love, in itself an emotive term, was even more blurred than it is in contemporary society.

Amongst the working classes where access to the romantic novels was somewhat restricted, notional interpretations of the meaning of love were not accessible to them. On the other hand, within the realms of the more educated middle and upper classes who had been exposed to whimsical images of idyllic, tender relationships culminating in the happy ever after syndrome, there was a more definite interpretation of love. However, even this was generally overcome by expediency, the irony being that the very people who were most influenced by these notions of love, that is young impressionable women, were in the main denied access to it.

Marriages amongst the upper classes continued to be dominated by male-stream ideology and were invariably unions of convenience. Security and enhancement of family wealth and prestige took precedent over misinformation offered by popular reading material of the time. If there were any practising 'love' relationships, it was invariably between married men and their mistresses and even those were under the control of male-stream ideology. It was usually a case of the older man being attracted to the younger woman and the younger woman in turn being attracted by the suspect promises of the older man. Florence had been given clandestine access to just such reading material by Harry Cropton and was currently absorbing and assimilating the definitive contents which lay therein.

It was not surprising, under the circumstances, that the community of Connington had already conducted the marriage ceremony of Clem Baxter and Florence Gallagher. It only remained for the church to give its blessing and authenticate the union. Both Clem and Florence were aware of the expectations of their friends and families and that somehow, when young Jimmy and Tom started work on the pit-top, the Gallagher family would return and be reunited within the community. Clem, for his part, made no effort to suppress the gossip and innuendoes – he felt that the general consensus would make it easier for him to ask Florence to marry him. Although he wouldn't admit it to anyone, he hoped that Florence would feel under some pressure to accept his proposal, should she be in any way unsure of her feelings towards him. He wasn't aware that Florence was reading a different book to the one he had written in his mind.

Clem was disturbed in his deliberations by the sound of rustling grass just beyond the brow of the bank behind him. He pulled himself to his feet lazily, his tongue suddenly flicking and caressing the end of the stem of grass more vigorously. As his momentum increased, he swivelled, excitedly, to encounter the figure of Florence appearing over the bank top. First her wide-brimmed, beige coloured straw hat, then her smiling face, shoulders, skirted waist and hips, and finally her whole self stood before him.

She was carrying a cloth-covered wicker basket which swung from her hand at her side. He whipped the grass stem from his mouth and held out his hand towards her free one.

"Hey up, love." A beaming smile had taken over the space where his face had been a few seconds earlier.

"Hello, Clem." Her response was not quite as enthusiastic as Clem's greeting. He drew her to him, wrapped his arms around her waist and kissed her full on the lips. "Careful Clem, you'll knock my hat off." She felt sure that her friendly admonishment would suffice to satisfy Clem that her rapid step back was purely for practical purposes.

"Sod the 'at." He made another grab for her. This time she acquiesced they indulged themselves in a lingering kiss which Florence actually found quite enjoyable.

In fact, Florence always enjoyed kissing Clem; she also enjoyed his company and his humour and affection. She knew that he would make a fine husband who wouldn't keep her short or beat her or be abusive to the kids but she didn't 'love' him. She knew she didn't love him because she wasn't feeling all the things that she had encountered in the books that she had been reading. Books, incidentally, which had been carefully selected by Harry Cropton.

Clem was blissfully unaware of the misgivings which Florence held and put her lack of enthusiasm down to the innocence and shyness of her youth. He felt that she was undergoing the same disturbing and uncontrollable urges to which he had been subjected and that she needed to be guided through this initial period of self-exploration. As their bodies separated, he took hold of her hand again, looked into her eyes and lingered, momentarily in the warm blue water.

"C'mon," he commanded and headed off along the top of the bank, tugging the reluctant Florence after him.

"Cleemm!" Her plea slowed him down and he turned to face her.

"What's up, love?"

She directed her gaze towards the houses further down.

"The village is that way."

"I know but I need to check some snares." His explanation was received with mixed feelings. She knew that the rabbits were a valuable source of meat and he regularly managed to send one over to her mother in Rotherham. On the other hand, she wished that he wouldn't go checking them when she was around. The sight of a skinned and gutted rabbit was one thing but to see the animal prostrate with its neck caught in a wire noose was an image that she would rather avoid.

"C'mon then, won't take long."

She followed reluctantly.

"Don't know why you can't check your snares when I'm not here, Clem."

"What's up, squeamish are we." His voice carried a tone of macho bravado in it. Florence raised her eyeballs to the top of her sockets and glanced up at the sky. This would seem to be a trait of the

Gallagher family, as it would appear, was the contrite audible gesture which accompanied the expression. She reconciled herself to accompanying him on his expedition whilst reminding herself of the benefits consequential to such a task. After all she did enjoy the taste of rabbit and never allowed her moral judgement to curb her appetite.

The first snare held nothing, although there were signs of activity around it – a rabbit somewhere nearby had lived to hop another day. The second had snagged a buck which now lay on its side and could easily have been mistaken for being asleep if it hadn't been for the terrified stare of its bulging eyes.

"Smashing, this one's for your Mam," Clem's enthusiasm overwhelmed any feeling of guilt or remorse which Florence might have been harbouring.

"He'll fill the pot nicely," she concurred and looked on in delight as Clem slipped the noose and released the limp carcass. He pulled out a small sack which he had tucked into his belt and dropped the rabbit inside.

"One more, and that's it."

As they approached the next trap, they became aware of a barely perceptible sound being emitted from its location.

"Hear that?" enquired Clem. Florence didn't bother with the formality of an acknowledgement.

"What is it?"

"Well, it's not a bloody rabbit," he winced at the sudden lack of control of his language. The Gallagher trait resurfaced. "Sorry." The discourse had diminished to the level of a whisper.

"S'alright, you're a miner." The grin on her face hid something somewhat more disconcerting.

During the short conversation their pace had slowed to a virtual shuffle and Clem assumed an almost instinctive protective posture. He stepped ahead of Florence and gently hustled her behind him, pressing his hand against her shoulder. As they approached the source of the sound in almost tandem formation (Florence was a reluctant follower), the sound became clearer and less threatening. Clem's feeling of trepidation began to give way to one of concern as he perceived the pathetic whimpering of a dog. His pace quickened.

"It's a dog!" The surprise and guarded relief struck them both simultaneously. They soon rounded the clump of bushes which concealed the next snare and the origin of what were now discernible as cries of pain.

Immediately the scene entered her field of vision, Florence rushed forward towards the distressed animal.

"He's caught in the snare!" Her exclamation held a tone of great concern.

"Careful!" His plea for caution did not carry sufficient pace to intercept Florence's flight of mercy. As she dropped her basket and reached out her arms, she was repulsed by a vicious show of teeth followed by an ear-piercing crescendo of barking and snarling. Although the dog wasn't very large, it triggered a formidable defence mechanism which sent Florence rocking back on her heels, Unfortunately for the animal, its spontaneous response had caused the snare to tighten up on its trapped paw and the pandemonium soon gave way to a painful whimper.

Clem instinctively attended to Florence – he was not sure whether she had been within striking range of the animal's teeth but he was reassured when she directed him to the plight of the dog.

"Never mind me Clem, see to the dog, will you." Her command was accompanied by a shrug of the shoulders directed more at her own perceived incompetence than at Clem's delay in tending to the dog. Clem applied the experience he had gained from working with the ponies at the colliery. He knew that despite the dog's anguish, he would have to take the softly, softly approach.

He moved slowly forward, talking gently and calmly to the dog, maintaining an assertive tone to his voice as he did so. When he reached the dog, he didn't immediately direct his attention to the trapped and bleeding paw, but sought to reassure the animal by stroking its head. At first it bared its teeth and emitted a low throaty growl but its apprehension soon subsided and Clem, still talking in a low but firm voice, turned his attention to the snare. He moved his hand carefully down from the head to the paw, all the time maintaining contact with the dog's body. He gently shifted its paw to apply some slack to the wire. The wire had sliced through the flesh just below the knee and he would have to ease it back out in order to slip the noose off.

"You'll have to help me," he beckoned to Florence to come over. "I'll hold his head and mouth while you slacken the noose and slip it off." Florence winced but she wasn't about to debate the methodology or division of labour suggested by Clem. She had observed him slipping the noose from around the necks of rabbits and felt sure she could do it just as well. "Make sure that the wire stays slack," he instructed. Florence became mildly annoyed.

"I can do it Clem, stop mithering will you?"

Clem adjusted his position and crouched at the head of the dog to allow Florence access to its paw. Her command of the situation was growing.

"Let me know when you're ready." He placed one hand at the back of the dog's head to prevent it from jerking free and cupped his other hand around its snout, all the while talking softly and reassuringly to it. At first it twitched nervously but then accepted its confinement and relaxed.

"Right... Now. Do it, quick Flori." She stroked the upper part of the trapped leg for a few seconds then grabbed it firmly, hooked her finger in the wire and slipped the noose open and pulled the paw out. The dog's body convulsed violently and it sprang up onto its hind legs before collapsing onto the ground.

Florence squealed with delight as the child took over from the woman. "Got it. Look I got it." Clem's admiration for her had reached new heights.

"Well done lass, well done."

The woman took over again.

"Look, he's still bleeding." She grabbed the tea towel from the basket and, with a sudden surge of strength fuelled by a rush of adrenalin, she ripped a strip off, down its full-length. Clem was soaring amidst the clouds. She wrapped the cloth tightly around the bleeding paw whilst Clem maintained his grip on the dog's head and snout. Then with a sudden sense of confusion she asked, "What now?"

"We'll have to take him home with us." The statement wasn't prompted by any rational assessment of the situation, it just tumbled from his lips.

"And then what?" Florence's grasp of the situation was becoming more apparent than Clem's.

"Well, we can't just leave him here, can we. He's probably from the village anyway. We'll take him home and get him right, Mam won't mind. Just a few days, till his leg gets better. Meantime I'll ask about and see if I can't find who he belongs to. If we hurry we'll still 'ave time to get over to your Mam's with this rabbit." She gave him a glance of acknowledgement. "C'mon then, best be off."

Clem lifted the dog and slung it under his armpit whilst Florence wiped the blood from her hands with the remainder of the tea towel, before discarding it in the shrubbery. She lifted the basket and marched off towards the village with a feeling of total satisfaction.

"Dare say he was chasing rabbits in the night. He's not very old. Still got a lot to learn by the looks of it," suggested Clem.

"Might be he's a stray, a runaway. Doesn't look much like a house dog to me. He's dead scruffy and skinny-like and if he was chasing rabbits he must've been hungry. Like as not he belongs to nobody." Clem considered Florence's observations for a few minutes as they walked down the hill.

"If nobody claims him then, we'll 'ave to keep him," he replied in a decisive tone. Florence was more cautious.

"You'd best wait and see what your Mam 'as to say about that won't you. When all's said and done, she's the one who'll have to look after it," she mussed for a few seconds. "Wonder if he's got a name. I'd like to choose one for him," again she paused and pondered.

Meanwhile Clem interceded, "What about Stupid?" His suggestion was, not surprisingly, treated with the contempt it deserved. Florence delighted in her quick and imaginative response.

"Don't be daft Clem folk'll get the two o' you mixed up."

She held her basket out at her side and gripped her hat in place as she started to skip and trot off down the hill in front of Clem. He could only marvel at her spontaneity and liberty of body and spirit. She left words trailing in her wake waiting for Clem to intercept them as he followed on behind.

"Lucky! We'll call him Lucky." The sound of glee still lingered in amongst her words and Clem wasn't about to argue with her choice. He fired a statement of confirmation back at her which sped through the air and skipped and trotted into her ears.

"Right then, Lucky it is."

Florence reached the top of Bank Street several seconds before Clem. He was fearful of jolting the dog and causing it more pain, otherwise he would undoubtedly have exerted his physical superiority and sped past her like an athlete competing in a race. She capitalised on the situation.

"You're nowt but an old codger, you are. Beat you dead easy. Lucky could have beat you even with his bad leg." She waited until Clem reached her location, then she lent forward to stroke the dog, and pursed her lips in an expression of affection. "Couldn't you Lucky? Beat an old codger like him. Yes you could." The dog looked up at her with its pathetic big brown eyes as if to enquire why Florence's speech had suddenly adopted the tone of a simple-minded dimwit.

Then it turned its attention to the bag which was hanging from Clem's other hand, intent on giving the contents a closer examination.

"You'll have to take the rabbit," insisted Clem, struggling to keep the one from the other. "He's a powerful mite for such a skinny little wretch." Florence took hold of the bag and its contents and led the way back to Clem's house, hotly pursued by the twitching snout of the short-haired mongrel which was precariously restrained under Clem's arm.

As they turned into the back lane, they were confronted by the sight of Jimmy and Tom arguing over a game of marbles, which was rapidly degenerating into a rough-an-tumble. Clem immediately exerted his authority.

"Steady up you two, else you'll both get a clip round the ear 'ole." The argument ceased, not, it has to be said, due to the intervention of Clem. Jimmy had noticed the presence of his sister. He broke free from the tangle of arms which had embroiled the two feuding youngsters and ran up to Florence, tugging at his ruffled clothing as he did so.

"Eh up Sis. What's in t' basket then?" The absence of the discarded tea towel enabled him to glimpse the contents as he approached. "Cor! Currant buns! Mrs Clary's sent some currant buns Tom." Mrs Clary was the cook at the Cropton household and was occasionally able to supply Florence with various items of home-baking by eking out the ingredients of batches of baking and producing a surplus of the final product. There was also the odd occasion when visitors to the house were offered an assortment of cakes and buns, some of which remained uneaten and were returned to the kitchen as leftovers. It would not be acceptable to retain them and serve them up the following day since they would no longer be fresh. So on this occasion, Florence was in possession of a dozen assorted fruit buns which were acquired through the means previously mentioned.

After fending off attempts by Jimmy and Tom to acquire part of the contents of the basket, Florence and Clem entered the house. It wasn't until then that the two boys noticed the stricken animal under Clem's armpit.

"Eh up! What you got there, our Clem?" Clem turned his head to peer behind himself intimating that, since his charge had not been noticed before, his younger brother must have been referring to something else.

"Under your arm Clem."

He turned back to address Tom. "Oh you mean Lucky." His faked surprise was wasted on the boys.

"No, I mean that furry thing on your 'ed." Tom pointed to Clem's hair and burst out laughing, his ridicule supported by Jimmy.

"Just watch it you two." Clem was about to lunge forward when be noticed the smile on Florence's face and checked his progress. "He got his paw caught in one o' the snares," he explained as the laughter subsided.

He moved towards the hearth and placed the shivering dog on the floor. His mother had been a passive observer up until then, waiting for Clem to reveal his intentions. He noticed the enquiring glance in her eyes and felt obliged to explain the reason for the presence of his new charge.

"I'd laid the snare over a fresh burrow on one o' the warrens and he must have got the scent. Probably started scratchin' or sumat to get into the hole and snagged the wire with his paw."

"Just as well he didn't stick his snout in first for a good sniff. Could've finished up with it round his nose or worse still round his neck." Florence reached up and placed her hand at her throat as she finished the sentence. "So we've decided to call him Lucky because that's what he is, isn't he?" May was sympathetic, but also quite sceptical.

"Well, I'll be blowed but I'm not so sure he's that Lucky to have ended up here. These two'll have him chasing his tail around. There's nowt so sure as that."

"Well, I couldn't just leave him there, could I?"

The plea of justification was met with a few seconds' silence then his mother spoke again.

"Better take a look at him then hadn't we." The moment's tension dissolved and the group set about finding fresh dressings and ointment to treat the wound. After establishing that it wasn't actually too bad and that the wire had only severed the skin due to the protection of the dog's hair, Clem and Florence suggested that they ought to be on their way. They left a bun each for Jimmy and Tom before setting off to deliver the remainder, along with the rabbit, to Florence's mother.

Whilst Clem and Florence undertook their weekly visit to Florence's mother, Jimmy and Tom would head off to the countryside on the outskirts of the village. This area was not common land, it was all owned by Lord Hase-Lore. He had allowed unrestricted access to certain areas, in the guise of a gesture of generosity, to the miners and their families. In reality, however, he had simply fenced off an area of disused grazing and shrub land, around the village to accommodate the expansion of the slag tips and the construction of new housing for his growing workforce. Since there was infinitely more profit in the mining of coal than the grazing of livestock, it was not a difficult gesture to make. It also reduced the likelihood of potential poaching since there was a fairly large population of rabbits on the 'accessed' land.

He had also been careful not to include access to the river in the neighbouring valley, again under the guise of a benevolent act. The tributary at the head of Connington valley had been diverted to the next valley in order to reduce the possibility of flooding in the mine. This meant that there was no access to any water which wasn't behind the fenceline and consequently no common fishing courses. There was fishing available to the miners and their families but they had to pay a levy for the privilege and were restricted to a course of water a good way further down the neighbouring valley. The best fishing was kept within the fenceline by a series of dikes and weirs which contained the breeding-grounds. The few fish which were available further down the river were there more by accident than design. It was a tempting proposition for the courageous to venture beyond the fencing and try their luck with the gamekeeper.

Clem had confided in Tom about the occasional trip that he and his father had made over the fence in the past when the getting of coal had become difficult due to geological problems and the wages had been reduced as a consequence. As a direct result of hearing about these daring escapades and especially since they had included his father, Tom had developed an urge to attempt the task himself. The fact that he had never tickled a trout in his life before did not deter him from his quest. He would often discuss the proposition with Jimmy who had an equally burning ambition to impress his mother by presenting her with the main ingredients of a fish supper. He also considered it his duty, being the eldest male of the family, to at least occasionally assume the role of provider to the family.

It was during their jaunts into the countryside that they plotted and schemed about how they would fulfil their ambitions. As they cleared the houses and emerged into the warm blue summer air, they gradually changed from childish eleven year olds into daring adventurers. As soon as they felt that they had put a suitable distance between themselves and the village, they each produced from their pockets a well-used sling. These weapons were, for the boys, essential prerequisites to facilitate their transition from boyhood to manhood. They gathered stones as they trudged up the hill and turned their pockets into bulging ammunition belts.

Every now and again they would encounter a suitable target – it might have been a tree-stump, a fence-post or a living one such as a bird or a rabbit. Sometimes they would let loose a volley which invariably missed the target, and then move on to the next. Or they would lock onto one and move progressively closer until the chances of hitting the target outweighed those of missing. A hit for one would prompt the other to suggest that he was too close and therefore the hit didn't count. As a result of constant practice they had become reasonably proficient with the sling and occasionally even scored hits on birds and rabbits when they were stealthy enough to approach within ten or fifteen feet of the poor unsuspecting creatures. Fortunately for the targets, this proximity was not a regular occurrence and hits which caused any visible injury to the wildlife of the surrounding area were few and far between.

Before very long the two lads had reached the outer fringes of the accessible land. The fencing which signified this point was more in the way of a marker than an insurmountable obstacle. It was merely a line of wooden poles driven into the ground at regular intervals and linked together by half a dozen lines of wire. The height was no more than four feet but the main deterrent to crossing this barrier lay within the text written on the signposts which appeared, periodically, along its length.

'TRESPASSERS WILL BE SHOT by order of the estate of his Lordship, Lord Hase-Lore.'

What other invitation would be needed for two such intrepid adventurers as Jimmy and Tom? In reality no one had actually ever been shot for perpetrating the misdemeanour although some intruders had been shot at by his Lordship's gamekeeper and aides. Anyone caught was usually prosecuted and always found guilty. The penalty was normally a fine and/or a short term in prison; naturally if the offender worked for his Lordship he would be dismissed from his position. The only instance of anyone actually being shot was when a poacher had been caught in the act and he had died of his wounds shortly afterwards.

Poachers were also prosecuted and found guilty but they received much harsher sentences. Imprisonment for several months or years was not an uncommon punishment, although it was not only until fairly recently that poachers could face the prospect of being hanged when found guilty.

Reports of such events were few and far between and Jimmy and Tom, although aware of the consequences, remained undeterred by the prospect. They regularly made excursions onto the estate proper and down to the river, keeping to the protection of the shrubbery and bushes and woods. They knew that poachers were nocturnal creatures and that the gamekeeper was at his most alert during the night. Still they plotted and schemed their plans in their *naïveté*, blissfully ignorant of the real consequences which might result from such an act of foolishness.

Chapter Six

Jimmy had only been over to visit the one-roomed tenement, into which his mother had moved, the previous Sunday. She had taken a job in a laundry in Rotherham town shortly after moving out of Connington Main, and managed to juggle her childcare arrangements with her sister. The elder of the two girls was attending school and would join various other unaccompanied mites on the journey to school from the tenement and from school to her aunty's house. The other daughter and her tiny brother would spend the day at their aunty's house, whilst Martha was at work.

Untidy as these arrangements were, they proved to be marginally better than the two families living under one roof. At night the three children and their mother would have to share a double bed, which was quite a suitable arrangement during cold weather. The arrangement, for all its obvious deprivation, relied heavily on Florence's contribution to the household income and the goodwill of Martha's sister and her husband in the form of free childcare.

As always, Jimmy had promised to present his mother with the rabbit which would signify his manhood and locate him firmly at the head of the family. He had emerged from the room somewhat despondent since most of the conversation had centred around the impending birthday of Florence who, along with Clem had accompanied Jimmy on his visit. He had grown weary of the innuendoes directed at the relationship between his two companions, and felt a degree of rejection, which made him all the more determined to go through with his promise.

His mother had made various intimations to Florence regarding the need to marry and furnish her with grandchildren, thereby offering her some distraction from the hardships of her existence. The concept of the passing of time was even broached.

"Before it's too late," was the exact statement. Of course this was purposely ambiguous, since she had drawn no distinction as to the identity of person for whom it might be 'too late'. Florence wasn't sure whether she meant that at seventeen she herself was heading for 'the shelf' or that her mother was questioning her own ageing process. Whatever the inference, Florence was not going to allow herself to be persuaded or cajoled into a marriage which she was not herself contemplating.

Having felt rebuffed by the concentration of conversation on the subject of Florence's birthday and her future, Jimmy was all the more determined to upstage her, only instead of a rabbit, the offering would take on a far more prestigious form, that of a fish. He had considered that a fish would have more impact since it was a more difficult commodity to obtain and required a greater degree of risk. Tom's assistance would be needed, of course, both for practical and supportive purposes. The acquisition of the bounty would be made today, being the night before Florence's birthday, so that presentation could be made on that very day thereby usurping her importance and ensuring maximum impact. The two friends had already established their plan of action several times, the insertion of a date and time for the expedition served to complete the preparations.

There were a couple of factors which supported the timing of their expedition. First of all, with Florence's birthday being on the Thursday, the venture would be undertaken during the week. The chance of detection would be diminished at that time since the estate workers were at their most alert during the weekends when most of the poaching was carried out.

The day had been a particularly overcast one and although there was no immediate indication of rain, nor was there any prospect of the cloud-cover dispersing. This would result in the obliteration of any moonlight which might expose their nocturnal adventure. In reality, the two intrepid hunters had not considered the consequences of being apprehended during the execution of their task – it was for them, an exciting, harmless prank.

As is the way within insular communities, various tales of daring deeds were told to bolster the cultural status of various members. Connington was no exception in this area. Clem's revelations regarding his own excursions with his father which he had imparted to Tom were in the main, gestures of bravado. He had, actually only once, ventured with his father onto the estate to procure brown trout for the dinner table. The venture had been a complete failure and although they had escaped with little more than dented pride, Clem had seen fit to distort the truth in his recollections. Not only had he himself successfully caught trout, using the 'tickling' technique, but his ambitious narratives had suggested that he had achieved success, on more than one occasion.

Naturally, Tom had retold these stories to Jimmy and the two had repeated them at school to their fellow classmates. The 'snowball' effect had been activated. By the time the interaction had run its course, everyone else's brothers, uncles and fathers had also been party to some form of poaching activity on the estate. Then, naturally, there were those children who had the uncanny ability to make up stories on the spot, the high number of their school pals who had themselves, allegedly, undertaken poaching expeditions only serving to fuel their own determination. Had the two scrutinised the data more carefully, they would have realised that their own expedition would have been pointless since there would have been no trout left in the river to poach.

Bolstered by the knowledge that so many other of the male members of the community were experienced and successful poachers, the two finalised their plans and proceeded to put them into effect. On the night of the mission they had retired early and waited patiently for the rest of the household to retire. In the meantime they laid out their sparse equipment on the bed and inspected it with the military thoroughness of two eleven year olds. Their 'combat' kit comprised of two balaclavas, one fishing-knife, one length of string, two well-used slings and two of Clem's rabbit sacks, one of which was filled with the other items. After hiding the filled sack under the bed, they pulled on their nightshirts over their clothes and climbed under the blanket into bed. They knew that they would have to wait a while and assured each other that neither would succumb to tiredness and fall asleep.

Clem had arranged to take the following day off from work since he had set himself the task of proposing to Florence, as promised, on her seventeenth birthday. He had taken the opportunity to visit the pub to partake of a quantity of courage-boosting beverage in order to support his endeavour. Though he hadn't intended to get drunk, the boys hoped that he would have consumed sufficient beer for him to fall quickly into a deep sleep, thereby ensuring their undetected exit from the bedroom.

When Clem did appear, not particularly drunk but certainly mellow, the two boys were fast asleep. So much for military precision! Fortunately, Clem tried not to disturb them. This was an act of consideration, which was usually unsuccessful even when he had indulged in only a light drinking session. Jimmy woke up, but was aware enough not to alert Clem to the situation. He waited.

Eventually the sounds which accompanied Clem's preparations for sleep, some of which seemed quite strange at times to Jimmy, subsided. In their place emerged the regular deep inhaling and exhaling which signifies the onset of sleep. During the previous few minutes of waiting, Jimmy had felt the build-up of nervous energy rising from within his stomach. For the first time during the meticulous planning of the past few weeks, he felt the onset of trepidation and fear. He embarked on a mental examination of the situation. It would be a simple matter to roll over and forget all about it. Tom was still fast asleep and would presumably remain so if he decided not to wake him up. He considered the repercussions of doing nothing.

In the morning they would wake up and face the criticism, each of the other, regarding whose fault it was that the expedition had failed. The inevitable result would be an acceptance of both parties that they were both to blame and would therefore both accept responsibility quid pro quo. There would be no perceived guilt applicable to either party so his only problem was reconciling his failure with his own expectations of himself. His personal honour and integrity were at stake.

It was as though it had developed into some sort of primeval tribal ritual act, a purging of his childhood and advancement into his destiny of attaining his manhood. He felt he owed it to his father's memory and needed to prove to his eternal spirit that he could assume the role of provider for the family. Then there was the cultural capital to be gained within the family and the community, his status would be elevated beyond expectation. Considering the youthfulness of the child, he had imposed upon himself a formidable array of influences which be found impossible to reject.

Almost involuntarily, he pressed his elbow into the small of Tom's back which was presently turned towards him, as he lay on his side. Tom's body responded still in the grip of sleep, so the reaction was simply one of a slight shuffle. Jimmy held his breath for a few seconds as though he thought that the sound of his breathing might rouse his friend. Tom hadn't stirred. A feeling of relief came over Jimmy, perhaps this was an omen not to proceed. Tom's negative response was a sign from his dead father's spirit to abandon this folly. He didn't need to prove himself, it wasn't necessary. He felt the nervous energy subside, the responsibility for the decision removed from his inexperienced shoulders and carried away into the night by the hand of fate.

He raised his arms to place his hands at the back of his head as he laid back, and stared up at the silent shadowy images on the ceiling. As he sighed with relief, his elbow struck something solid. Tom's head. He froze.

"Must've dropped off." He desperately tried to prevent the whisper from entering his head. He even pretended that he didn't hear its drowsy lethargic drone. There was a silence which he wished would last forever, his stomach muscles starting to tighten up again. "You ready then?" This time the utterance was a more alert whisper. Jimmy squeezed his eyelids tightly together and clenched his fists at the back of his neck. He could hear a groan of despair inside his head. He heard himself whisper a reply.

"Been lying 'ere ages, waiting for you to wek up." The agitation was obvious but it was not due to Tom having been asleep, as he assumed. Still, he apologised softly.

"Well, I'm sorry then."

"Doesn't matter. No 'arm done." Jimmy was gradually coming to terms with the situation, he just wished that he hadn't been awake long enough to have second thoughts. "Best be getting off then."

The two of them quietly and gingerly eased themselves out of bed and removed their nightshirts. Tom retrieved the sack containing the 'equipment' before the two of them exited the room and descended the stairs. As Tom pulled the door to, he listened for any sign of his older brother stirring. The sound of inhaling and exhaling was steady, deep and regular and there was no indication that Clem had been disturbed. They carried their boots in their hands in order to minimise the noise as they descended the wooden-treaded staircase.

When they reached the backdoor they quietly put on their boots. As they did so, a head lifted from the midst of a small pile of old rags which lay on the floor in the corner of the scullery, a snout twitched enquiringly and a pair of big brown eyes scrutinised the proceedings before returning to its previous position on top of a pair of outstretched paws. Jimmy opened the backdoor before realising that they had to negotiate the flagstones of the backyard. They left the door ajar while they removed their boots in order to carry them again, and eventually proceeded into the night, closing the door behind them. The two lads turned to one another and silently acknowledged the successful completion of phase one of the operation. Nothing was said as they strode cautiously along Bank Street to the fields at the end of the terrace.

Jimmy glanced up at the dark night sky, the nervous energy in his gut gradually being replaced by the bolstering effect of adrenalin. The cloud cover had held and even though their eyes had adjusted to the darkness, they could see no farther than ten feet or so ahead of themselves. Having traced their path many times during rehearsals they knew instinctively which route to take. As they went along, they began gathering suitable pieces of ammunition, in the form of pebbles and small stones, for their slings.

Now that they were out of audible range of the village, they considered it safe to resume communications with one another, though they kept the volume down to a strained whisper. Macho bravado fuelled by adrenalin was beginning to emerge.

"This is gunna be a doddle." The tone of the remark almost suggested a question rather than a statement of fact, but any linguistic analysis was squashed by the emerging confidence of the two lads. Jimmy's reply to Tom's statement was more to confirm his own growing nonchalance towards the proceedings.

"Wonder what time it is then?" he said casually, knowing full well that there was time enough to undertake the expedition twice over.

Within the space of half an hour they had reached the fence but not even the encounter of this significant psychological boundary gave them cause for concern. They paused only to negotiate the flimsy obstruction and were soon heading off down the other side of the hill into the valley below. Getting to the river would take them about twenty minutes, coming back up would take a little longer, about half an hour.

There was no well-trodden path on the estate side of the fence which served to heighten the excitement of the two lads. It was as though they were the first humans to enter the wilderness beyond the fence. Even though they had made the trip down to the river on several previous occasions in the daylight, their current foray became all the more exhilarating in the dark. They varied their pace depending on the lie of the terrain – where the bank became steep, they would scurry down, sometimes sliding almost out of control as tufts of grass broke loose beneath their boots – when they encountered cover, such as a clump of bushes or shrubbery or a cluster of trees, they would pause in its midst to catch their breath and to check their direction of travel.

It wasn't difficult to maintain the right track. After about fifteen minutes they could hear the sound of flowing water as long as they followed the sound and kept going downwards, they would eventually reach the river. Suddenly there was a shriek of surprise immediately in front of Jimmy and he froze in his tracks. He could just recognise the outline of Tom's back, through the gloom a few feet in front of him. Tom had also stopped moving, almost simultaneously, and with the halt in progress, came the first rush of fear to Tom's senses. They had been discovered, Jimmy tried desperately to suppress the thought but it kept surging to the forefront of his mind.

"Why wasn't Tom moving? What was happening?" He took a deep breath, grasped at his fear and wrenched it from the back of his throat.

"Tom! What's up Tom?" There was no reply from the figure in front of him, it just turned towards him in one swift movement. Jimmy needed no further prompting – he dropped the sack, dug his heels into the ground, whipped himself round and started scrambling up the bank.

"Jimmy! You silly beggar, 'old up a minute." The instruction felt like a warm blanket being thrown over him and wrapping him up in a safe cosy bed. He collapsed with relief.

"What the 'eck's up wi' thee Tom? Scared the living daylights out o' me you did."

"It wor a bird or sumat, one o' them grouse things I think. It just flew up in front o' me from out o' t' bushes, nearly pissed misen, I can tell thee."

"Me too, you pillock. Where's the sack? I just let go on it." Tom scanned the ground around his feet and bent down.

"Got it. Come on then, ger off your backside and we'll ger on down t' river."

A few minutes later the intrepid pair were on the riverbank, having progressed gingerly down responding to the slightest sounds *en route*. They found a spot a little further on, under the cover of a cluster of trees which overhung the water.

"Right then, best get at it." The note of uncertainty was perplexingly obvious for Jimmy to pick up.

"You sure you can do this trout ticklin' thing Tom?"

"Course I can, easy peasy. Our Clem told me exactly what to do. An' he's done it loads o' times." Jimmy's acknowledgement and feeling of reassurance was more self-imposed than generated by Tom's comments.

"What's it taste like anyway, this 'ere trout fish?" The question was a genuine enquiry and not in any way meant to test out the truth of Clem's claims. It did however generate a sensation of puzzlement inside Tom's mind.

If Jimmy could have observed the expression on his face through the gloom, he might have detected some cause for concern. For all the fish Clem had supposedly caught, he couldn't actually remember eating any. Standing as he was on the bank of the river in the middle of the night, trespassing on Lord Hase-Lore's estate, he wasn't about to allow even the slightest semblance of doubt enter his head.

"'Ard to say really, it dun't taste like rabbit though," he paused, "'ant had any for ages anyway, so I can't really remember." He almost convinced himself that he must have had some trout at some time in the distant past but had forgotten about it. Out of expediency, he diverted attention away from the subject of taste and towards the task at hand.

"Right I'll get in the water an' tickle the trout. You stand 'ere next to me on t' bank and catch 'em as I throw 'em out." Jimmy was impressed by the use of the plural in Tom's statement. He had visions of an abundance of fish flying through the air and cascading into his arms as he tried desperately to cram them into the totally inadequate sack. "Bloody 'ell. Water's freezin." The spell was broken.

"Keep your voice down, will you? You could wake the bloody dead." Jimmy had pinched the cliché from his mother's wide repertoire which she used to call upon when reprimanding him for various acts of misconduct. Tom acclimatised himself to the temperature of the water and spread his feet apart before bending forward and slowly lowering his hand into it.

"Right shur up now else you'll scare t' fish away." Jimmy concurred, assuming what he considered to be an appropriate catching posture. They waited in silence. Tom peered into the water and Jimmy peered at Tom. They maintained their respective poses for a few minutes until

"Gotcha!" Tom thrust his cupped hands through the water and scooped upwards as he turned his body towards Jimmy who responded immediately. He reached out his hands and caught the fish in a crescendo of cascading water and euphoria and immediately dropped it. He lunged forward just in time to see the slimy creature slithering down the bank and into the river, laughing all the way in. "Bloody 'ell Jimmy." Tom once again illustrated his semantic economy.

"'T were like a bloody piece o' soap," Jimmy insisted, "slimy thing just wriggled out o' mi grip." They looked at each other, bemused and frustrated. "I know I'll catch 'em in mi shirt." The use of the plural had now become a matter of course. He dragged his shirt over his head and cradled it in his hands. "Come on then, ger on wi' it." The whispering had long since broken loose from its restraints and they were now communicating at the volume of normal speech.

Tom resumed his posture and Jimmy returned to his waxwork-like catching position, the two of them waited impatiently. After a few long minutes Jimmy spoke.

"Like as not, bloody things warned its mates off."

"Don't be stupid. More like it's gone to fetch 'em round, so they can all 'ave a good laugh."

The volume of speech had once again reduced to that of a whisper, possibly a subconscious reaction to the subdued sound of the flowing water as it wound its way between the riverbanks. Jimmy's thoughts began to wander as he considered the reaction of his mother on receiving the trophy in the morning. He felt sure that his offering would signify acceptance that he was able and capable of assuming the coveted role of provider within the family. His position in the community would be elevated, and he would overtake Tom in the scramble to achieve manhood. He would be recognised and acknowledged as the 'man' who took on his new responsibilities with great authority.

"Now!"

Jimmy was suddenly jolted from his ruminations and only just regained his composure in time to glimpse the growing shape of a fish flying through the air towards his head. With the sharp, instinctive reactions that only children possess, he rocked back and threw up his shirt-cloaked arms, towards the homing missile. The spray of cold water, which accompanied its trajectory, showered his face and naked upper body. He felt the thump of the fish as it fell into his grasp. He lowered his arms to the ground, engulfing his charge in the sodden shirt as he did so. The garment had assumed a life of its own, wriggling, thrashing and contorting in an effort to throw itself back into the river.

Tom had followed the fish's flight path and was grappling, alongside Jimmy, with the shirt soon after he had grounded the thing.

"Keep it in the shirt, keep it in the shirt." The direction was totally unnecessary since Jimmy had fallen upon his captive and had virtually covered it with the whole of his body. Had Tom not placed himself between the grappling duo and the river, the roll of captor and captive would almost certainly have been reversed as Jimmy's efforts left him precariously poised on the edge of the riverbank.

Eventually the pandemonium subsided as the shirt's objections to its confinement diminished. They slowly released their grip around it and retreated, remaining ready to spring forward again as it persisted in giving the occasional twitch of defiance.

"Blinkin' 'eck!"

"Little devil!"

Several more expletives were uttered whilst the duo regained its composure and lifted the bedraggled garment to examine their spoils. The fish lay motionless, its death throes over, with its mouth open and its eyes bulging from their sockets.

"Is it a big un?" Jimmy enquired. Naturally, never having encountered a brown trout before, he was unable to gauge the level of satisfaction he should show. He looked at Tom and waited for his definitive assessment of the fish's size. Tom felt cornered, he fumbled to construct a sentence in his mind which would relieve him of the possibility of making the wrong judgement. All he could come up with was,

"Not bad. 'Ard to say 'till we catch another and match 'em up." The tone of his voice was unconvincing, but the renewed prospect of obtaining a second handsome trophy was enough to redirect Jimmy's attention away from the inadequacy of the answer.

"Come on then," Jimmy's enthusiasm was re-emerging and he grabbed at the trout, intending to remove it from his shirt and stuff it in the sack. He had forgotten how difficult the previous one had been to handle and it insisted on slithering free of his grasp each time he tried to accomplish the transfer. Tom intervened.

"Come 'ere," he had regained his perceived authority. "I'll hold the sack open, you slide it in off of your shirt. You don't 'ave to try to pick it up." Tommy obeyed gratefully and they had soon resumed their 'catching' positions ready to receive another victim.

It was some considerable time before they were able to capture another fish. Tom had encountered a couple of wily ones which had proved unreceptive to his attentions and managed to escape. By the time the second trout had given up the ghost and been fumbled into the sack, they had grown concerned about the passing of time.

Each trout weighed between one and a half and two pounds, either one of which would have provided a meal for the Gallagher family. Since Tom had no idea what size or weight of fish would be suitable for a family meal, he insisted that Jimmy should take both of them to his mother's later that day. Jimmy's shirt was in no fit state for wearing due to its dampness and the pungent odour that had begun to emerge from it. However, the night was a warm one with the cloud cover holding the humid air down at ground level and Jimmy was not concerned with the exposure of the upper part of his body. He stuffed his sodden, stinking shirt into the other sack, with the string and knife, which Tom had volunteered to carry whilst Jimmy slung the trout-filled sack over his shoulder.

They were well chuffed with the night's work and looked forward to the day ahead. "Told you it'd be easy," Tom confirmed. He dwelt on his words as a sign of reassurance for his own misgivings, as much as to confirm the proposition to Jimmy. Encouraged by their success and keen to return to the notional safety of the other side of the fence, they scrambled with some urgency up the hillside towards the snarling, slavering, growling outburst which suddenly erupted in front of them. They froze in their tracks, terrified by the blood-curdling rage which suddenly blocked their retreat to safety. They could barely distinguish the words which formed the directive that accompanied the ferocious outburst.

"Stay just where you are, you two." The deep-throated command bludgeoned its way through their ears and into their startled, panic-stricken minds. Their reaction was purely instinctive, stimulated by the terror which engulfed them. The instant their minds had assimilated the situation before them, they fled, each closely pursued by their own horrified screams.

By some quirk of fate, each flight assumed a different direction. Tom scrambled to his left and Jimmy turned on his heels back towards the river. There was no reasoning behind the choice of direction, it just happened. Jimmy immediately found that his legs were unable to keep pace with his acceleration, the top half of his body rapidly overtook the bottom half and he found himself tumbling uncontrollably down the slope. Then he stopped abruptly.

His mind was urging his body onward, but being barely perceptive of his predicament, he had not yet realised that he had rolled into a thicket of bushes. As he struggled to free himself, his orientation returned only to stimulate his awareness of the terror which had pursued him down the hill. First, the hysterical sound of homicidal mania, immediately followed by the growing shape of a monster hound, emerging from the gloom and baring down on his prostrate figure.

Jimmy was trapped, not only by the physical restraints of the bushes, but also by the paralysis imposed upon him by the terror which had gripped his whole being. All he could do was look on, wide-eyed and open-mouthed; he wanted to scream, but his paralysis prevented it. In an instant his whole frame of vision was filled by a display of shining white teeth and bulging black eyes. There was no escape – in seconds his head would be crushed by the evil power of the jaws which had opened to receive their victim. He started to cry convulsively as he felt the stench of the hot, foul breath of his nemesis on his face. He shut his eyes, tight-closed, in a final futile attempt to obliterate the inevitable, and waited.

Jimmy didn't see the monster dog stumble, its charge halted in midflight. Nor did he perceive it turn its attention to the source of the pain, which was now afflicting its ear. He hadn't noticed the sharp alien sounds which had intermingled with the savage snarling, and growling of the monster dog. With his eyes closed he couldn't have seen, in the corner of his peripheral vision, the shape of something smaller flying through the air from his right. It appeared to latch onto the ear of the monster dog and pull its head across and away from its target as it tumbled to the ground. The missile, meanwhile, had resumed its feet and embarked on a deluge of verbal abuse, in canine language, hurled at the monster dog. The massive hulk lunged across towards the source of this new irritation but inevitably its lolloping pace was no match for Lucky's swift, twisting motion. He darted backwards and forwards taunting and teasing, snapping and snarling, all the while drawing the monster dog further away from its original victim. Within minutes, the two adversaries had dissolved into the gloom further down the hill. All that signified their proximity was the dwindling sound of their doggy interaction.

Scratched and bleeding from the effect of hitting the bushes at speed, Jimmy quickly seized the opportunity to head off in the opposite direction to the pandemonium further down the hill. There were no incredulous expletives to be uttered, all he felt at that moment in time was a numbed feeling of relief. He had long since relinquished any attachment he previously had to the sack and the fish inside it and had no inclination to search for it. As he hauled his exhausted body back up the hill, he could detect evidence of a further commotion higher up and to his right.

He couldn't distinguish any meaning in the words, just that it was obviously more than a heated discussion between a child and an adult. He immediately altered his course and headed for the source of the new sounds, the content of which was rapidly becoming discernible.

"You're coming with me you, little brat. I'll show you what we do with poachers around here." The word 'poachers' amplified and repeated itself inside Jimmy's mind and for the first time, he realised the magnitude of their predicament. He proceeded forward gingerly, searching all the while for any cover in which he could conceal himself and eventually he reached a point where he could identify the shapes of the two adversaries.

The gamekeeper had gripped Tom's upper arm, and was beating him with his stick whilst Tom in response was swinging the sack at the gamekeeper's head with little effect other than to increase the rage of his captor. Jimmy's actions were now driven by a resurgence of adrenalin, accompanied by the need for both of them to escape this nightmare. He thrust his hand into his trouser pocket and pulled out his sling along with a couple of reasonable-sized stones.

Without considering the consequences of his actions, he loaded his sling and lunged forward into firing-range. Jimmy's sudden appearance startled the gamekeeper but not as much as the stone that hurtled against his cheekbone. He released his grip on Tom as be reached up to attend to his injury. Tom didn't need the encouragement screamed at him by Jimmy and he immediately sprinted over to join his friend as the two of them charged relentlessly up the hill and away.

"Come back here you little brats. I'll get you for this," the threat had nowhere near enough pace to catch up with the fleeing youths. The only sound they could hear as they reached the fence, on the edge of the estate was the doggy interaction below. Tired deep-throated barking interrupted by excited, teasing yelps.

"What the 'ecks that?" Tom's enquiry was enclosed in an envelope of sharp, deep breaths as they scrambled through the fence and continued down the other side of the hill.

"Lucky, it's our Lucky." Jimmy's reply was accompanied by the same gasps to fill his lungs as Tom's. "He saved my life. That monster was just about to 'ave me and 'e jumped in to save me. Bit its ear I think an' then took off down t' river. That monster just took off after 'im."

"Bloody 'ell!" Tom's response stimulated an echo from Jimmy.

"Bloody 'ell!" The exclamations were accompanied by huge sighs of relief. They had escaped, not only the clutches of the maniac gamekeeper, but also the slavering jaws of the monster dog.

"Must 'ave got out while we were tekin our shoes off at the back door and followed us down to t' river," Tom's assumption was acknowledged by Jimmy who turned to him and nodded his agreement.

It was not an unusual occurrence for Lucky to take the opportunity, when possible, to venture out into the hills. After his rescue he had been adopted by the Baxters who made feeble attempts to locate his owner and soon reconciled themselves, not too reluctantly, to keeping the new addition to the family. Tom and Jimmy would regularly take him out with them but on several occasions, when they were involved in plotting and scheming, they would leave him behind. This was not a problem for a dog which had spent the early part of his life fending for himself.

At the first opportunity, he would escape the confines of the house and follow the scent of his young friends. He would never make his proximity known to them but would just maintain a reasonable distance and go about his own business, sniffing around the rabbit warrens and investigating the inhabitants of the clusters of flora in the vicinity. He would invariably make his presence known as the two lads returned back to the village but at this point any reprimand would be futile. So, it seemed that this particular night the dog's covert presence had saved Jimmy from a certain savage mauling, or worse.

The two didn't dwell on their experience, though the relief at having escaped was tinged by regret for the loss of their trophies. The release of all their physical and nervous energy had left them drained and exhausted – all they wanted was to reach the sanctuary of home and crawl into their bed. They didn't even consider the safety or eventual outcome of Lucky's decoy activities. The commotion behind them melted into the blackness of the night as they put more and more distance between themselves and their little adventure.

Chapter Seven

The two lads were awoken a few hours later by a barrage of demands from May and Clem, who leant menacingly over either side of the bed. May was clutching a sodden, slimy, stinking shirt and holding it with demonstrative venom in front of Jimmy's face, whilst Clem was emptying the remaining contents of his rabbit sack onto the bed on Tom's side.

"What, the 'ecks been happening in the night wi' you two?" Clem's outrage hurled the question from the back of his throat and thrust it angrily into the ears of the two recipients. The two lads, at first shocked out of their sleep, clutched at the blanket as though it could protect them from the ongoing verbal onslaught. Still wrestling to escape from the drowsiness of sleep, they sat up displaying a look of total confusion and disorientation.

As their eyes gradually rediscovered their ability to focus on the images before them, the stark recollection of their nocturnal excursion began to unfold inside their minds. May was growing impatient.

"Well, come on then, just what have you two been up to?" The higher tone of her voice seemed somehow even more menacing than Clem's deep-throated attack. They cowered, desperately trying to achieve some coherence from the jumble of words in their minds, in an attempt to organise for themselves a decipherable sentence. Tom spoke first. It was a pathetic effort.

"What's up? Don't know what you're on about." Jimmy turned his head and looked at his friend in disbelief, a feeling reinforced by the expression on his face. He adopted the Gallagher trait once again (eyes rolled up accompanied by that familiar 'tut' sound).

Tom's mother's response was totally predictable.

"Don't you start acting the goat with me, my lad. I'll knock your block off." Jimmy interrupted with a somewhat more comprehensible though equally unconvincing remark.

"We went to check the snares to mek sure we 'ad some rabbits to tek to mi mam's today," his voice began to tremble as he realised the inadequacy of his statement. Clem's sarcastic reply smacked Jimmy straight between the eyes.

"That's nice," the utterance bounced around inside Jimmy's mind mocking his feeble explanation, "I bet your mam would've liked a couple o' fish flavoured rabbits." He hadn't finished yet, "So how is it that your shirt reeks o' fish then Jimmy?" May's gesture supported Clem's interrogation as she thrust the shirt further towards Jimmy's face.

"Well! We're waiting mi lad,"

Their resistance was, not surprisingly, totally destroyed. They had neither the presence of mind, nor the inclination, to attempt any kind of fabrication of the truth. They retold the events of the night, emphasising at regular intervals that the act of folly had only been undertaken because Jimmy wanted to surprise his mother. The only part of the incident which they omitted was where Jimmy had let loose with his sling at the gamekeeper. There was no conspiracy behind this exclusion, it was as though they had subconsciously wished it hadn't happened, and could somehow erase the incident by declining to mention it.

When their story had ended, May insisted on examining Jimmy's back, she had already noticed several scratches on his arms. The evidence that he had been entangled in bushes was irrefutable. Fortunately, none of the scratches were deep enough to warrant any treatment other than the application of some of Mrs Cook's home-made ointment. Then a realisation occurred to them all although May was the first to translate it into verbal concern.

"So where's Lucky now then?" Her enquiry was met with silence at first. After some consideration Tom answered with another question.

"Hasn't he come home yet then Mam?" Clem's agitation was increasing.

"She wouldn't have asked where he was if he'd got back, would she, stupid?" Jimmy interrupted, detecting the rising tension between the two brothers.

"Well, he's probably still givin' that monster dog the run around. He'll be rate." It was too late, Tom went on the offensive.

"You've some need to talk anyway. All them times you've been down 't river nickin' fish when Dad wor alive." It's funny how the chickens eventually come home to roost.

May stared at Clem with a serious look on her face.

"Have you been telling stories and putting ideas into the lad's head?" Clem's response was feeble and totally inadequate, which is what you would expect from someone who had suddenly had the tables turned against him.

"Blinkin' 'eck it were only a yarn. I didn't think he'd tek it serious like."

Tom was amazed at his own ability to divert the attention, even momentarily, from the main issue and place the blame, or at least some of it, on his brother's shoulders. He even managed a wry smile till he felt the nudge of an elbow in his side. He recovered a serious expression before being discovered.

"Sometimes I think I'd been better off with a pair o' lasses than you two. A lot more sensible than a couple o' stupid lads." The latest discourse had reduced the urgency of the situation and diluted the reprimand. May could see no good reason for pursuing the matter further, apart from to remark. "Well, at least you're all right. You probably got away with it, what with it being so dark an' all and with you leaving the fish behind. Let's just hope Lucky gets back in one piece."

The confession didn't make Clem feel any better – he felt a great responsibility for his charge. After all, it had been he who had suggested that Jimmy come to live with them. The possibility that Florence would blame him for the incident was beginning to take precedence over the other issues.

"Right, best be getting yourselves up then, we'll need an early start to get over to Rotherham."

It had been decided to hold the gathering to celebrate Florence's birthday at the house of her Auntie in Rotherham. Since Mrs Gallagher only lived in one room, they would meet up at her sister's house where there was more space. May and the two lads would go directly there whilst Clem had arranged to meet Florence on the way and escort her to collect her mother before meeting up with the others. It was during his walk with Florence over to Rotherham that he had planned to ask her to marry him. He had hoped that Florence would see the announcement of their engagement as having some therapeutic value for her mother, whose spirit had been extremely low just lately. The opportunity to offer her some good news, he hoped, would be seized by Florence and would encourage her to make a positive response to his proposal.

May didn't have time to wash out Jimmy's soiled shirt, so whilst the two lads were washing and dressing, she filled a bucket with water, sprinkled some salt into it and immersed the shirt, leaving it to soak. She was attending to this chore in the scullery when she heard a welcome sound in the yard outside. Short enquiring yelps interspersed by spasmodic scratching at the door indicated that Lucky had returned from his adventure. A relieved smile quickly replaced the expression of seriousness on her face. She wiped her hands on her apron-front and, as she straightened up from her stooping posture, opened the back door. The smile immediately gave way to a look of astonishment and dismay, which began to embrace the whole of her being. It suppressed any effort she may have been tempted to make to comment on the sight before her.

As she stared out beyond the door frame, she felt the attentions of the dog springing up at her legs, blissfully unaware of any impending trouble. Before she could regain her composure, a deep-throated voice wrapped in a tone of authority commanded her attention.

"This your dog Missus?"

"Yes, why? Is there a problem, officer?"

"We're investigating a very serious complaint. You are Mrs Baxter." This was not a question but a statement of fact. The police officer continued, "And you have a son called Thomas and another lad in your care called James." May could barely utter a response.

"Yes, that's right officer." By this time she was able to distinguish the members of the trio which stood before her. The speaker, a police sergeant, stood in the middle and was flanked by the other two. On his left, stood the local constable, Mr Peters, who was well-known in the village. On the right, stood a man dressed in country tweeds with a large dressing on his left cheek and holding a sack in his right hand.

"I have reason to believe that your son, or the boy in your charge, or for that matter, the two of them, is responsible for a serious physical attack on Mr Darbast, the estate gamekeeper here." He turned to his right and nodded his head towards the tweed suit. "Also that both of the youths are guilty of the criminal act of poaching on

Lord Hase-Lore's estate. I am here to apprehend the two of them and take them to the police station in Rotherham where they will be charged with the said offences. Also, I am instructed by his Lordship's estate, to search your property for any evidence which might be used to secure a prosecution in this matter. Now let me in please so that I can carry out my duties. Constable." He ushered the constable forward into the house past the distressed woman and followed him in along with the gamekeeper.

The two lads were sitting at the table eating their breakfast, totally unaware of what had just transpired. Clem had been upstairs quietly preparing himself for his forthcoming proposal to Florence but was disturbed by the activity downstairs. By the time he reached the backroom, the three men were busy interrogating the bewildered lads.

"What the 'ecks goin' on here?" His intonation converted the question into a demand which immediately put the sergeant on his guard.

"Keep out of this Mr Baxter if you please, we are in the process of a lawful arrest here and I won't take any bother from you." Clem reluctantly halted his intervention; he had been taught to respect the law in much the same way as he had been taught to respect religious dogma, through a kind of blind acceptance. Any misgivings regarding either seemed to be suppressed by some mysterious, inexplicable persuasion from within his consciousness. The sergeant redirected his speech to the gamekeeper who remained a shadow-like appendage on his right-hand side. "Now then Mr Darbast, can you point out the one who inflicted the injury upon your person for me please Sir?"

The gamekeeper stepped forward, still attached to the invisible umbilical cord which connected him with the sergeant, and commenced a detailed examination of the two accused. May had, in the meantime, shuffled over to Clem's side and taken hold of his arm; he placed his hand over hers in a futile gesture of reassurance.

"Stand up, you two ruffians and let me get a closer look at you." They deferred to the gamekeeper's command and reluctantly rose to their feet, each of them clutching the edge of the table with trembling fingers. The man seemed to delight in prolonging the visual interrogation and he could sense the fear rising inside the lads. The dog also sensed the tension and emitted a low prolonged warning snarl, as it curled its lips back and bared its teeth at the man, from the corner of the room. The sergeant detected the threat.

"Keep that dog under control, if you please Mr Baxter. Things are serious enough without further trouble." Clem intervened.

"Lucky, shut it, be quiet now." His voice was firm and forceful and the dog deferred to its perceived pack-leader after directing a final defiant growl towards the gamekeeper.

"That's all right sergeant, me and that scruffy mongrel there have got an understanding. If it wasn't for the dog, I might never have caught up with these two little thugs." His face contorted into an expression of glee and he produced a sickly scoffing smile. Still his stare alternated between the faces of the two lads. "Aye, led us straight to your door, he did, couldn't have been any more helpful if he'd a tongue in his head."

He turned away from the boys and directed his next remark to the dog, still maintaining the sickly smirk. "That's right, isn't it you tatty mongrel?" The two lads once again became the subject of Mr Darbast's gloating. "After you two ruffians scurried off last night, I followed the sound of the dogs down to the river and called Jasper to heel. Naturally he obeyed immediately. Now that's what you call a dog, full-blooded Rotweiller, don't come any better for doing the business. When I called him over, he came all nice and obedient-like and let me just slip his chain on. I went to give that one a taste of my boot but as we walked back to the house, he just kept on following us. At first I got a little riled but then I realised that he might just come in useful.

When I arrived back at the house with your dog still in tow, I found a piece of Mrs Darbast's meat loaf and a bit of Yorkshire pudding and threw it into the shed. Sure enough, the stupid animal ran in after it and I just slammed the door shut behind it. First thing this morning I reported the attack to the constable here and suggested that he contact his superior on account of the seriousness of the offence, like. So he went off and fetched the sergeant here and it was a simple matter of putting a rope around the dog's neck and fetching it down to the village. It wasn't long before he was straining at the tether and leading us right up to your backdoor step. So you see, you've him to thank for being found out."

Mr Darbast continued to intimidate Jimmy and Tom by constantly alternating his gaze from one to the other without saying anything further, and obviously deriving a great deal of sadistic satisfaction from doing so. Clem was becoming annoyed.

"Just how much time do you need man? Do you see 'im or don't you or are you just mekin' it all up, eh?" The venom which accompanied the enquiry snapped the man into a decision and he pointed his finger at Jimmy.

"That's the thug, sergeant, that's him, wants locking up, little hooligan." At the same instant Tom released his pent up anguish. It was a damning indictment of himself and his friend.

"What did you expect, you old codger, when you were beating on me wi' that bloody rod?" he screamed.

"Shur up Tom, for Christ's sake," Clem's blasphemous intervention could only chase around the room, incapable of preventing Tom's revelation from imprinting itself indelibly on the minds of all those present. The sergeant's trained and disciplined mind seized the moment and exploited it to the full.

"Perhaps you can tell us all what happened in the night then, will you lad?" Tom looked every bit like the eleven year old child that he was. He directed a pathetic glance over to his mother and felt his chin and lower lip start to tremble; then he simply burst, into tears. His mother reacted instinctively. She rushed over to the distraught lad, wrapped her arms around his head and drew him to her bosom. She tried to reassure him with verbal gestures of consolation but she knew herself that if there had been even the slightest violence that the penalty would be severe. Jimmy felt isolated – he too was beginning to realise the gravity of the situation and spurred on by his friend's breakdown, he also burst into tears. May released one arm from her embrace of Tom and pulled Jimmy towards her in a further act of consolation, She turned to the gamekeeper.

"How dare you call these lads thugs and hooligans? If they've done wrong, it's only because they didn't realise..." She curtailed her appeal when she realised that her words were having no impact on the accuser, and diverted her attention to the two lads. "Best sit down nice and calm now and tell the sergeant what happened, and if you don't mind sergeant, if that man's said his piece, I'd sooner he waited outside." The sergeant acknowledged May's request and asked the gamekeeper to wait outside now that they had established the perpetrator of the attack. The man reluctantly agreed but remained adamant in having the last word.

"Aye and we'll see who'll be listened to in court," he pointed his finger again at Jimmy. "You're going to jail, you... mi' lad."

After the gamekeeper had left, the sergeant adopted a more sympathetic attitude though he still presented an air of authority regarding the proceedings. Tom and Jimmy took it in turns to recount, once again, the night's incidents. They emphasised the attack by monster dog and the beating that the gamekeeper had administered to Tom. They also, this time, included Jimmy's use of the sling in rescuing his friend.

The sergeant indicated that the act of poaching on its own, and as a first offence, might not have warranted too severe a punishment. However, the assault on the gamekeeper was an entirely different affair. Even when Clem intervened and suggested that the action was one of self-defence, the sergeant pointed out that no act carried out during the course of trespass would be excused by the court. The only hope that they might have regarding a lenient outcome would be for the gamekeeper to drop the charge of assault. Even the sergeant looked dismayed as he suggested such an act of humanity coming from someone who was so obviously vindictive. There might have been some cause for hope when the sergeant suggested that the injury to the gamekeeper was only minor and that the dressing was hardly necessary but no one was prepared to speculate on that fact.

During the course of his not so thorough search, the constable had recovered the shirt, still reeking from the smell of fish despite May's efforts. The gamekeeper's statement, the evidence and the confession all pointed to the need for the lads to place themselves at the mercy of the court. They would have to be arrested and taken to the police station to give a statement and they would be held in custody pending the Magistrate's hearing at which they would have to confess their guilt and await the outcome.

May naturally insisted on accompanying the two lads, a proposal to which the sergeant had no objection. Clem had the unenviable task of breaking the news to Florence and then to Jimmy's mother. His feeling of guilt and failure to undertake his responsibilities had an overwhelming impact on his confused thoughts. The group eventually left the house and proceeded to the waiting police wagon where May sat with the lads and the constable inside, whilst the sergeant and the gamekeeper took their places on the driver's platform. Clem waved them off with a few meaningless words of reassurance before commencing by foot on his journey to rendezvous with Florence and try to explain the terrible sequence of events.

Clem's thoughts were in total disarray; he could only conjure negative responses to his mental probing. He dreaded the prospect of confronting Florence, though his motives were actually quite selfish. He was concerned enough about the plight of the lads but he couldn't help letting his own self-interest interfere with his deliberations. One thing he had definitely reconciled himself to was that now was not a good time to ask Florence for her hand in marriage. That would be one subject which he would not be addressing to her.

He had to determine just how much he was going to tell her. Certainly he couldn't tell her about the stories he had told since they inevitably had had some influence on the decision of the lads to proceed with their act of folly. Nor could he, at this juncture in time, bring himself to tell her of the gravity of the accusation of assault. It was not many years earlier that such an offence combined with that of poaching would have been punishable with transportation to the colonies or even the imposition of the death penalty. His emotions were more easily definable – he was angry, but he couldn't pin down his anger to just one cause or even two.

He was angry at himself for promoting his male macho image and telling stories about imaginary exploits which he portrayed as being real, and for putting ideas into the head of his younger brother and his friend. On that basis, he was angry with the two lads to the extent that they were foolhardy enough to undertake such an irresponsible act. Finally, he was angry with the gamekeeper for making such an issue out of the minor injury which he had sustained. He knew full well that even if it could be proved that he had been viciously beating Tom, it would hold no sway in a court of law.

Clem's own impression of the British justice system was that it favoured and supported the upper classes and those people who were the representatives of those classes. If a situation arose where a verdict hinged on the difference between the word of a member of the working classes and that of the upper classes, the latter's would always be accepted as the truth. He continued to prepare himself for his meeting with Florence and the explanation he had to give regarding the current traumatic change of circumstances which had just transpired.

Instead of checking his snares and recovering any trapped rabbits to present to Mrs Gallagher, as he had intended, Clem proceeded directly to his meeting with Florence. Normally, there would be a spring in his step and a lightness in his heart, spurred on by his impending encounter with the person he loved, but all he felt was the burden of the weight of the awful news which he was compelled to impart to her. Today was supposed to represent a milestone in his life, it may well yet prove to be, but not for the reasons that he would have wished.

The cloud cover was breaking by the time he reached the brow of the hill occasionally the sun would indicate its presence by emerging into a patch of deep blue sky. He could tell from its position in the sky that it was by now midmorning and he knew that Florence would have been awaiting his arrival for some time. This did not present any great concern for him since it was not an unusual occurrence for either one of them to arrive late for their liaisons. He knew that while she waited, she would be indulging herself in the exuberance which these excursions into the local countryside always evoked. An additional stimulation was that today was her birthday. When he reminded himself of this fact, his depression became total.

He eventually encountered the track which served the two country houses in the next valley and linked them with the road to Rotherham further on. Florence would have walked down the spur from the Cropton residence and waited in the shade of the beech tree further along the track... He could make her out in the distance, she was leaning back against the trunk of the tree. Her head was turned up towards the sky as she allowed her face to be caressed intermittently by the gentle warmth of the summer sun. As he approached, he could see that she was totally relaxed, her mind meandering amongst the clouds and thinking only about the things which made her feel happy.

He almost felt like turning round and heading off back towards the village, such was his reluctance to decimate the scene of tranquil serenity which invaded his vision. Even as he considered such an act of cowardice, she sensed his presence and turned her untroubled smile towards him. He acknowledged her by forcing his mouth to form the contours of a poor example of the same gesture. She noticed the awkwardness but didn't detect the desperation.

"That's a funny look Clem," her gleeful remark reflected the radiance of her smile and he struggled to maintain his composure. He needed to take control of the conversation.

"Oh! Is it? Sorry I'm a bit late love, there's been a bit o' bother at home." He could see no point in delaying the inevitable as he took her hand and placed a light kiss on her cheek.

As she drew back, he saw the smile slowly evaporate from her face to be replaced by a look of consternation.

"What's up Clem?" Her intonation of concern was prompted by the distressed expression which she was now able to perceive on Clem's face. His response was immediate.

"Jimmy and Tom 've had a bit o' bother wi't gamekeeper." Before Florence could interrupt he proceeded to recount the events of the previous night and morning; he was anxious to reveal the story as soon as possible.

As Clem's disclosure unfolded Florence's countenance altered spasmodically. Her initial expression of concern changed into one of disbelief, as the story unfolded. This was followed by one of relief when he confirmed their escape. Then there was the anger in response to Clem's description of the gamekeeper's act of vindictiveness. Finally she reverted to a look of concern tinged with a trace of sadness. The whole episode took about half an hour to retell, after which time she felt totally drained and helpless. The relaxed happiness which she had felt earlier had completely evaporated and the major event of the day had been relegated to the back of her mind.

They strolled slowly along Clem trying desperately to comfort and reassure Florence who in turn gradually diverted her attention to the impact that such knowledge might have on her mother.

"I don't think we should tell Mam about it." She wasn't sure herself whether she had uttered a statement of intent or a question. She looked at Clem, her eyes appealed for some guidance in the matter. He didn't respond immediately he was still experiencing the mild relief he felt as a result of unloading his burden. His mind slowly came round to dealing with the statement, at first he addressed the disadvantages of such a proposition.

"She's bound to ask after him, and Tom for that matter. Then there's Mam she won't know that we didn't tell your Mam. When she finally turns up she'll be well cheesed off." He considered an alternative. "What if we tell her about the fish bit but not the sling business with the gamekeeper. Mam'll know more what's happening when she gets back I'll..." he paused and pondered for a minute or so. "No, I know. We'll tell her what I just said, then I'll shoot off to the police station and see Mam before she gets round. That way I can let her know what we've told your Mam."

Florence's disturbed mind couldn't compose itself sufficiently to offer any opposition to Clem's proposal. She was currently diverting her thoughts away from analysing the situation and towards the formation of a procession of probing questions.

"Yes, all right. What on earth possessed them to do such a stupid thing, Clem?" If she had been looking at Clem when she asked the question, she would have perceived a facial expression which she might well have interpreted as a look of guilt. Fortunately for Clem, she was staring down at the floor and he was able to adjust the grimace which would have communicated his guilt to Florence.

"Seems like Jimmy just wanted to surprise his mam wi'somat he'd got himself."

"But why a blinking fish? He could've got a rabbit for her. Why did it have to be a fish?"

This time she looked at Clem, her eyes echoed the question and inexorably drew the look of guilt out of Clem's conscience and onto his face again.

"Cleeem?" Her voice stretched the syllable until it reached all the way from her vocal cords and took hold of his guilt, intent on shaking it loose from his face. He was helpless and completely subjugated by the power she held over him.

With total disregard for the consequences of his verbal outburst he commenced to explain his influence over the lads' decision to go 'fishing'. For a further fifteen minutes he recounted the fictitious yarns about his poaching expeditions with his father and how he had sowed the seeds of their exploits in the minds of the gullible youngsters. Expressions of anger and shock scrambled over each other to assume the position of prominence on Florence's face, eventually merging into one intense look of abhorrence.

"Sometimes you can be so stupid, Clem. I suppose it was all to do with showing them how brave and manly you are. Well, I hope you're satisfied with yourself, you make me sick." He thought, for an instant that he could feel a turbulence in the air around him, brought about by the force of the oral onslaught, directed towards him. If emotions could be sliced through and chopped into little pieces, by the knife edge sharpness of such a viscous verbal attack, then Clem's had experienced just such a dissection. He was gutted, he had never before heard Florence display such venom to anyone, let alone himself.

He just hoped and prayed that it was a gut reaction to the situation and that she didn't actually mean what she had said. Although it wasn't so much what she had said that concerned him but the way she had said it. The statement had been honed by her expression of contempt and its point driven home by a malicious intent. He would sooner have faced the knuckle missile from Sam Jackson, than the verbal battering which he had just experienced. If Florence had ever harboured the slightest feeling of love for him it had surely just been totally vanquished from her heart.

For the remainder of the journey the two of them remained silent. They were each deliberating and debating with themselves the destiny of the two lads. They both knew, from the stories they had heard of men from the village and surrounding area, that being convicted of poaching could well lead to imprisonment. The punishment for the crime of assault would certainly be far more severe. The difference would lay between a few weeks for the former to several months or even years for the latter, the discretion for the harshness of the sentence would be left totally in the hands of the court.

By the time they had reached the outskirts of Rotherham, Florence had already formulated a plan of action in her mind. She would ask Harry Cropton for his help, she knew that he had grown fond of her, and so too, had she of him, for that matter. With the Cropton family being close friends of the Hase-Lore's it would not be impossible for Harry to persuade the gamekeeper to drop the charge of assault against Jimmy. If he were not able to approach the man personally, he could surely request that Lord Hase-Lore intervene in the matter. The gamekeeper would certainly then be made to co-operate. There would still be the question of poaching to address but, considering the age of the two young offenders, it might be that they would only be made to pay a fine and not be sent to prison.

Her mental manipulation of the situation put Florence in a satisfying and determined mood, although her feelings towards Clem had not mellowed in any way. She held him entirely and solely responsible for the whole state of affairs and was not inclined to allow him any further consideration.

During the journey, Clem too had been giving the matter some consideration. He felt that if he could resolve it then he would re-establish his position in Florence's affections. It had also occurred to Clem that the dropping of the charge of assault would eliminate much of the distress and concern which was being experienced. Unlike Florence, Clem had no direct access to anyone who might be in a position to influence the gamekeeper's decision to press charges and there was no way that the man would listen to a direct appeal for leniency. The only course of action that Clem could contemplate involved a little 'friendly' persuasion.

One thing that there was no shortage of in the community was the spirit of unity, especially against those who held the power to affect adversely the lives of its members. He knew that there would be no shortage of volunteers ready and willing to seek out the gamekeeper and convince him that it would be in his own interests if he were to drop the charges against Jimmy. Like Florence, he felt quietly confident of the outcome of his plan of action but considered it prudent not to reveal it to her at this moment in time.

As they entered the town of Rotherham, Clem thrust a previously clenched fist into his jacket pocket. He had completely forgotten about the present that he had brought with him and his intention to present it to Florence as they walked along. It might have offered a way of at least re-establishing communications between the two of them. Unfortunately, he did not consider that the production of an engagement ring at this time would serve to smooth over the troubled waters. He closed his fist around the small package inside his pocket and at the same time, for an instant, squeezed his eyelids tightly together. He cursed quietly to himself.

Chapter Eight

The relationship between Harry Cropton and Florence Gallagher had developed somewhat haphazardly over the previous six months. A week after attending her father's funeral, Florence had found herself on the periphery of an alien world composed of opulence and privilege. Naturally she was not a part of this new-found domain, merely an observer of its rituals, in a role of servitude. She was the newest and youngest member of a staff of six and took up the appointment of scullery-maid. This was the most menial of positions, her designated role within the household being, effectively, to serve on the other servants.

Florence's duties consisted of the scrubbing and cleaning of the stone floors, steps and window-sills in the kitchen and scullery areas. She was also responsible for the washing of all dishes and utensils, and including those used by the staff, she also assisted with the laundering of all the household linen. Other duties involved the fetching and carrying of sundry items as and when required. Excursions into the main part of the house were, at first, few and far between and would only consist of standing in occasionally for other staff, who for various reasons might have been temporarily unavailable to carry out their duties.

For her pains, she was allowed Sundays off, after her compulsory attendance at chapel. By prior negotiation with Mrs Winston, the housekeeper, she might manage to swap her rest-day for another day of the week, should the necessity arise. The Cropton household was forward-thinking in this respect and often regarded as being too liberal with its arrangements for staff by other households in the area. One of the main bones of contention was that all staff members were allocated their own individual bedrooms. Staff at other households considered this to be something of a privilege but their concerns were driven more by jealousy and envy rather than reasons relating to household standards.

Brigadier Cropton, Harry's father, did in fact have what he considered to be a good reason for these arrangements. He felt that by isolating the staff, each from the other, there would be less likelihood of any breakdown in discipline. They would be unable to confide their concerns and worries to each other beyond the listening range of the butler Mr Slater or Mrs Winston. The Brigadier believed earnestly in the military concept of 'divide and rule', his escapades throughout the Empire having confirmed the effectiveness of this strategy. So Florence enjoyed the dubious privilege of having her own bedroom and enduring an isolation which only served to reinforce her naïveté and vulnerability.

When Florence took up her duties at the house, Harry Cropton had not yet returned from his sabbatical in Paris. She had heard of his existence from other members of staff in general conversation and had seen his picture on various family photographs, which she encountered on her rare sortie into the main house. They adorned various walls and sundry dressers and sideboards in the living areas of the house. Even before she met him, she had generated for herself an aura of mystery around the verbal and visual images to which she had been subjected.

She imagined a dashing, well-educated young gentleman of great charm, whose worldly travels would only serve to enhance his knowledge and depth of character. Certainly, the female members of staff, regardless of age, were quick to relate his virtuous disposition and amiable manner. They each seemed to have a more intimate knowledge of the young man than the other, even though he had spent most of his childhood and youth at boarding-schools and university. The short periods of time that he had spent at the house actually revealed very little to the staff of his character and temperament. The person who knew him best, his nanny, had only enjoyed close contact with him until he reached the age of seven when he departed to attend his first boarding-school. So most of the reports regarding any aspect of his being were based more on flamboyant speculation rather than definitive knowledge. Even so, Florence had generated an image which had raised her expectations of the young man to such a height that it would be difficult for her to acknowledge even the most obvious of faults in his countenance.

It is true to say that Harry Cropton was a good-looking man by accepted standards and could be said to possess a high level of intelligence, having secured a first-class honours degree at Oxford (that is, if such an accolade is acceptable as a measure of one's intellect). He had taken the accepted route to privileged manhood via the public school and Oxbridge university systems, courtesy of the family wealth accumulated over centuries of royal bequests and investments. The family history was a military one, dating back to feudal times when the value of men was based on their ability to kill and oppress others.

His ancestors were fortunate enough to have been on the winning side of conflicts more often than on the losing side and, consequently, had been the recipients of several bequests of land from whatever man assumed the role of monarch at the time. The land yielded rents which later provided the finances to convert comfortably from the feudal system to the capitalist one.

The establishment of the Empire offered rich pickings through investments in precious minerals and resources which were readily available to the diplomats and ranking officers on the spot to take advantage of. Meanwhile, in Britain, the construction of the railways generated income and an investment potential for landowners who possessed ransom strips and could command the highest possible price for the right of passage of a rail-route. The Cropton dynasty had enjoyed all of these things and even though there was talk of reserves of coal being located under his estates, the Brigadier had no inclination to blight his landscape with the establishment of working class communities and the like.

Harry Cropton was the sole heir to the vast wealth of the Cropton estate and had no hesitation in living his life the way that he saw fit. His father saw that his dynasty was secure with Harry and was, in turn, not disposed to interfere with the way in which he conducted his life. The only area in which he insisted on having any influence was in his son's choice of a wife. He had no objection to his son choosing his bride himself as long as she met with the Brigadier's approval. The word 'she' is used loosely here, since 'she' was merely a representative of the family which would be fortunate enough to marry into the Cropton lineage. Other than this minor imposition, the Brigadier had neither the time nor inclination to interfere with either his son's choice of career or his social life.

When Florence finally encountered Harry about a month after she had taken up her position, he had fulfilled all her expectations and even if he hadn't, he would have. She had no control over the situation – her upbringing, the way she had been taught at school and the influence of religious ideology combined together to create a certain working class impression of the members of the upper classes. There were certain exceptions to the rule as there are with all consensus opinions. Compulsory education of the working classes had generated enquiring minds and some of these minds questioned the blind deference which permeated through the ranks of the lower classes but had only a sluggish impact on shaking off the acknowledgement of their own inferiority.

Since most women were doubly subjugated, by both the class structure and male domination, then it is not surprising that Florence was no class rebel. Her expectations and aspirations in life, whether courted or not, remained entrenched in the traditional female role as wife and mother of her prospective husband's children. In insular communities such as mining villages, this tradition maintained its stranglehold on the members. The only concession to this imposition was the aspiration held by many young women, that they might at least marry into a higher status than their present one. Improving one's class status through social institutions, such as marriage, was actually more accessible to lower class women than it was to the men, though it was more usual for women of the lower classes to become mistresses rather than wives.

Florence held just such aspirations, and her naïveté and inexperience would not allow her at the time to consider the rationale of such desires. She had heard stories of young lower class women being 'rescued' from their dismal existence by men of substance who had, as it were, broken the mould and married beneath themselves. Some were actually true but those that were, in the main, signified marriages between some wealthy, ageing man and a much younger woman. The kind of relationship that Florence craved was very much the exception rather than the rule. This would not however deter her, since she remained blissfully unaware of the obstacles which lay before her.

Not being an unintelligent person, she had planned her route carefully and had decided, as a girl, that she would take up employment in domestic service. The reasoning behind this was that it would give her access to the more privileged classes. In mining communities there had generally been three courses of action for girls of working age. In households with large families and where the income allowed, a girl might continue to assist in the rearing of her siblings until such a time as she married. For others, usually where an income was required, there would be one of two options available.

A girl could start work on the pit-top in the screening sheds, sorting coal, whilst again waiting for marriage, although pit-top jobs for women were becoming harder to obtain. Or she could enter domestic service but this was not, as it might appear, the most popular option. A pit-head worker would be better paid than a domestic and would remain at home. The domestic, although of higher status, would have to leave home and sometimes live a great distance away from her friends and family. The latter option was usually taken up by girls in Florence's situation, where circumstances had dictated that staying at home with the family was not an option. She had been fortunate in being located within walking distance of friends and family and, it seems, in being allocated a post at the home of an eligible young bachelor.

Florence need not have been concerned about making herself known to Harry Cropton. When he returned home, the full complement of staff were required to present themselves in the entrance hall of the house to receive the young gentlemen. It had been supposed by staff members that this ritual was a throw back to the Brigadier's military days, something resembling a military parade of honour awaiting inspection. There had in fact been a number of staff changes of which Harry had not been aware and this was seen as being the most appropriate way for him to acquaint himself with the new recruits.

He arrived with a flamboyance that even Florence had not expected, his approach being heralded by the uncommon, or common (as his father believed) rumble of the internal combustion engine. He had procured for himself a motor car, much to the disdain of his father who was convinced that they wouldn't catch on. He was a horseman of some repute having been a commander of cavalry and he refused to acknowledge the growing impact of the internal combustion engine on the development of society. Needless to say, any argument was completely wasted on Harry who had already experienced the boost in image which a modern motor car had bestowed upon him. The younger members of staff were suitably impressed, the men for different reasons to the women, whilst the older ones remained more sceptical.

Since Florence was the most junior member of staff, she was located at the end of the parade and waited impatiently for the butler to usher Harry along to her location. She constantly rubbed the palms of her hand down the front of her starched white apron trying to eliminate the beads of moisture which insisted on forming on them. Occasionally, she would reach up and feign adjustment to her hat. The reason for this gesture was a complete mystery, since it was firmly pinned onto the compressed hair of her head. When he was introduced to her, she knew immediately that there was some kind of chemistry between them, and even if there wasn't, to her, there was. The words he spoke to her caressed her ear-drums with the softest touch of a pure silk scarf being drawn gently across her mind.

"Florence, now that's a delightful name." The diction was perfect, as was the comment itself, and she blushed as the child in her resurfaced. For Harry's part, he too had been smitten by the contrast revealed between her deep blue eyes and the wisps of dark brown hair which peeped from under her maid's hat.

"Thank you Sir," the response was spontaneous, as was the neat little curtsy which she performed before him. He wanted to take her hand and explain that there was no need for her to defer to him, but in such company he had to maintain his dignity and posture.

That first meeting was significant enough for Harry to establish a series of contrived liaisons between himself and Florence. It was essential that he remained discreet, so it was to facilitate this that he appropriated a store-room on the first floor of the house which he proposed to convert into a private study. He insisted on clearing it himself but required the services of the scullery-maid to dust, clean and wash down the room and generally prepare it for habitation. It was during the course of the ensuing encounters that Harry and Florence's relationship developed from more than a straightforward employer-employee relationship.

At first he had difficulty in convincing the housekeeper of the necessity to employ, so frequently the services of the scullery-maid. She protested that Florence's other duties would be neglected, so he simply instructed her to redistribute any outstanding work between the rest of the staff. She had considered referring the issue to the Brigadier but, since she recognised the fact that Harry was his father's son, she could see no advantage in that course of action. Although she wasn't one to prejudge the intentions of the young gentleman, she was well aware that such unchaperoned meetings between a worldly gentleman and a naïve young maidservant often resulted in regrettable indiscretions. At the outset, indiscretions were the very thing that Harry had in mind.

Harry was well aware of the power he had at his disposal should he require it. However, he had no desire to effect a relationship which would be anything other than a mutually gratifying one. The pleasures derived would be so much more satisfying if Florence were to become a willing participant in the proceedings. He soon realised that Florence was in fact a most amiable and co-operative helper, though her own reasons for her acquiescence were somewhat different and based on a longer-term arrangement than Harry's. If moral judgement were to be applied at this juncture, it might be reasonable to suggest that both parties in this intrigue had intentions to deceive the other.

On the one hand, Harry's quest to impose his lusty intentions on the unsuspecting young woman could be described as being despicable. On the other hand, Florence's marital ambitions, although more honourable, might be considered equally despicable. The difference being that Harry's agenda was driven purely by his carnal desires, whereas Florence's was driven by the need to escape from the hardships of poverty. In the final analysis, both parties had agendas which were derived from self-interest. The first meeting between the two proved to be satisfactory for both of them.

The room which Harry selected, virtually at random, since he had no intention of making use of a study, or not at least for studying purposes, was, if nothing else, intimate. It was situated at the end of the first floor landing and measured approximately eight foot by ten with wood-panelled walls and a small high-set window with a westerly aspect. He had spent a day, with the enlisted assistance of the footman, clearing out sundry boxes full of various household items and cleaning materials which required a man's strength to relocate. What remained was a dust-ridden shell which required, he was sure, a substantial amount of time to convert into a room suitable for his intended purposes. The following day he sent for Florence to assist in the washing-down and cleaning, whilst he effected the transfer of certain reading material, to be removed from the library and relocated in the study. This he considered would give the room an air of authenticity. He hadn't at that stage realised the interest that Florence would develop in the novels which formed part of the consignment.

Florence was busying herself, washing down the wood-panelling, when Harry entered the room, his legs buckling under the weight of a box full of texts. He placed the box on the floor and swung the door shut with the heel of his foot.

"We had better keep the door closed, Florence, otherwise the dust will create havoc with Mrs Winston's breathing processes," the humorous remark was not lost on Florence who responded with genuine appreciation of Harry's wit.

"Best not let Mrs Winston hear you talk like that, Sir, she might get a bit upset." What she wanted to say was 'annoyed' but during the construction of the sentence, she realised that Mrs Winston couldn't possibly show anger towards the master of the house. She managed to insert the alteration to the statement before it reached her vocal cords and the adjustment was undetectable within the finished utterance. Of course, there was an ulterior motive for keeping the door closed, which was to ensure privacy. Harry was not disposed to allow the slightest possibility of unwanted interference or interruption, nor did he want anyone to overhear the ensuing conversation.

When Harry began to unpack the box, Florence offered to help and he didn't object since it necessitated a closer proximity which could only prove advantageous. Whilst she was handling the books, she remarked on her own inaccessibility to literature of such quality. She had heard of the likes of The Brontë sisters, Dickens, Hardy and George Eliot and she had read a small selection of the work of one or two of them and marvelled at their contents. Harry seized the moment – he offered for Florence to take her pick and suggested that he would supply her with various suitable reading material which would be selected and recommended by himself.

Whilst Florence was pondering over her choice, he intervened and chose for her a copy of *Jane Eyre* which she gratefully accepted.

"Not a word to the rest of the staff, wouldn't want them to think I was opening a library." Without trying, he had stumbled on a way of endearing himself to her and nurturing her vulnerability by supplying her with an abundance of 'informative' romantic literature.

For the remainder of the encounter, they indulged each other in a discourse designed to achieve maximum impact relative to their respective agendas. They were both unaware of the emotions which were gradually being awakened from within the consciousness of their beings. Subsequent encounters were to stimulate these emotions until eventually one of them, at least, would become aware of a sensation which wasn't part of the agenda. After several weeks, Harry found his lust for Florence mellowing into something more associated with affection and admiration. He had been careful to stretch the work on the study out over a period of times limiting the work to one day a week. In the meantime, he made just such arrangements which would maintain occasional contact with Florence, relative to her household duties.

There was little doubt that her own initial agenda was also being steadily eroded, not only as a result of Harry's impeccable persona but also as a result of the influence of the contents of the novels which he had selected for her. Being produced, mainly, for the consumption of the middle and upper classes and being written in the main by members of those same classes, she found herself immersed in a world which she perceived to be real but had no way of confirming its existence.

In the isolation of her bedroom she had inadvertently become a prisoner of her own fantasies, fuelled by the selected diet of Romantic Realism to which she had been subjected. She became increasingly convinced that, despite any obstacles and hardships she might encounter, in the end she would fulfil her destiny and live a fruitful and happy life. It was as though she was assuming the role of a character in one of the novels which she was reading and she found herself feeling the same emotions about which she had read, emotions of which she had no inkling before she had read about them. Harry had remained the same person but she was also gradually, transforming him into a character of the sort about which she had read.

Late into the night she would become absorbed in her reading and during her working day she would imagine herself a heroine, and Harry a hero, the two of them falling deeply in love and overcoming the bigoted pride and the prejudices of others, who would render asunder their inevitable unity.

She had no reason to doubt the authenticity of the texts and narratives which she had ingested. If such households as the Croptons acquired such a vast library of this literature, then its quality and status was unquestionable. These authors were established, well-respected people whose work was admired by those far better equipped to analyse it than she was. She would pursue her fate, guided by the experiences of those people about whom she read. She knew that she was falling hopelessly in love with Harry and he with her and that their love would overcome any barriers which might be placed in their way. Their first kiss would be the most wonderful experience which would transcend their human frailties and transport them to a higher plain, a fusion of pure emotions.

Florence didn't even consider other, more physical, aspects of the relationship between a man and a woman. The only knowledge which she possessed of the sexual act was when her mother instructed her on the mechanics of reproduction at the time when she was experiencing her first period. She did not dwell on the instruction but she did consider it somewhat distasteful. Certainly there was little direct reference to the act in the novels which she had read. The only references to love-making were clouded in imagery and ambiguous phrases like 'their bodies melted together in a loving embrace' or 'they became as one, oblivious to the world around them'.

The implied significance of such narratives was lost on Florence's innocence. If she hadn't lived such an isolated existence, she might have considered discussing their meaning with a room-mate, who may have been somewhat more experienced than she was in the ways of the world. It was as a result of these somewhat dubious literary influences that Florence became convinced of Harry's willingness to assist her in rescuing her younger brother from the fate which awaited him. When Jimmy's plight was revealed to Florence, she felt certain that Harry would come to the rescue with all of the heroic flair which she now associated with him and his social status.

The refurbishment of the store-room had been completed for some time. Harry had made arrangements for a new lock to be fitted to the door in order to ensure privacy and had seen fit to supply Florence with a spare key. This facility enabled Florence to ensure a continuous supply of reading material; she would simply leave a finished novel on the desk, to be replaced shortly after by another. It also enabled them to communicate and arrange meetings by leaving notes to one another in the new study.

Harry, of course, did not actually need to indulge in this clandestine mode of operation, he needed only to summon Florence and she would be compelled through duty to respond. He did, however, for reasons of his own, wish their liaisons to remain as secretive as possible. He also received quite an adrenalin rush from the *risqué* nature of the proceedings, even verging on a degree of sexual stimulation. For her part, the mystery and intrigue of the situation tied in beautifully with her new-found romantic inclinations and expectations. Illicit meetings and secret letters left for lovers to discover stirred the emotions and intensified the desires.

The day after her birthday Florence left a note on the study desk for Harry, requesting an urgent meeting. It read:

> *My Dearest Harry*
> *We must meet urgently. A most terrible thing has happened which I cannot reveal to you in this note. It needs your immediate attention and assistance which I am sure you will give willingly once you realise the terrible nature of what has happened.*
> *Florence*

Six months earlier, Florence could not have conveyed her plea so eloquently. She applied all of her newly-learned vocabulary to emphasise the importance of her communication. Harry was impressed and somewhat endeared by the entreaty for he could perceive the effort and emotion that had generated such a request for help. He felt sure that whatever the problem was, he would certainly be in a position to solve it, and in doing so, to intensify the relationship between himself and Florence. He wrote a reply which could have been lifted straight from any one of the romantic texts with which he had, so liberally, showered Florence's mind.

> *My Dear Florence*
> *I was deeply moved to learn that you are so obviously the innocent victim of some dreadful event which has occurred. Naturally I will do everything in my power to remove this heavy burden from your conscience. I will meet with you here, this evening, at seven o'clock. If you have not arrived by ten past the hour I will assume that you are delayed by your work. Should that be the case, then I will send for you directly under the guise of requiring certain duties to be performed. This issue is obviously of such magnitude*

that it must be dealt with without delay. My whole being is at your disposal.
   My fondest Love, Harry

Florence received the reply early enough to arrange her duties in such a way that she would have enough spare time to allow for the meeting with Harry.

During the intervening hours, he tried to generate a scenario which might have been the cause of such an emotional outburst. There was no reason why he should have heard of the incident through any of his channels of communication. The estate managers and gamekeepers had *carte blanche* regarding the prosecution of trespassers and poachers and the landowners were seldom alerted to such trivial matters. He was not therefore able to consider any situation which might have brought about Florence's misery.

When Florence arrived at the study, she found Harry sitting on the edge of the desk and musing over the note that she had written. She entered the room in a subdued manner and approached him with her head hung low. Harry's cultivated eloquence immediately emerged to soothe and caress her troubled mind.

"My dear Florence," he reached out his arms towards her, and she floated gently into his embrace. The soft, gentle tone of his voice massaged her sorrow and immediately began to ease the pain.

"Now tell me all about it, I can't bear to see you so full of such sadness. I'm sure that whatever it is that causes you so much distress can be sorted out," he placed his hand under her chin and lifted her face towards him, as he did so he placed a kiss on her forehead. She smiled sheepishly and felt a drop of moisture form in her lower eyelids, as she spoke it spilled out and traced two glistening trails down either cheek.

"Oh, Harry," her voice trembled as the words flowed from her mouth. "It's so terrible I don't know how to tell you. It's Jimmy, my little brother Jimmy."

Harry braced himself for the worst, he felt sure that her brother had died or had been maimed in some terrible accident.

"He's been arrested for assaulting the gamekeeper and he's going to prison."

He suddenly felt confused, he replayed the dialogue in his mind, she did say 'little brother' and 'assaulting the gamekeeper'. The two statements were not compatible, little boys don't assault grown men, he thought. He needed clarification. Still revelling in the embrace, he suggested that she tell him the whole story, hoping that the mist, presently engulfing his comprehension, would be lifted as a result.

Florence proceeded to relate the poaching incident to Harry who listened attentively, periodically caressing her arms, and stroking her hair. As the tale unfolded he became more and more confident that he could effect some simple solution to the predicament, he also became more and more aware of a certain sensuality that was emerging from within their embrace. Having established in his own mind the simplicity of rectifying the problem he found his attentions being inexorably drawn to the sensations which he was now experiencing.

The physical and emotional proximity between the two of them was becoming a form of arousal over which neither of them had any control. For Harry the deep distress which Florence was feeling had been caused by a mere triviality, which be would eradicate simply by instructing the gamekeeper not to proceed with the prosecution. He wouldn't need to act through the Hase-Lore family, his personal status would ensure co-operation from the gamekeeper, even though be was not his employee. Such was the power of the those at the top of the class structure. He was not disposed, however, to convey the simplicity of his solution to Florence at this juncture. He felt that to do so would decrease her reliance upon him, which would in turn diminish the closeness which had materialised between them.

Harry's sharp, responsive thought-processes were co-ordinating a response even as she was finishing her story.

"That's an awful predicament, Florence. I'm sure I can persuade the gamekeeper to drop the charges, though I'll have to make some enquiries first. I'll visit the police station tomorrow and have a word with the sergeant to clear up the legalities of the situation. Then I may need to speak with you further," Florence interrupted, impatiently.

"Tomorrow, Harry. We'll meet here again tomorrow, so that you can give me the good news."

"The only problem I may have is that I may not return home early enough to meet with you. I have one or two appointments to attend. It may be better if we meet the day after tomorrow." Harry's dilemma was a genuine one, since he really did have other appointments to keep the following day, which would cause him to return home late. In his own mind he was confident of the outcome of his intervention which, consequently, for him, diluted the urgency of his quest. Florence, on the other hand, was totally committed to an early resolution of the problem and was quick to offer a solution.

"Come to my room tomorrow evening, Harry, after you return." Her voice was insistent rather than pleading.

Even Harry's quick, perceptive mind was momentarily stunned into inactivity. He needed to confirm the meaning of the request.

"You mean your bedroom?" his gaze repeated the question.

"Yes, Harry. I need to know that everything will be all right." He was totally unprepared for such a request, he certainly had in mind a seduction but he never thought that the circumstances which may allow it would be created for him. Least of all by the very person for whom his seduction was meant. He would never have suggested a liaison in her room, that would have been far too presumptuous. He was as yet unable to tell whether Florence had made the suggestion because she too was falling in love just as he realised that he was, or because she really felt that the urgency of the situation warranted the alternative time and venue.

She had given him no alternative, he had to discover the depth of her feelings towards him.

"You do know that I'm falling in love with you, don't you Florence?" he surprised himself with the genuine sincerity of his confession. If he had harboured any doubts previously that his intentions were driven by no more than lust, he had just convinced himself otherwise. He really was falling in love with Florence. He waited nervously for her to reciprocate.

"Yes, I know, Harry." Whether or not she was aware that she had taken control of the whole proceedings, her incomplete remark certainly convinced Harry that she had. She smiled, a smile of innocence or maturing wisdom?

Chapter Nine

As Harry proceeded up the back stairway of the house the top floor of which was occupied by the staff's quarters, he wrestled with his conscience, trying to erase the guilt he felt concerning his deception of Florence. He hadn't attended the police station to talk to the sergeant, nor had he approached the gamekeeper to instruct him not to press charges against the two lads. There was no need. He was fully aware of the power at his disposal and knew full well that his bidding would be carried out, the intervention could wait for a day or two. In any case, he was far too preoccupied with the prospect of an intimate liaison with Florence. He had reconciled himself to acknowledging his love for her, and it was this love which generated the guilt. He had pursued her vigorously with the intention of seducing her but now his emotions were dominating his lust and he was deriding himself for his dishonourable intentions. All he needed to confirm at this stage was that Florence would return his love.

While he was making his way up to her room, Florence, also, was deep in thought. She was sitting on her bed waiting for Harry to arrive and, although she was excited at the prospect of any news which he might offer to alleviate her concern, she was apprehensive about having invited him into her room. She had only considered the implications of her invitation that same day, during the course of undertaking her duties, and was as yet undecided as to the prudence of such a request. At the time, she had been swept along by the emotion and passion of the interaction; she had experienced an intimacy with him which was unfamiliar to her and the invitation seemed to be an acknowledgement of that intimacy. There was no sexual connotation implied or even considered at the time, but now she was beginning to recognise the intimation of her action. On the one hand, she felt certain that Harry would act like a gentleman and be completely honourable; on the other hand, she harboured an inexplicable feeling that she would succumb to his very appealing and persuasive charms.

It was due to this anxiety that she had made a conscious decision to remain fully clothed and not to dress in her night attire. She had, however, instinctively removed her apron and cap, the absence of the latter allowing her hair to hang freely about her shoulders. In order to avoid discovery, they had arranged for their meeting to take place after midnight, ensuring that the whole house would have retired to bed. As a consequence of this, she had divided the previous two hours between her fitful deliberations and a somewhat futile attempt to read the new novel that Harry had given her as a birthday present.

She had found the leather bound volume on the desk in the study the day before her birthday. It had been accompanied by a note from Harry.

> *My Beloved Florence*
>
> *Please accept this gift as a token of my love and deepest affection. The book holds, for me, a certain emotional significance, since it was bequeathed to me by my mother and was in turn bequeathed to her by her mother.*
>
> *The novel had been presented to my grandmother in a gesture of friendship by the author. Inside there is an inscription, laid down by the hand of that same person. It relates the depth of friendship between the author and my grandmother, which in turn, I humbly offer to you, in the form of my undying love. Please accept it as yours to keep forever, and I implore you to do the same with my love.*
>
> *Have a Wonderful Birthday*
> *Love Harry*

The house was now in total silence and she sat quietly in the dim, flickering glow of the bedside candle. She had contrasted the affection of Harry with the lack of the same from Clem, whose failure to present her with a present had not gone unnoticed.

She became aware of Harry's proximity when she noticed the sound of the door handle being turned from outside the room. The action was accompanied by a gentle tap on the door. As it slowly swung open, she heard Harry's subdued voice.

"It's only me Florence," the whisper reached her ears at the same time that her eyes observed his shadowy outline entering the room. She placed the book on the bed and without acknowledging his arrival, impatiently enquired as to his progress.

"Did you see the sergeant, Harry? What did he say? When can you talk to the gamekeeper?" The urgency in her tone seemed to generate a kind of whispered shout. Although the volume was in reality quite low, Harry's reply was filled with concern.

"Keep your voice down Florence, otherwise you'll wake the others. Everything is under control. I've been to see the sergeant and he cannot envisage any difficulties provided that the gamekeeper withdraws the charges." The lie struggled to free itself from his conscience, but by the time it reached Florence, it had been transformed into a shining ray of hope and reassurance.

As he spoke, he noticed the semi silhouette of her upper body, highlighted by the hazy glow of the candle-light. He had never seen her with her hair loose before, on the few occasions that she had not worn her cap, it had been pinned up in an unflattering bun. The sight of her half-illuminated, half-darkened face, framed as it was in the natural veil which cascaded from above her brow, radiated an aura of mysterious sensuality. He marvelled at the vision before him.

"Florence you're beautiful, and I love you." He stood before her and reached out his arms in a gesture which beckoned her to accept his embrace.

Florence too was witnessing a revelation, as he stood before her, in the yellowy haze of the flickering candle-light. He was dressed in a white blouson shirt, opened at the neck and tucked into tight black breeches at the waist. The breeches were in turn tucked at the bottom, into a pair of black leather boots. The image exuded masculinity and stimulated a sensation which she had never before experienced. She rose, without hesitation from the bed and fell helplessly into his arms. Their embrace became a catalyst of their emotions, the kiss which followed was inevitable. Verbal communication melted into the intimacy of the moment to be replaced by a proclamation of love indicated purely by vision and touch. A mutual sensuality was being transmitted, passionately, between the two of them as their lips fused together and conveyed their innermost emotions. All the while, the touch of their hands proclaimed their desire in a way that words could not possible emulate.

Neither Harry's experience nor Florence's naïveté had any bearing on the proceedings. They acted and responded to one another with an instinctive, impulsive urge which eclipsed any notion of control which might have been imposed upon them. When their lips eventually parted the momentum was such that it urged them on towards the abyss of their desires. In one swift movement, Harry bent low and swept her up, so that her petite frame was cradled in his arms, all the while his eyes reassuring her of his love. He took two or three short strides over to the bed where he bent forward and placed her gently down. Her face radiated the full impact of the candle light. For the first time he was smitten by the hypnotic mystique of her deep blue eyes, set like precious stones in a cushion of soft, iridescent silk and intensified by the dark brown waves which caressed and framed her beauty. In that aspect there appeared just the slightest hint of red, in her hair, highlighted by the candle glow which served to generate a warm inviting aura about her person.

She slowly released the grip around his neck, which she had effected during this manoeuvre and let her hands fall unobstructively by her side. Harry placed one knee on the edge of the bed, and leaned forward, reassured by her lack of resistance. He lowered his shoulders towards her face and cradled her head in his hands, he kissed her again. She yielded completely in passive compliance to his attentions, as he released his hold and moved his hands from her face down to her shoulders.

Once more their lips parted, their physical fusion being replaced by a visual one. As his hands continued to move down below her shoulders his eyes constantly sought permission from hers to proceed, all the while her response was one of total acceptance. Eventually, after what seemed to be a perpetual suspension of time she felt his touch move over her breasts, her breathing quickened for an instant as their passion transmitted through the flimsy barrier of fabric which restrained their desire. She felt the need to eliminate this barrier and proceeded to undo the fastenings which held them apart.

As she opened her blouse Harry's hand shifted under the cotton camisole at her waist and moved slowly but steadily upwards until it rested gently upon a warm, soft mound, the signifier of her womanhood. Her breasts were not large or voluptuous like those of the women he had know in Paris, but they were firm with the fullness of maturity, and he marvelled at the immense feeling of privilege which he was experiencing. He wondered at the intimacy of the moment as he explored that part of her body, to which no other person had previously been allowed access. This was not the same sensation of lust that he had encountered with the women in France. This was undoubtedly something else.

Florence, in turn, closed her eyes and absorbed the sensuality of his tender caresses. They kissed again before his mouth moved round to her ear and whispered the gentle request.

"Shall we undress, my love?" The intrusion of the attention to such practicalities might have indicated a final opportunity to put a halt to their actions but, the strength of their passion maintained the momentum. As Harry lifted himself from the bed, Florence pulled up her knees and slipped the bed clothes over her body. Her modesty prevailed, for some inexplicable reason, and she proceeded to remove her garments from beneath the security of the bedclothes.

Meanwhile, Harry exhibited no such reservations and removed his clothes in a full and open expression of his manhood. At first, her gaze was attracted to his nakedness in a gesture of curiosity. Then, again as a result of inexplicable modesty, Florence averted her eyes away from this display of aroused masculinity. Within a few minutes they were both naked and Harry, having become aware of her embarrassment, slipped quickly and quietly under the covers and into her bed, alongside her nakedness.

Had Harry not been experienced in such matters, their lovemaking might have been more clumsy and uncertain. Although he had only in the past indulged in self-satisfaction, and in that respect this encounter was no different. He was not able to transform his emotional responses towards her into a mutual physical gratification and their union ended soon after his gentle invasion of her maidenhead.

For her part, Florence had no idea what to expect from this physical confirmation of her feelings. After the initial pain, she did become aware of a sensation of arousal but unfortunately the event terminated too rapidly for her to pursue it any further. At first she thought that Harry was also in pain since he was moaning so vigorously, but soon realised that he was experiencing something else. His climactic explosion and ensuing exhausted collapse gave her a feeling of great fulfilment which went some way to alleviating any disappointment which she may have experienced. From being a passive participant she felt for a moment that she had taken control. It was she who had caused such an explosion of passion from her lover and that notion gave her an immense feeling of satisfaction.

He rolled his spent frame over onto the bed by her side and settled his head on her bosom. She, in turn, cradled him in her arms and detected a vulnerability in him which seemed to satiate her own desires and any mild sensation of frustration of which she might have become aware. Harry's breathing became deeper and the weight of his head on her bosom seemed to increase as it did so.

Florence sensed that he had succumbed to his exhaustion and fallen asleep. She felt comfortable and relaxed as she kissed the top of his head before leaning her own head back on the pillow and staring up, through the tranquillity of the moment, towards the dimly lit ceiling. Her thoughts drifted up and away from the confines of her conscience, and hovered above her. She could see the words and read the contents of her mind – it had opened up, like the text of a book and invited her into a world of promises, transporting her and her lover to another place.

They were no longer entwined in the confines of her single bed but their embrace had become engulfed by fine silken sheets which caressed the nakedness of their bodies. The dingy ceiling above her had been transformed into the curtained canopy of an immense four-poster bed, the flowing fabric tinged with the most delicate lace. Against one wall there stood a fireplace from which radiated the flickering glow of warm hypnotic fingers of flame, dancing to the tune of their own firelight. She could even detect the sound of the spitting and hissing of coal gas, as the fuel consumed itself, and became the source of its own disintegration...

She felt totally relaxed and secure in their newly-consummated love. Now she was the mistress of the house, the pit village rapidly disappearing into the distance beyond her fantasy and being replaced by a new reality. A reality which had been offered so appealingly from within the confines of leather-bound promises, which had become the confirmation of her destiny. She was convinced, and had been convinced, by nothing other than her own vulnerability and isolation, the victim of processes which have influenced and will continue to influence as long as access to the written word continues to be made available. Even her name had changed, it was no longer Florence but Jane, and she found herself being gently jostled and guided by a myriad of life-sized letters into which she had tumbled.

As she lay contemplating her fate, she began to drift slowly and inevitably into the deep uncertainty of sleep.

Florence awoke just in time to witness the door of her attic room being pulled shut by the departing hand of her lover. The flickering glow of candle-light, long since extinguished by its own disintegration, had been replaced by a different light. This new light was more uniform, more definite, it penetrated through the small window, defused slightly by the flimsy material which hung limply before it. Her thoughts returned immediately to those over which she had pondered during the night and she smiled to herself, certain in the knowledge that her love was now secure.

As Harry retraced the route of his previous journey he too contemplated his love. He had not wished to disturb Florence's slumber. He would leave a note reaffirming his love for her and arrange to meet with her as soon as it was humanly possible. There was now no question in his mind that he loved Florence and that she loved him, he was already making plans to secure their future. Before he arose from the bed, he had lain awake for some time deliberating the complexities of a future with Florence as his wife and the mother of his children.

He was well aware of the difficulties which lay ahead but after all this wasn't the nineteenth century anymore. Queen Victoria was dead, King George signified a new modernist era. It was a time of tolerance and liberalism. His father would embrace his desire to marry Florence despite the enormity of the chasm between their class status. The Brigadier was an understanding man – after all, he had not tried to influence Harry's choice of career. He had always encouraged him to take a commission in the army but had never put him under any pressure. To best suit the situation, a position in the diplomatic corps would be most appropriate. He would apply for an overseas posting to India or the West Indies and Florence would accompany him as his wife. Her lowly station would not be detected there and he could instruct her in all the finer points of being the wife of a diplomat. Then, whenever they returned to England, she would fulfil her new role admirably and integrate easily into society.

At the same time that Harry pulled the door closed behind himself, another door at the end of the landing also clicked shut. Stevens was the butler to the Cropton household and ex-valet to the Brigadier, and as such, he enjoyed the trust and status of a companion rather than a servant. He had served with the Brigadier for over twenty years and had fought by his side in the Boer War and other skirmishes throughout the Empire. He was a dependable and honourable sort in whom the Brigadier regularly confided over a bottle of brandy at the end of the day. They would often recall their escapades before entering into retirement together and returning to the somewhat boring environment of the estate. It was this unwritten and unacknowledged camaraderie between the two men that was the stimulus for the rapid chain of events which was about to take place within the Cropton household.

After breakfast that same day, Harry was summoned to the Brigadier's study. He had not found the time to compose a note and leave it for Florence before presenting himself to the Brigadier. When he entered the room, the Brigadier was sitting behind his desk and Stevens stood by the door in attendance.

"Come in Harry, sit down." Harry became aware of a distinctly hostile atmosphere. "I don't want you to attempt to interrupt what I am about to tell you. These instructions are not for discussion, they are issued solely for your compliance and implementation. Is that clear?" Harry was about to speak but read the echo of the statement in his father's eyes and simply nodded.

"Now, Taylor is packing just so much clothing and personal items that you will require for the next few days. The bulk of your belongings will be sent on to you in due course. While you are travelling down to Sandhurst, I will arrange for accommodation to be provided for you and for your commission and training to proceed immediately. You will not attempt to contact the object of your lustful attentions. If you make any attempt to do so or decline to carry out my instructions, I will disinherit you and cut off your allowance. Is that clear?" Harry was dumbstruck. If he had wanted to make any comment, he had become totally incapable of doing so. Once again he simply nodded his compliance.

The Brigadier continued his verbal onslaught.

"The girl will remain in my employ until we discover whether or not there are any consequences of your actions. Whatever the outcome, arrangements will be made to deal with them, arrangements to which you will not be a party or over which you will not have any influence. Stevens will escort you to your motor car and oversee your departure. Mark my words, young man, if you disobey me in any of these directives, I will disown you. There's a good chance that there will be a war soon, there's nothing like a good war to develop a man's character. Honour and Glory, me boy, something that you obviously know nothing about. Right off you go. You'll be kept informed of the situation as and when I deem necessary. Goodbye. Stevens!" He beckoned to the butler to escort Harry out.

As the two men proceeded to the main entrance hallway, Harry recovered his composure sufficiently to mumble some vague enquiry.

"What the hell's going on Stevens?"

"Not for me to say young Master Harry. I just carry out the Brigadier's orders. Now come along, you heard what he said – you wouldn't want to lose all this, Sir?" Stevens's arm gestured a panoramic sweep of the main hallway and Harry acknowledged with a dejected shake of the head.

When they stepped out into the warm summer air he found his car waiting for him. Taylor, the footman, was loading his bags into the boot of the vehicle, Harry, still escorted by Stevens, climbed into the driving seat. He had a glazed expression of disbelief in his eyes, Taylor closed the boot and walked round to the front of the car.

"Ready, Sir?" Harry reached out and pulled the ignition switch on. Taylor stooped low and took the crank handle in his hands. A few short minutes later, Harry was being transported out of the leather bound promises of his imagination and into the distant reality of his future. The person, who he was only a few hours earlier, had been dissolved and scattered into the past, by the harshness of his father's words.

Shortly after Harry's ignominious departure, the Brigadier sent for Florence. She had been conscientiously performing her duties, totally oblivious of the events which had occurred during the course of the morning. Her mind had been absorbed in thoughts concerning her future with Harry and her escape from the squalid existence that was pit-village life. When the housekeeper approached her, she was smiling to herself and busily writing the script of her own novel in her mind. It would be a classic tale of the rise of a young woman out of the pit of depression and into the heights of society. The path would be difficult and often strewn with obstacles but, in the end, love would conquer all and she would fulfil her destiny.

"Florence!" The pronoun was crammed full of curious connotations. She looked up, at first intrigued, but then a wave of concern flowed over her. "The Brigadier requires your attendance in the study, he wishes to speak with you regarding a most disturbing matter." Her manner and tone of voice carried a stern urgency about it. Florence soon became aware that she was about to be reprimanded for the only thing that she could consider would warrant such a formal and foreboding instruction. She closed the pages of her mental manuscript, not realising that it may never again be opened to accept any more narrative.

Mrs Winston didn't speak again during the short walk to the Brigadier's drawing-room. Florence didn't dare enquire of her escort as to the nature of the impending interview. She was afraid that it would only confirm her worst fears. As they approached the large, polished door, Mrs Winston finally spoke again.

"Tidy your cap and your apron Florence, it's the least you can do, to smarten yourself up, under the circumstances."

Florence obeyed in total subjugation, she was now certain that the night's occurrences had been discovered and that something dreadful was about to take place. The housekeeper tapped firmly on the door, the deep-throated response caused a shiver to surge through her whole being.

"Enter." It remains an amazing phenomenon how some words can be fashioned and transmitted in such a way as to convey so much more than the sum of their parts. Florence experienced an involuntary shudder as the two women entered. She felt some slight relief when the Brigadier instructed Mrs Winston to remain in the room.

The Brigadier rose to his feet, to create an imposing, powerful figure towering over Florence's slight, suddenly almost diminutive frame. When he spoke, the words emerged from his mouth in thick, solid globules of sound which forced their way in, brutally, through her ears. It was a verbal assault.

"Right, young woman, what I have to say won't take long. I suggest that you listen very carefully. I am fully aware of your reprehensible conduct during the night and have already acted accordingly regarding the punishment of my son. As for you, you will remain in my employ until any consequences of your actions become apparent. Should, God forbid, there be any issue from this unholy union between the two of you, then the following action will be taken."

Florence became paralysed with fear, she hadn't contemplated the fact that she might become pregnant as a result of their love-making. Suddenly the Brigadier's words became dense and muddy, they seemed to merge into a meaningless drone which pounded its way into her mind but was too coagulated to penetrate her senses.

"Should you be with child, then you will go to a place where you will be attended to until its birth. Upon its birth, you will give the child up to the care of those who have attended to you who will in turn pass it on to a God-fearing, Christian couple for its adoption. You will never have any contact with the child but rest assured that it will be brought up infinitely better than you could possibly hope to manage."

Although she could barely decipher the significance of the statement, she was aware of the magnitude of the situation. She felt totally isolated. She gripped the sides of her apron and bowed her head, not in shame, but in fear. The tension and anxiety combined behind her eyes to cause drops of moisture to form in the well of the lower lids, a condition to which she had recently become accustomed. She sobbed, all the while trying desperately not to, which only served to cause her whole body to tremble uncontrollably.

The Brigadier continued, unmoved.

"Should there be no such consequence of your actions then you will be dismissed from the household without references except for appointments which you might apply for outside the county. He paused, but only to acknowledge Florence's distress.

Since you have brought some certain distress upon yourself, you will be relieved of further duties today on the premiss that you are unwell. I do not wish the rest of the staff to be alerted to the events of last night. You will tell no one of it, if you do then the consequences will be most severe. Mrs Winston will escort you to your room where you will be confined for the remainder of the day. Now get out of my sight."

Florence glanced up at the Brigadier, her eyes glazed and vision misted by the moisture of her tears, whilst her cheeks glistened from the trail of misery which traced down her face. All she could make out, looming ominously before her, was the vague outline of the source of her feeling of complete and utter hopelessness. The housekeeper reached out a hand and placed it on her shoulder, gently pulling her round to face the door.

Once in the hallway, any modicum of restraint was lost. She pulled the hem of her apron up to her face and wept uncontrollably into it. Mrs Winston guided her to the back stairway and led her up to her room. As she ushered her inside and pulled the door shut, there were no words of sympathy or consolation. She simply commented,

"Oh, Florence! What a silly girl you've been." The statement repeated itself over and over again inside her mind as she hurled herself onto the bed, face down, still weeping in anguish. Whilst the bed's physical structure arrested the flight of her body, her emotional being continued to fall beyond its restraint, beyond the fabric of the bedcovers, through the mattress and the floor of the room and on into the room below. Her spirit plunged downwards, beyond control, spiralling into the bottomless chasm which was the terrifying unknown of her own perilous future. Eventually, the physical composition of her environment evaporated into the deep dark depths of her own intense despair and her consciousness deserted her, to make way for the comforting embrace of sleep.

As she fell, her hand had encountered something on the bed and without examining its form, she grasped it in her fist and hurled it into the corner of the room. If she had read the words on the page at which the book lay open after landing on the floor, she would surely have realised her foolishness. She remained prostrate on the bed for the rest of the afternoon. After a short while, she awoke to a stark awareness of the nature of the predicament in which she found herself. She bombarded herself with the same questions and problems over and over again, but could find no answers or solutions to any of them.

During the Brigadier's verbal barrage against Florence, a motor car was travelling along the road, leaving the house behind it to diminish steadily in size as it proceeded. Inside the vehicle there sat a man who carried with him a baggage of shattered dreams and aspirations. Harry eventually recovered his senses sufficiently to attempt an analysis of the situation. The emotion which he felt most of all was that of anger, not, as one might expect, directed against his father but against himself. He hated himself for his shallow insensitivity and lack of courage and conviction.

For all of his expensive education and assimilation of knowledge and moral values, in life, it all boiled down to one thing, wealth. He had allowed his love for Florence to be summarily dismissed by the threat of losing his inheritance. The notions of valour, truth and courage had been buried beneath an onslaught of verbal oppression. Surely be couldn't let his father, a man whom he hardly knew, after all, dictate the course of the whole of the rest of his life.

He considered the options which lay before him, should he resolve to disobey his father and go back for Florence. The loss of his allowance and inheritance would leave him penniless but for a small balance in his bank account. It was true that it would be sufficient to purchase a small house somewhere, but then what of an income? He had spent his twenty two years of life learning how to spend money, without any consideration as to how he might earn it, should the need ever arise.

Any position of employment that he might take up would be based purely on its interest and prestige value and any access it might offer to other men of influence. When his father eventually died leaving the estate to him, there would be professional people employed to ensure the security and growth of the family wealth. There would be accountants, lawyers, stockbrokers and estate managers, as there were now to advise his father. His culture based entirely on privilege had taught him nothing of the methods of working for a wage or earning an income.

He had never turned his hand to anything remotely resembling physical labour. His degree in Ancient History had equipped him for nothing, which might produce an income. Access to the professions, such as teaching or the military, would be barred, he was sure, by his father's influence. Yet, for all of this, he couldn't bring himself to feel any hatred for his father. After all, he hardly knew the man. Nannies, boarding-school, and university had all combined to distance his relationship with the man who spawned him.

Even after his mother's death, they were brought no closer together. He was only nine years old at the time and boarding at a school in England whilst his parents were in Africa. His mother died after contracting a tropical disease, the details of which he was unaware and having secured his heir, the Brigadier saw no positive reason to remarry. For Harry, his father was more of an institution than a man, a signifier of a life embroiled in wealth and power. His father would live on after death through his son, thereby ensuring the continuity of the Cropton dynasty as it thrust its way through history. It was this notion alone that gave Harry some small crumb of comfort.

Would his father really terminate the Cropton lineage by disowning his only son or was his threat merely a bluff? Of course, at forty six years of age, the Brigadier could remarry and produce another heir to replace Harry. All the while he continued to examine his predicament and the motor car was drawing further and further away from the source of his torment. Yet, still he hadn't generated the conviction to pull over and turn around and return to the embrace of the one he loved.

Chapter Ten

A week had passed since Florence's elevation to the heights of sublime happiness and subsequent decline to the depths of misery and despair. She had not made any effort to contact her family or anyone in the village. Her attention was given up entirely to a desperate attempt to make some sense of recent events. The committal, to appear before the Juvenile Court at Rotherham, of her little brother and his friend and her own enforced separation from her lover, all combined to demand the whole of her attention. Then there was also the possibility of her having conceived, and all the horrific consequences that would be imposed upon her if such an event were to come to fruition.

Clem was not surprised by her lack of communication since she had made it abundantly clear that she didn't want any contact with him, at least not in the immediate future. She wasn't due to visit her mother until the next day, this being Saturday. Whether or not she could muster the courage and presence of mind to undertake such a meeting was not yet apparent to her. Meanwhile, Clem had been plotting and scheming over his plans to confront Darbast and persuade him, by whatever means necessary, to drop the assault charge against Jimmy, in an effort to regain Florence's affections. The sooner that he could generate some good news concerning the plight of the two boys, the sooner he could continue with the wooing process which had been so abruptly halted.

Clem knew that there was no point in pursuing his plan to persuade the gamekeeper to drop the charges until he was sure of an attentive and sympathetic audience. It was for this reason that he waited until the following Saturday night to prime the situation in a place with an atmosphere conducive to generating maximum impact. The male clientele of the Queens on a Saturday night was always receptive to the raising of macho bravado. He had already received feedback during the working week, below ground, that his mates were angry and anxious to help in any way they could. The whole village knew within forty eight hours of the incident, and that the two boys had been arrested for what was acknowledged as being quite a trivial offence.

There were, naturally, differing degrees of accuracy regarding the substance of the telling and retelling of the events of that night. Some stories told of the severe battering that Tom had received at the hands of the gamekeeper, including broken limbs and deep lacerations. Others told how they were now languishing in a rat-infested dungeon being fed on stale bread and water. Clem didn't mind the exaggerations, he considered it suitable fuel to stoke the fires of anger and revenge which had been kindled in the community. Mrs Baxter had journeyed over to Rotherham twice during the week to attend to Mrs Gallagher who was still unaware of the charge of assault made against her son. She was in the process of recovery from the initial shock of the arrest, and it was considered prudent to delay the conveyance of such disturbing news until as late as possible.

Florence's absence was not seen as being unusual since she was not yet due to take her rest-day, and was therefore not unduly missed. The hearing for the young offenders had been set for six weeks hence, when the next Juvenile Court sat, which would allow time for all concerned to prepare, each in their own way, for the proceedings. Clem was therefore confident that some arrangement could be made to ensure that the assault charge was dropped before the date of the hearing.

It was about eight thirty when Clem entered the public bar of the Queens. It was a warm muggy August evening, the yellow orb was completing its arc and the brightness of the day was giving way to the more mellow, twilight glow of the setting sun. The natural light inside the pub was never brilliant, even in the most intense sunlight due to the diminished size of the windows. Such buildings were constructed more to repel the ravishes of the harsh winter weather than to accommodate the life-enhancing effect of full blown sunlight. The windows were small and the beamed ceilings low in order to retain any heat emitted from the large inglenook fireplaces which served as the focal point of the individual rooms.

The Queens had three such rooms, the Public Bar, the Snug and the Smoke Room. Each room catered for a different section of clientele. The Smoke Room is self-explanatory, although smoking was actually permitted throughout the whole of the establishment. The Snug was conducive to the entertainment of female companions or groups of females who occasionally availed themselves of the pub's hospitality.

It also boasted an Off Sales lobby where drinks could be purchased for consumption outside the premises. Young women would often make use themselves of this facility since it ensured a certain degree of anonymity. It was not considered appropriate for women, either alone or in groups, to enter the premises without a male escort. In this respect, the Off Sales lobby provided access to alcohol without the stigma attached to the prospect of young women entering a public house unaccompanied.

On his entrance into the Queens, Clem was greeted with various comments and gestures of concern from those already settled in the convivial atmosphere. The air was invaded by the smell of tobacco smoke which prompted him to squint in an effort both to improve his vision and restrict the irritation to his eyeballs. As he acknowledged the assorted greetings directed towards him and shook sundry outstretched hands offering solace, his eyes scanned the room searching for particular individuals, one such individual soon entered his field of vision. Josh was leaning on the edge of the counter at the end of the bar deep in conversation with Sam Jackson.

As he approached the two men, Josh caught sight of him and acknowledged his presence by raising his half-empty glass into the air. Sam, whose broad back had been turned towards him, spun round as he recognised Josh's gesture as a greeting to a third party. He too lifted his glass but only as far as his lips – in one hefty gulp he downed the contents of the pot, over half a pint of bitter.

"Na then young Baxter, thas got rate good timin' you 'ave lad." He placed the empty pot on the bar, at the same time wiping his mouth with the back of his other coal-dust encrusted hand. "I'll just manage a pint o'bitter wi' thee then." The pint pot was unceremoniously shoved along the bar in front of Clem as a broad menacing grin appeared on the face of its owner.

"Sam. Josh. All rate? Josh, same again?" He nodded his head and directed his gaze towards the glass in Josh's hand.

"Aye, don't mind if I do Clem, cheers." The drink in his glass immediately suffered the same fate as that of Sam's, only a minute earlier, though not quite with the same enthusiasm as the former. Sam placed his massive, hairy forearm across the top of Clem's back and gripped his shoulder with his hand.

As he yanked Clem towards him in a friendly gesture, (it would have been foolhardy to consider it otherwise), he remarked on the conversation he had been engrossed in with Josh.

"Josh 'n me 'ave been having a chat with regards to this little problem thas got Clem lad. Why dun't tha tell us what tha's got in mind then?" Clem ordered three pints of bitter and distributed two of them along the bar, one for each of his friends.

"Best sit somewhere a bit quieter, out o' the way," he suggested and pointed towards a vacant table in a corner of the room. The three men shuffled over to the table and sat down as Clem commenced to explain the situation to the two others. "Don't know what you two've heard about it other than the bits I told you at work but I'll give you the general idea of what's gone on."

He proceeded to impart the saga of the adventure and subsequent catastrophe to the two men who listened attentively with only the occasional interruption. Sam had developed a habit of repeating a certain expletive every time Clem mentioned the name Darbast.

"Bastard, shit," he would say before taking a deep gulp from his beer, as if to flush the remark back down his throat ready to be repeated at some suitable moment in the future. After Clem had completed his description of events, he paused for any comments from his audience. Sam was quick to respond, but for the wrong reason, unfortunately.

"Right then Josh, your round in' it?" The verbal request was supported by the waving of an empty glass in front of Josh's nose. "Can't gi' this matter our full attention wi' out some more lubrication can we?"

For all Sam Jackson's brash, heavy-handed approach to life and people, Clem and Josh had a guarded admiration for him. As long as you were prepared to accept the worst scenario, such as Clem had encountered when he was making his collection, then he was an easy person to get on with. It was true enough that he had a short temper and usually preferred the threat of physical violence to verbal persuasion in any disputes in which he was involved. He had been known to beat his wife on occasions, but it was always behind closed doors, never in public.

The general consensus in the community, at least amongst the men, was that what a man did in his own home was his own business. He wasn't, after all, the only miner to beat his wife. When they'd done a hard shift underground, possibly knee-deep in water, and gasping for breath in the foul, stale air which they had to breathe, they considered it was little wonder that some men took out their frustration on those nearest to them. They were usually repentant afterwards and the women were generally quite tolerant, knowing as they did what harsh working conditions their men had to endure.

There was less tolerance for those men who beat their children. Of course, it was acknowledged that a good slap or a belting never did a child any harm. However, some children were the victims of severe and regular beatings and the community did not condone this abuse. Not that there was much that they could do to prevent it except to ostracise and alienate the perpetrators. Domestic violence was largely ignored by the law and it was left to the community to take whatever meagre action it could to persuade men against committing these acts of aggression.

For all his highly-strung, aggressive tendencies, Sam was considered a good sort who was always willing to defend his mates and their families against others. He was a good worker and would often tackle faces underground that others found too difficult or hazardous. If these pockets of obstruction were not cleared they could hold up the job for some considerable length of time, which would inevitably mean lost output and lower wages. Not that Sam's main driving force behind these gestures of good will were motivated by any sentiment towards his mates. It was more a question of emphasising his physical attributes and superiority in a macho display of strength. If Clem was going to persuade the gamekeeper to drop the charges against Jimmy, he could have enlisted no better a man for the task than Sam Jackson, provided, of course, that Sam would agree to help.

As yet, Sam appeared to show a degree of enthusiasm to help which gave Clem good reason to rely on his assistance.

"So the idea is to get this Darbast fella' on his own and persuade him that it would be in his interests to drop the charges against Jimmy," explained Clem to his attentive audience.

"And if he dun't we beat him to a pulp," interrupted Sam. He looked decidedly excited at the prospect of such an outcome. Josh saw the look of disdain on Clem's face and intervened, in an effort to dampen Sam's fuse.

"I think what Clem's trying to say, Sam, is... well... the idea is, that we don't 'ave to touch the pratt, we just threaten 'im a bit." Clem took control of the interaction again.

"Thing is Sam if he du'nt back down, we won't know 'till after the hearing and there'd be no point in beatin' 'im up after Jimmy's been done. It'd be too late by then si' thee."

"Aye lad, but it'd mek me feel a lot better." Sam insisted. That familiar sadistic grin slowly emerged as he contorted and reformed the muscles in his face.

Josh and Clem stared at each other, the look of concern in their eyes confirmed their dismay. Clem was beginning to wish he hadn't allowed Sam to get involved. He felt sure that they would all finish up in more trouble if Sam was to have his way. Clem needed reassurance from Sam that he wouldn't actually get violent with the gamekeeper, whatever happened.

"Now look Sam, if we go beatin' up this fella it'll only make things worse. All we need is to make him think that if he goes ahead with the charges he's going to get a thumping. All right?"

"Aye. If that's what tha wants young Baxter." Once again he finished his drink. This time it was his own round but he had shrewdly timed his acquiescence with the emptying of his glass. "You could do a bit more persuading though, couldn't you?" As he spoke he directed an intense and deliberate stare towards the pot as he held it up in front of himself Clem needed no further gestures or hints – he stood up, collected the glasses and went over to the bar.

When he returned with the newly-filled glasses, the conversation had moved on. Josh was already coming up with problems which would need to be addressed, and solved.

"Just sayin' Clem, where're we going to find this pratt of a gamekeeper? We can hardly go routin' round the estate looking for him, can we?" The three men paused to consider the problem, surprisingly, it was Sam who offered the solution.

"Far as I know he goes drinkin' in Rotherham. Not sure which pub, but if we can find out, we can like as not pay him a visit and have our little chat." Josh took up the momentum initiated by the revelation.

"Ned Walters 'll know. I've seen him in here tonight." He drew back from the huddled group and started to survey the rest of the room.

Ned Walters was a farm labourer who along with the other labourers would drink in the Queens, as and when they could afford it, that is. They mixed furtively with the miners. Most of them had things in common, such as a mutual hatred for the pit and landowners and their associates. Ned owed no allegiance to Mr Darbast. He saw him as an instrument of oppression and authority and he despised him for the way in which he deferred so readily to his masters and betters.

Like Stevens, the Croptons' butler, Darbast was ex-army, a retired N.C.O. who had spent his life ordering the ranks around and deferring to his superiors. He knew very little about the land and how to care for the flora and fauna, which lived upon it. He seemed to delight in searching out trespassers and poachers and applying the full weight of the law, even if it seemed hardly appropriate. The more he thought about it, the more Josh became certain that Ned would offer his discreet assistance regarding the matter at hand. "I'll go see if I can find him. Dare say he'll help, if he can, for the price of a pint." He shuffled out of his chair and wandered off into the drifting smoke and hazy gaslight.

A few moments later he returned, closely followed by Ned.

"Sit thee sen down Ned. A pint o' bitter is it?" No sooner had Josh uttered the statement than he felt a sudden urge to draw breath and suck it back into his mouth. It was too late, an empty glass was thrust up in front of his face as he stood waiting for the acknowledgement. "While you're at it Josh. It's all rate, I'll get next uns in, lad." Josh was not convinced but Clem intervened, suddenly detecting a degree of frustration within Josh.

"Sit down Josh, I'll get 'em. Ned?"

"Aye. Thanks Clem, don't mind if I do." Filled with renewed confidence brought on by the implementation of his idea, and to some extent the drink, Sam took over.

"Has Josh told you that we're in need of some assistance with regards to a bit of a problem we're having, Ned?"

"Well, he's mentioned some'at to do wi' Darbast."

"Well, wi'out going into too much detail, like, we've taken a bit of an interest in his drinking habits. What we need to know from you is, where he drinks and when he drinks, see."

The total lack of subtlety and menacing tone in Sam's voice raised a certain degree of inquisitive interest from Ned.

"Aye, rate then. So what's all this in aid of then Josh?" Ned addressed his remark to Josh because he was already feeling the full weight of Sam's presence bearing down on his mind. The problem with Sam's presence is that it occupied a wide field of influence and a mere redirection of conversation was never going to be sufficient to avoid it. He leaned forward towards Ned onto his massive bristling forearms which he folded in front of himself on the table. His next statement grabbed Ned's full attention. By the throat.

"Well, that's somat you don't need to know, in' it lad?" The question was tightly wrapped in a deep-throated growl and did not expect to receive a response.

"Aye rate, Sam," Ned paused and swallowed nervously. "Well, you know as how old Darbast's ex-military, like." Sam nodded an acknowledgement as he sat back in his chair. Ned felt a sudden surge of relief as the previously compressed space between his face and Sam's slowly expanded with Sam's retreat. Ned went on to explain the gamekeeper's drinking habits.

Being, as he had indicated, a military man, he had developed a precise ritual regarding where and when he would embark on a drinking session. He always drank in the same pub in Rotherham, he never visited the Queens because he had no desire to mix with the local rank and file of the village. The King's Arms in Rotherham was frequented by the iron and steel foundry managers, pit managers and estate managers and those others with whom they wished to associate themselves. These might include members of the town's commercial sector, local traders and shopkeepers and sundry professional people,

He would only drink one night a week, on a Thursday. He avoided Friday and Saturday nights since these nights were popular with the lower classes and tended to be somewhat boisterous for his liking. Since pay-day was on Fridays, the town's streets would understandably be deserted on Thursdays, and he wouldn't have to face the prospect of sharing them with the local riffraff. He always set off at seven in the evening, allowing an hour to complete the five mile march to the town. *En route*, he would meet up with Stevens, the butler, from the Cropton household and their estate manager who was not ex-military but whose job status made him acceptable as an acquaintance.

They would terminate their session at quarter to eleven and follow the same route home. If the weather was bad they might occasionally take a cab but being trained as they were, this was a very rare event. Clem had returned to the table with the drinks at the beginning of Ned's monologue and so didn't miss any of the information. It became apparent that there would be a period of time within the gamekeeper's excursion during which be would be alone, this being the last mile between the Croptons and the Hase-Lores households.

"So this happens every Thursday night then?" Clem wanted to confirm certain elements of the story.

"Aye, every Thursday night, unless the Master has any special duties for him which int very often." Sam was satisfied that they had now gleaned sufficient information to dispense with Ned's presence.

"Rate Ned, tha's been real helpful, so tha can piss off now lad and tha won't be spoutin' off to anybody about our little chat now, will you?" Again the question was conveyed with the answer already inserted in its context and intonation.

Ned nodded and then shook his head, not sure which gesture would be appropriate under the circumstances. As he rose to his feet, Josh thanked him with a somewhat less intimidating choice of verbal communication. Clem thought for a few minutes and then spoke.

"Rate then. Next Thursday then." He looked at the other two in turn. "Josh? Sam?" They both nodded in agreement, then, to Josh's amazement, Sam stood up and collected the three empty glasses from the table.

"Rate then, same again, is it?" This time the question hung appealingly in the air and floated patiently around Josh's head, waiting for an answer.

"Bloody 'ell! Aye Sam. Cheers mate, thanks very much." Sam's grin reflected the mood of the threesome and they spent the remainder of the evening discussing their plans for the following Thursday. And getting drunk.

By the time the following Thursday had arrived, Clem had still not had any communication from Florence. He had heard from his mother during the week that she had been to visit her own mother in Rotherham on the previous Sunday. Other than that, he know nothing of her well-being or her current feelings towards him. Her regular visits to her mother were the only occurrences of which he could be certain so he had made the decision to intercept her that coming

Sunday with some good news regarding the fate of her brother. The plan was that he himself would check at seven o'clock that evening on the movements of the gamekeeper.

It would be a simple matter for him to secrete himself in some adequate foliage and observe the man embarking on his usual excursion to the King's Arms in Rotherham. He had arranged to meet up with his two accomplices later in the Queens where they would stay until closing-time. It was simply a matter then of intercepting the man on his homeward journey after the departure of his two acquaintances.

He had worked a hard shift, for two reasons. First of all, he had been determined to release all of his aggression so that he would be in full control of the evening's proceedings. Secondly, he wanted to boost his dwindling funds for the previous Saturday's drinking session had left him a bit short. By teatime he was physically exhausted but mentally stimulated by the prospect of performing the task at hand.

May was surprised that he intended to go for a drink that evening but considered that he was seeking solace in response to Florence's rejection of him. She had no knowledge of the nature of the forthcoming night's events. She was aware of Florence's anger towards her son but hoped that the passing of time would heal the rift between them. For his own part, Clem was certain that the healing would require far more than the passing of time and was therefore desperate to succeed in his self-appointed mission.

He arrived at the edge of the track which wound its way across the fields to Rotherham shortly before seven o'clock that evening. Soon afterwards, and with a punctuality honed by years of military precision and indoctrination, Mr Darbast appeared. He was a stout-looking man, having gained some weight after his retirement from the army, but not so stout as to appear portly. In actual fact, he was a solid well-proportioned man who looked well capable of taking care of himself should the occasion warrant it. Clem had encountered the man before at village fêtes and harvest festivals but had never taken much notice of him. There was also his intrusion into his home with the policemen but the nature of the situation was not conducive to any recognition of the man's physical appearance.

Now that his attention was directed specifically towards him, he became aware of the formidable presence of the man. He reassured himself with the silent confirmation that Sam Jackson formed part of his means of persuasion. As he concealed himself in the luscious summer growth of the flora which bordered the track, he observed the man head off on his ritual visit, to meet up with his friends. He mentally congratulated Ned on his accuracy of information and turned back towards the village and his meeting with his two accomplices. Neither Clem's confidence nor his resolve were diminished by the brief encounter – the perceived rewards for his actions were far too great for him to give any consideration to abandoning his quest.

As he entered the public bar of the Queens, Clem glanced at the clock on the mantelpiece above the fire. He had marked the time when he left the place of his observation of the gamekeeper and confirmed to himself a lapse of thirty minutes. Sam and Josh were at the end of the counter, as they had been on their previous meeting, and again acknowledged him as he approached. The bar was sparsely populated, only the more hardened drinkers were present. Most of them were still in their working clothes and liberally covered in sweat-soaked coal-dust which had dried and clung to the contours of their exposed skin. Their appearance was a depiction of their abominable existence.

The landlord of the pub had considered barring unwashed men from his premises but when he voiced his considerations, he was confronted by a barrage of opposition. After all, the coal dust which encrusted itself on the bodies of his clientele was the stuff which burnt in his hearth and supported his livelihood. No one else complained, all the other men lived with the stuff for eight or ten hours a day, six days a week. For a fleeting moment, Clem was reminded of his desperate need to break out of his environment. All he required was some indication, some manifestation to point the way forward, out and beyond his present hateful predicament. It didn't have to be anything particularly better, just something that was different and offered the potential for him to break the chains of his parochial existence.

He had often considered moving to Rotherham or Sheffield and taking up work in the iron and steel mills. At least he would be living in a large town or even a city instead of the stifling confines of village society and the claustrophobic atmosphere of the pit-bottom. He had commitments, however – until Tom was earning a man's wage, he couldn't escape for he would have to take his family with him and that would be restricting. If he left the pit, his mother would lose the house, so he knew he would have to defer his plans for another four or five years. Who knows what other commitments he might have by then? He was jolted out of his day-dream by a sharp jab inside his ears.

"He's at it again young Josh, a million miles away. Na then Baxter, get thisen back down to earth lad. What's wi't this pratt Darbast then? Is he out and about tonight or what?"

"Sorry lads, miles away. Aye Sam, he's on his way, just like Ned said. All we've to do is wait till about eleven o'clock and make our way up to t'track and intercept him like."

"Well, I hope thas got some brass then, cause I've nowt, and I can't stay here for nigh on three hours wi' out some liquid refreshment to concentrate the mind."

"As it happens Sam, I thought we might all nip off home and meet up later. Got to keep our wits about us, too much beer..."

The interruption was like a boulder being rolled over the mouth of a cave, heavy and solid.

"Aye well you two piss off home and mek yoursens a nice cup o' tea and I'll just settle misen down 'ere and wait for you to come back later. Just put a few coppers on t' bar like a good lad Clem and don't fret none about me, si thee." Clem thought for a minute and considered the proposition. If he left Sam on his own, there was every likelihood that he would be much the worse for wear by eleven o'clock and could easily become a liability rather than an asset. If he stayed on with Sam, he might at least be able to influence the rate of alcohol consumption and keep it down to a reasonable amount.

He glanced at the smiling face at the end of the bar.

"Rate then, we'll hang around here then, shall we?" It was another one of those questions which answered itself. Josh intervened.

"That's what I like about you Clem, once you make up your mind, there's no changing it, is there?" Clem fumbled through his mind for an adequate response in a feeble attempt to save face.

"Well, you don't think I'm sitting at home suppin' cups o' tea' while Sam's here downing pints, do you?" At first Clem couldn't read any meaning into the expressions which began to emerge on the faces of his two companions. Suddenly it dawned on him and he turned to the landlord.

"Three pints o' bitter down this end Lenny, when you're ready like."

As the evening progressed, a dialogue, of sorts was constructed and memorised which Clem hoped would persuade the gamekeeper away from pursuing his vendetta against Jimmy Gallagher. It was considered prudent for Sam to play the strong, silent, intimidating type. Two elements of this criteria, he fitted perfectly; the third, silence, would be a more difficult proposition, although he did promise faithfully not to intervene unless required to do so. Clem would do all the talking and Josh would serve as a back-up to reinforce the threat. All the while, Clem was vainly attempting to suppress the rate of beer consumption but finding it more and more difficult as the evening wore on.

By the time eleven o'clock arrived, the trio were well-prepared for the task at hand. Certainly they were relaxed and confident but whether they could prevent the whole episode from degenerating into an irresponsible farce was another issue. The evening was a cool one, resulting from a sparsely clouded sky which allowed the warmth of the day to rise into the oblivion of space. On occasions, the earth would be bathed in the white glow of moonlight, on others it would disappear into a black hole as the clouds engulfed its source. Sinister shadows appeared and disappeared creating an atmosphere of foreboding. The imminence of the occasion was also becoming apparent to Clem and he began to consider the various scenarios which might be consequential to such an encounter.

He hadn't previously contemplated the possibility that the gamekeeper would refuse to co-operate. If he declined to withdraw the charges, what would be the next course of action? As he deliberated the issue with himself, he found that he was becoming more concerned and uncertain as to the suitability of such a course of action. The relaxing affect of the alcohol was beginning to wane and he was becoming more and more sober as the journey to the rendezvous progressed. In the meantime, he was aware of a rising bravado between his two accomplices who were proceeding in front of him engrossed in light-hearted conversation buttressed by the occasional outburst of laughter.

By the time they arrived at their predetermined destination, Clem had become decidedly apprehensive about the whole affair. Sam detected the anxiety which Clem was feeling.

"Eh up lad! Tha's looking a bit sheepish, what's up? Not got cold feet have we? Look at it this way, in an hour's time you'll be tucked up in bed, slapping thi sen on t' back, for a job well done."

"Aye, thas rate Sam. Can't help wondering, what if he won't co-operate? You're not going to do owt that'll make things worse, are you Sam?" Sam stepped over to Clem and thrust his massive, hairy arm around his shoulder and squeezed. Clem felt as reassured as a grape in a winepress.

"I'll do nowt without your say so, lad. All rate?"

"So if I say we're off then, you won't be wishing him goodnight wi' a parting smack in the teeth? Rate."

"Aye. It'll be rate lad, don't fret." Clem felt the pressure of the winepress ease, just slightly, but not completely.

They hadn't long to wait until they detected the emerging presence of someone walking briskly along the track. They split up. Clem and Josh quietly made their way through the cover of the hedgerow at the side of the track to emerge at the rear of the gamekeeper. When Sam saw through the intermittent brightness that they were in position, he moved his huge frame into the path of the oncoming figure. The man was startled but not frightened by the sudden appearance of Sam. Before he could enquire as to the reason for such an intimidating presentation, a voice from behind him caught his attention.

"A word, Mr Darbast, if you please." Clem injected as much authority and menace into the statement as he could muster. The gamekeeper, again startled, turned sideways on in an effort to keep the two sources of distraction within his peripheral vision. He clutched the stick he was carrying in a firm resolute grasp as he gradually began to recognise one of his confronters.

"You're that Baxter fellow, aren't you? You're the guardian of that brat Gallagher who assaulted me."

"Assault! That was no assault. That was a nick from a stone, slung by a scared young lad whose mate you were beatin' on wi' that bloody stick. And since you've mentioned it, don't you think, on reflection like, that you were a bit hasty with your assault charge?" Clem paused, realising that his tone was more threatening than persuasive.

At this stage he was hoping not to have to use coercion to convince the gamekeeper to withdraw his charge. He adjusted his tone accordingly and continued with the discourse in a manner which was more appealing than demanding.

"Don't you think that being done for poaching is enough to convince them not to try anything like that again, Mr Darbast?" The gamekeeper was about to propose a deluge of reasons why he should proceed with the charge but paused himself to assess the situation. He looked more closely at the figure which had initially barred his progress and then diverted his attention back to Clem and the third person. His military mind weighed up the situation with speed and precision. He responded in his best sergeant major diction.

"So, what you are suggesting then is that I show a little mercy for the lad? Well, you've picked a funny time and place to come appealing to my better nature, young man." Uncharacteristically, Clem's mind was absorbing, assimilating and amassing a response almost as the gamekeeper spoke. He also detected a mellowing of the atmosphere and acted accordingly.

"Well, to tell you the truth Mr Darbast, it only dawned on me this evening, whilst socialising with my two friends here, that you might reconsider your decision to press charges. That is, of course, if you received an assurance that the same thing wouldn't happen again and that the lads would in future be kept under the strictest supervision."

He amazed himself with the structure and content of his appeal and even managed a subtle smile, Mr Darbast detected some relief in the tension and was not disposed to disturb the emerging restraint of the situation.

"Well, since you appear to be a man of some integrity and since you are prepared to keep the lads under some sort of control, I think I might be able to accommodate your request." He scanned the immediate vicinity and detected some sign of relaxation from the disposition of the three men.

"Just, out of interest, how did you know I would be passing this way at this time of night?" The question stunned Clem; he rummaged through his mind, sifting his vocabulary in an effort to construct an adequate response.

"You're a man of regular habits Mr Darbast." The words flew past Clem's left ear, and confidently headed towards Mr Darblast. Josh took over the conversation. "Bein' of a military background, like. It's well known that you frequent the more select pubs in Rotherham and that you make the same journey every Thursday evening, like."

"Well, you can rest assured that I'll be withdrawing the charge of assault against the lad but the poaching charge stands, is that clear?" The gamekeeper was keen to end the proceedings on a note of authority. Clem was unconcerned, he had received the assurance he had wanted and was happy to defer to the man.

"Right then, Mr Darbast. We'll be on our way then and thank you for being so understanding."

Sam cringed at the sound of Clem's closing statement but he clenched his fists and held his tongue as he had promised he would.

Chapter Eleven

Another two weeks had passed before Clem encountered Florence again. He had been anxious to give her the good news regarding the withdrawal of the charges against Jimmy. However, despite dispatching several messages to her via various visitors to the Cropton house, he had not received any response from her. None of the tradesmen or delivery men had managed to make personal contact for some reason and there was no guarantee that the notes which they left had even reached their intended target. He was desperate to see Florence again, his emotions running a reckless course of peaks and troughs.

On the one hand, be missed her terribly and longed to hold her and repair the damage he had done to their relationship and move on with his intended proposal. On the other hand, he bolstered his flagging morale by constantly recalling the positive outcome of his meeting with the gamekeeper and contemplating the reaction of joy that the news would bring to Florence. For her own part, she had been in a state of constant and unremitting despair. She had lost her lover and been thrust into a situation which was far beyond her youthful ability to comprehend or to cope with. The impact of Florence's predicament was intensified by the isolation within which her life functioned.

Although none of the staff other than the housekeeper and the butler were aware of the situation, she had withdrawn away from any group gatherings which might occur. She had visited her own mother only twice since that fateful day because she found it far too painful and difficult an effort to hide her emotions. She had sent word that she was unwell or detained by extra duties as excuses for not visiting. The only close human contact which she maintained was with the housekeeper and this was strictly on a need to know basis. Mrs Winston had instructed Florence on the various tell-tale signs which, if they occurred, would eventually indicate that she was pregnant the most significant being that of a missed period which would, usually, be closely followed by morning sickness.

Mrs Winston's attitude and demeanour towards Florence varied between that of an authoritative instructor and that of one who had a degree of guarded sympathy for her vulnerability and *naïveté*. Occasionally it generated an almost *déjà vu* quality to the interaction between the two women. That is, on the part of Mrs Winston. Sometimes Florence got the distinct impression the housekeeper had encountered this situation before. She was too preoccupied with her own situation to dwell on the intrigues and implications which occasionally emerged from their conversations.

Clem had eventually resolved to contrive a meeting with Florence. He was aware that she had not visited her mother the previous Sunday, this non-event having been reported by his own mother. On that basis, he made the assumption that she would not miss two weeks in a row and would resolve to journey to Rotherham on the following Sunday. His plan was to intercept her on the track between the Cropton House and the town. In an attempt to minimise any awkwardness or embarrassment, he had decided to take Lucky along with him. The dog, be hoped, would help to clear any tension from the atmosphere. He was quietly confident that, once Florence had received the news about Jimmy, she would welcome him back into her affections.

He set off early in the morning to be sure that Florence would not avoid his interception. The late summer morning penetrated his mind and instilled in him the brightness of hope and the determination to fulfil his quest of love. He located himself within the cover of a thicket of lush green bushes from which he could survey the entrance to the grounds of the house. The emerging day seemed to be offering its support, the still air was steadily becoming warmer and the shrill sound of the birds bolstered his resolve as he waited. After about an hour, his vigil was brought to an end.

He observed the figure of a person whom he knew immediately to be the subject of his love. Florence was, as usual, carrying a basket under her arm and was dressed in the same outfit that she had worn on their last encounter. As she turned out of the entrance onto the track, Clem moved forward from his hiding-place. To avoid startling her, he called out her name in as convivial a tone that he could muster.

"Flori! Wait up a minute love." She turned her head in order to identify her pursuer; she already knew from the sound of the voice who had called her name.

"Go away, Clem." Her retort flew at him with a vigorous intent. It was not anger that propelled it but more of a stern assertiveness. Clem dodged the full impact and refused to be diverted.

Even as she quickened the pace of her steps, he had almost caught up with her. He fired off a salvo designed at least to slow her down if not to halt her in her tracks.

"Flori! Please wait. I've some good news for thee about your Jimmy."

'Good news' was a phrase that she hadn't heard for some considerable time and was suddenly ready to allow herself some exposure to the calming effect it might bring. She slowed down and, without looking at Clem, gently urged him to continue as they walked along. As she did so, Lucky emerged from the thicket at the side of the lane. His appearance caused her to come to a complete stop and she crouched down to receive his playful attentions. The incident had relieved the tension sufficiently for Florence to offer Clem the chance to explain the interruption to her visit to her mother, though her response remained one of defensive acquiescence.

"Go on then Clem, what is it? But I warn you, it won't change things. I'm still angry with you."

As soon as the last word of her remark rolled from her lips, she realised that she was lying.

She wasn't still angry with him, she was angry with everything and everybody and Clem's presence was beginning to become a useful diversion.

He commenced to explain the gamekeeper's decision to drop the assault charges against Jimmy, with the whole story being carried along on a wave of relief. He was however, careful to eliminate any indication that the capitulation was brought about by anything other than friendly persuasion. The news really did have a positive affect on Florence. For the first time in weeks the contours of her face reformed into a fragile smile. Without thinking she stood up, turned towards Clem and flung her arms around his neck and hugged him. It was not however, an embrace of the person but more an embrace of the news that he had just imparted to her.

Even if Clem had been aware of this unintentional subterfuge, he would have ignored it and interpreted the gesture as one of reconciliation. He returned her embrace with increased enthusiasm and felt sure that their reunification was now complete. Even as she realised the impetuousness of her action and withdrew sheepishly from his arms he was mentally preparing his statement of proposal. There was no way that he would detect any regret that Florence might have felt for her actions, how could he, he was in love with her.

"Marry me Flori. Please marry me, I really do love you." His proposal was cocooned in a display of deep affection and sincerity, but for Florence they were words which she had dreaded hearing. At first she tried to ignore them as they penetrated her mind and dwelled, impatiently awaiting an answer but the pleading tone of his request almost prompted an unqualified acceptance from Florence.

At that juncture in time she could have asked for nothing more than to be loved and cared for by another person. The prospect of having Clem as her spouse had never been a distasteful one for her, there had, even been occasions when she had considered him a good potential choice. Certainly there were other women, in the community, who would have regarded a man like Clem Baxter an extremely good catch. However, not all of the other women had been exposed to the influences which had invaded Florence's mind and life during the previous months.

Her present understanding of the concept of love, was currently in total disarray. At that moment in time, she had no idea whether or not she could ever love Clem. She had thought that love was a spontaneous feeling which overwhelmed all other considerations and conquered class barriers. It could bring prejudices crashing down and warm even the coldest hearts but the past three weeks had verified her growing disillusionment.

Harry had failed to contact her and, indeed, she could discover no evidence that he had even tried to communicate with her. The housekeeper, Mrs Winston, although generally stern and somewhat officious, had at times shown a little compassion towards Florence's plight. Sometimes it was almost as though there was an affinity between the two women, although she had not herself detected this revelation. She had enquired regularly whether or not there had been any attempt at communication from her lover – an intercepted message or letter, a telephone call diverted by those who would wish to maintain her desolate isolation. Mrs Winston had always given a negative response and she had no reason to believe that she was keeping the truth from her.

Then there was the other distraction which had occupied her gravest deliberations. The notion that such a fleeting union might have such enormous consequences and impact on her life was still beyond her comprehension and that those same consequences could not be immediately apparent only added to her anguish. The good news which Clem had brought was virtually negated by his ensuing proposal which resurrected these other considerations. Her reply was, under the circumstances, the only one she could give.

"I can't marry you, Clem, I'm sorry. I can't marry anyone." This was a response he hadn't expected. He picked at the statement, analysing each word carefully but kept returning to one in particular.

He couldn't somehow relate the word 'can't' to his selection of possible replies. He had reluctantly prepared himself for rejection on various grounds but none of his explanations had allowed for the word 'can't'. Eventually, it became the only part of her reply which remained, suspended inside his head, constantly repeating itself and increasing in magnitude. Finally, it became so immense that he had to release it from the confines of his mind.

"Can't! What do you mean 'can't'? I don't understand Flori, why 'can't' you marry me?" Her reply did nothing to alleviate his affliction, it only served to increase his bewilderment.

"I just can't Clem. I'm sorry." That word was there again, it felt like a wedge being driven into his consciousness by the hammer-blows of her voice.

"You've said it again, that word 'can't'. Don't you mean won't? You don't want to marry me?" His attempt to alter the semantic structure of the statement was accompanied by a distinctly agitated tone in his voice.

Florence detected it immediately. She didn't want to make Clem angry for she realised that he was her only ally and didn't want to lose his friendship. At the same time, she couldn't possibly tell him the reason why she had to refuse his marriage proposal. She had to divert the conversation and blame her answer on something other than the truth.

"I'm sorry Clem. When I say I can't, I mean I can't just yet, not while Jimmy's still got this poaching thing hanging over him." The explanation emerged as a lie but was received as the truth.

Had Clem not been willing himself to believe her explanation, he might have noticed the lack of conviction in the tone of her voice. However, being the victim, as he was, of all the vagaries associated with being in love, he accepted her explanation wholeheartedly. Florence instantly realised that she had effectively accepted Clem's proposal of marriage and, before he could generate a response, she qualified her statement.

"That's not to say that I accept your proposal, Clem. I still need to think about it." Clem's confidence was soaring, he received the statement and its accompanying smile as though she had actually accepted.

"Well, why didn't you say so, Flori? I mean, it's not as if there's someone else, is there?" He didn't expect an answer to his question. After all in the close knit community which embraced their lives, he would have known immediately if she had been seeing someone else.

The fact that she needed time to think about it was, for him, indicative of a woman's prerogative to be evasive and coy. All the same he felt the urge to press her further for a more definite answer in an attempt to confirm his aspirations.

"So what's there to think about lass I'll look after you rate well, and we'll 'ave a dozen kids, all wi' brown hair and blue eyes. I'll not be a miner all me life you know, I've got plans." She cut him short, she couldn't bear to listen to him rambling on about the future and having children.

"Hang on Clem, one thing at a time. I've told you I need to think about what you've said. You'll get my answer after the court hearing, so you'll just have to be patient won't you?" She needed to change the subject and divert their attention to something else. "So are you going to escort me to my mother's or not, Clem." As the words reached his ears, he held out his hand to her. At first she withdrew, still not wanting to raise his hopes about their future relationship but she did desperately want to cling on to his friendship. After a moment's consideration, she took hold of his hand and they proceeded on their journey,

As if exhausted by the tension and verbal gesticulations of the previous interaction, they continued to walk along in silence for a few minutes, each rearranging and reorganising their own thoughts. It was only now that Clem became aware of an apparent change in Florence. The problem was that he couldn't identify it. There was something distinctly different about her and it was starting to prey on his mind. It wasn't the way she looked or dressed – to him she always looked beautiful and dressed in a way which emphasised her femininity. Nor was it the way she acted or her demeanour. As he probed and searched the different aspects of her personality, he eventually realised what it was that had made him so perplexed.

It was her voice, or more precisely, the way she spoke. She had very slightly dropped certain aspects of her dialect. He recalled, for instance, the last statement which she had made. Instead of saying 'mam's' she used the term 'my mother's' and he recalled other snippets of conversation which confirmed his discovery. He suddenly felt a compulsion to enquire of her the reason for this refinement, as he saw it, in her diction.

"So how is it that you've suddenly started to talk all posh then, lass?" The interpretation was a total exaggeration of the extent of the change in her dialect but it generated a nervous and guarded reaction from Florence.

"Pardon! I mean, what!"

"There you are you see." Clem was treating the incident as a flippant interlude in their journey and was not aware of Florence's apprehension and growing agitation.

"You've gone all posh like. Must be living wi them toffs that's done it, you've caught the 'posh disease' wot ho, golly gosh."

"Shut up, Clem. I haven't caught anything of the kind and anyway what's wrong with improving the way you speak? I've been doing some reading, which is something that you know nothing about."

"Reading! Reading what?"

"Books. Books of quality, if you must know."

"So how do you come by these books then?" Clem's enquiry was meant in an innocent inquisitive way but the conversation was beginning to close in on Florence. What had started off as a light-hearted observation by Clem, drifting harmlessly between the two of them, was now taking the form of an interrogation.

She felt cornered, almost panicky. She couldn't understand how she had been manoeuvred into such a position of vulnerability. She suddenly wanted to tell Clem everything – to confess her relationship with Harry, to reveal the fact that she might be pregnant. It was an overwhelming desire to unburden herself, to confess her sins and release all of the pent up tension and guilt which had accumulated inside her. She could feel her grasp on the situation begin to loosen and slip from her hands. Unable to hold herself back, she opened her mouth as if opening the flood barriers to some great reservoir full of pain and anguish.

"You've been sneaking in the library and nickin' books. I'll bet you 'ave, you bad lass." The revelation accompanied as it was by the deep-throated laughter, emitted by Clem, immediately slammed the floodgates shut.

"Well, they let us take the older books, as long as we return them of course." She had no idea where she had plucked her response from, it just sailed from her lips and into the air. Clem accepted it without further enquiry.

"Well, I think it suits you. I think it's lovely." His laughter continued to weave its way through the words as they walked on towards Rotherham.

Chapter Twelve

The journey to the court buildings was undertaken by the group, for the majority of time, in silence. There had been an abundance of reassurances showered upon the two lads at the outset, none of which was entirely convincing. The feeling of fear which pervaded their spirit had not been alleviated. Jimmy sat on one side of the cart huddled in the embrace of his sister whose arms wrapped protectively around his shoulders, his head resting gently but fitfully upon her bosom. Likewise, young Tom Baxter was comforted in a similar manner by his mother. Clem had hired the cart specifically for the purpose of transporting them all to the court-house in Rotherham. They would naturally detour to the tenement occupied by Mrs Gallagher where she and her sister would join the group and proceed to the court-house for the hearing.

When they arrived at the court and entered its huge lobby, they were greeted by the usher who took the names of the two children and the accompanying adults. None of them was surprised or concerned when he suggested that they accompany him to an office to meet with the police sergeant. Had any of the adults present been more alert, they might have realised that in cases where charges of trespass and poaching, which have been admitted by the defendants, are concerned, proceedings were usually quite straightforward. However, where more serious charges such as assault are pressed, then consultation with the authorities was not unusual in order to arrange for someone to speak on behalf of the offenders.

It wasn't until the sergeant proceeded to confirm the charges laid against the two boys that the worst scenario emerged. He affirmed the charges of trespass and poaching but then proceeded to address the charge of assault. This charge, he confirmed, was a most serious one which could result in detention for the luckless child. He went on to suggest that the plea of guilty was under the circumstance the most appropriate one and that the saving of the court's time and resources would be taken into consideration when sentencing was made. During the latter part of the sergeant's explanation of the formalities, the group was noticeably hurled into a state of shock though the policeman himself was oblivious of the fact.

When he had finished his summary of the situation, Clem spoke up.

"Excuse me sergeant, but we were all of a mind that the gamekeeper had dropped the assault charge and that the two lads were only to answer for the trespass and poaching charges." All the while that he spoke, his mind was assessing the implications of the situation. His gaze alternated nervously between the face of the sergeant and that of Florence. He was constantly feeding the rim of his cap, which he held, in front of his body, through his fingers illustrating his obvious anxiety. By the time he had completed his statement, Florence's facial expression had changed from one of disbelief to one of contempt.

For her part, her gaze was transfixed on Clem's face.

"I'm sorry, Mr Baxter, but that is not the case. The charges remain the same as they were at the initial hearing. There has been no alteration to them." His voice was a monotone, devoid of any compassion and full of the indifference of officialdom. "Now, can we move on please. Because of the charge of assault, sentencing will be imposed in the court chambers in the presence of all the court officials. Only members of the family, including yourselves as guardians, and one or two newspaper reporters will be allowed to attend the hearing. You will be given the opportunity to speak on behalf of the two boys regarding their general good character and any mitigating circumstances which may serve to influence the court's sentencing. Now you'll have to wait in the entrance area whilst I prepare my summary for the superintendent. You will be called into the court-room in due course." The bewildered group filed out of the room and into the corridor. As soon as they reached the waiting-area, Florence beckoned Clem over to one side.

When she was satisfied that they were out of hearing-range of their companions she proceeded to question Clem regarding the assault charge. Her voice was stern and uncompromising.

"Clem, you said that the gamekeeper was dropping the assault charge. What's going on?" Clem didn't know what to say, he hadn't bothered to check with the police that the charge had been dropped. He wasn't even aware that such a route of confirmation was available to him. One of the disadvantages of living within the insularity of a mining village was that it restricted access to the wider workings of society. People were preoccupied with the essentials of existence and this anomaly bred a certain kind of naïve ignorance. The sergeant would not have had reason to communicate with the Baxters regarding the status of the charges since, for his part, there had been no change. Justice for the lower classes was in any case carried out on the most basic principles. There was, at that time, no provision for legal representation to be given by the state on behalf of the defendant and once a date had been set for the hearing, the case would be filed away and forgotten until it was due for consideration.

The sergeant hadn't given any attention to the case, apart from having it entered in his diary of engagements, since the date of the hearing had been set.

"He said he was going to drop the charge." Clem was getting the distinct impression that Florence was of the opinion that he had fabricated the story. He made a desperate attempt to qualify it. "You can ask Josh and Sam Jackson, Flori. They were there when he said it."

"So what exactly happened Clem, how was it that Josh and Sam became involved. It's got nothing to do with them." She was constructing her own mental scenario of what had happened and why the other men had been involved. Clem's feeble resistance was collapsing and he could see no alternative but to explain the whole episode to her. Nor could he see any way in which he could sink any lower in Florence's estimation of his character.

"It just seemed a good idea at the time – that the more of us there were, the more likely old Darbast was to co-operate. It just seemed like a good idea, like I said."

"Oh Clem." Florence reached out a hand and touched his arm. She was fully aware, from the tone in his voice, that he was feeling extreme guilt for his actions. "You can't threaten these people, Clem, you know that. They have the power. If Darbast couldn't be persuaded to drop the charge, he certainly wouldn't have bowed to pressure or threats." He was pleasantly surprised to detect a subsidence in the tone of anger in her voice. There was emerging a definite mellowing of her emotions and her tone was becoming more sympathetic.

Had Clem been aware of the true reason for Florence's more amiable disposition towards him, he might have found cause for hostility himself. In her relentless quest to relieve the plight of her brother, she had ignored her own indiscretions and deceit. Only now, as the futility of the situation was emerging, could she relate to the foolishness of her own actions. She was beginning to realise that the ill-considered acts carried out by Clem were somewhat insignificant compared to what she now perceived as her own foolishness.

"I'm sorry Clem, I'm not really angry with you. I know you've done the best you can for Jimmy. Why is it that men, even boys, have to try to impress other people by wanting to look brave and manly?"

"I don't know Flori. I suppose it's because sometimes we think it's all we've got to hang on to." She squeezed his arm reassuringly and smiled for a fleeting moment and he felt things were back the way they had been nine months ago.

The sound that broke the spell was like a knife piercing his eardrums.

"James Gallagher and Thomas Baxter, make yourselves known to the usher, if you please." The group reformed from the various breakaway factions which had developed during the waiting period. As they came together, they exchanged tentative glances between one another, all the time maintaining a nervous silence. The police halted the group at the door to the court-room and took charge of the two terrified lads. They were led away past the entrance to the gallery and further along the corridor to another doorway. The adults were the first to enter the room, directed by the usher to occupy the seating in the public gallery.

The entrance through which the two boys were led opened into a confined area cut off from the rest of the court-room by a timber-panelled barrier through which there was no access to the main chamber. A handrail immediately to the left of the door guarded the opening of a stairwell which signified the other exit to the dock. This exit led inevitably to the court-cells beneath the building where convicted prisoners would await their transfer to the various places of incarceration, imposed upon them. The only furniture in the area consisted of a straight-backed wooden bench permanently fixed to the floor in front of the barrier.

The two boys were escorted to the bench and directed to be seated by the accompanying police officers. Jimmy slumped onto the seat and bowed his head in total dejection. Tom clung to the rail at the top of the barrier, his wide-eyed stare projecting a pathetic plea of desperation to his mother in the public gallery across the chamber. A large powerful hand pressed down on his shoulder and guided him backwards towards the bench. He could hear the statement which accompanied the act but it didn't register in his bewildered mind, it just hung there and then dissolved into oblivion.

"Come on now, sit yourself down. There's a good lad." As he sat back next to Jimmy, his last semblance of security disappeared from his vision. It was as though the panelled barrier had been raised to obliterate any remaining connection with their loved ones. The all-important though minimal comfort gained from maintaining eye contact with their families had been withdrawn from them. They could see nothing over the barrier which had caused this sense of total rejection and isolation.

After what seemed to be an eternity, a voice was heard coming from the front of the chamber.

"The court is in session, all rise before the bench." As if by premonition of the lads' inability to interpret the request, the two officers moved forward and gestured the lads to stand. Their attention was drawn to an opening door in the far corner of the chamber. A black suit topped by a grey beard emerged and proceeded up a small flight of steps to take its place behind an enormous bench positioned as the highest structure in the room. Without hesitating, the suit and its accompanying beard seated itself behind the bench. The voice discharged a further instruction. "The court will be seated. The accused will remain standing." Unable to function independently, the two lads took their cue from the remainder of the chamber and proceeded to sit down. Once again the officers were moving ahead of them, as if they were already aware of the confusion which pervaded the senses of the boys.

Before they could regain their seats the officers had intercepted them and held them in the standing position. The instinctive expression of confusion from the lads soon changed to one of unconscious compliance and they remained standing, staring blankly at the black suit and grey beard which towered above them. The clerk's voice boomed as he directed the proceedings and guided the court through the details of the case and the charges laid against the boys. The magistrate then ordered the clerk to offer a plea on behalf of the accused and accepted that of guilty. He then directed that any person representing the defendants should offer any mitigating circumstances or additional information which might be taken into account when imposing sentence.

Clem rose to his feet and offered to speak on behalf of the two boys. He was prompted to come forwards by the clerk and told to address his remarks to the magistrate's bench. He was nervous but determined and fully aware that it wasn't just the fate of the two lads which might be affected by his monologue, but also his own standing with Florence. He was holding, his cap in front of his body and as he started to speak, he began to feed the rim through his fingers. His solid South Yorkshire accent permeated his address and it became some source of aggravation to him that the suit had to interrupt it in order to clarify certain utterances with the clerk.

Despite Clem's attempts to highlight certain elements of the incident, such as the act of defence of his friend and the fact that the two boys had not offended previously, there was no indication on the expression behind the beard of any sympathy. As he drew to the end of his disclosure, he was experiencing a distinct feeling of disdain and despondency. His tone was gradually changing from one of perceived authority and confidence to one of disillusionment. As if he had become aware of the futility of his remarks, he ended his address with a plea for mercy on behalf of the lads but could detect no discernible response from the figure to which it was directed.

The magistrate thanked Clem for his deliberations and proceeded to address the two boys.

"Having listened carefully to the plea for clemency on behalf of the accused, I have come to my decision regarding sentencing. I will first of all deal with the lesser of the two cases, that concerning Thomas Wilfred Baxter. You have pleaded guilty to trespass and the criminal offence of poaching. The magnitude of your crime lies not in the act but in the person against whom you perpetrated the act. The fact that you have trespassed and poached on the estate of Lord Hase-Lore gives this offence a particular significance. Lord Hase-Lore is an upstanding and righteous leader of the community, he has provided work for hundreds of people in the area and your actions have been an insult to his good name. I have no hesitation therefore in sentencing you to be detained at His Majesty's pleasure in a suitable Industrial School to be selected by the superintendent, for a term of not less than six months. I feel sure that during this time, you will realise the seriousness of your crime and be dissuaded from offending in the future."

There was a gasp of amazement from the immediate family whilst the rest of the court room remained silent. The grey beard then turned in the direction of the sounds and silence was restored to the room.

"I now turn my attention to James Patrick Gallagher. You have committed the heinous crime of assault. This, however, is not just any assault, it is not an assault on someone of the same rank or station as yourself. It is an assault on the gamekeeper in the service of Lord Hase-Lore. In carrying out this attack on the representative of Lord Hase-Lore, you have effectively carried out the attack on his Lordship himself. I can think of no deed that can be any worse in magnitude. I have observed that you are a child without a father and whose mother is obviously incapable of giving you a decent upbringing without the guidance of a husband.

"You have spent your time recently in the charge of a family which is also without the authority of a father. It is blatantly obvious to me that you have lacked the discipline and authority that only a father and husband can impose on such a delinquent as yourself. In order to restore this absent discipline to your life, I have decided to sentence you to be detained in the local Reformatory School until you are of an age to take up work and earn a wage which will instil in you the sense of responsibility which you presently lack. You will therefore not be released for three years. In order that you appreciate fully the seriousness of your crime against his Lordship, you will first receive six strokes of the birch to be administered by the constable. Take them down."

This time the whole chamber gasped, that is, apart from one or two totally unmoved and intransigent men. Even the journalists of the local newspapers joined in the expression of disbelief which permeated throughout the court-room. Jimmy Gallagher's reaction was not, however, prompted by any realisation of the severity of the sentence which had just been imposed upon him. It was in response to the gasps of horror which infiltrated his ears and filled his mind. He had not actually understood or realised the gravity of the sentence which had been imposed upon him by the grey beard and black suit. Whilst his hands gripped the top of the barrier with a fierce, terrified determination, his stare reached out across the dispassionate void in an effort to receive the comfort of his mother's warm embrace.

Instinctively she threw out her arms and released an anguished cry.

"Jimmy! Oh Jimmy!" So frantic was the appeal that it penetrated the whole being of her son and caused a reaction of equal emotional intensity.

"Mam! Mam! I want to go home Mam." As he released his response, the terror which had surged through his consciousness burst out in a flood of tears. He loosed his grip on the barrier and threw out his own arms in an effort to receive the gesture of consolation. As he did so, the same firm hands, which had directed him previously, reached out and seized him by the shoulders. Once again he was oblivious of the words which entered his ears and hung unacknowledged inside his mind.

"Now come along lad, we can't be having this rumpus in here. Do as you're told and come along with me."

There was no resistance from the youth, just a numbed compliance as he was led to the top of the stairs and escorted down into the certainty of his fate. He could only continue to gaze, through tear-hazed eyes, towards where he knew his mother to be, until the court-room disappeared from view above his head. During the few moments which constituted this emotional outburst, the grey beard and black suit which had so effortlessly and dispassionately inflicted such pain, disappeared quickly and silently into oblivion, beyond the door in the far corner of the room.

Florence grasped the trembling body of the woman, who stood weeping next to her and attempted to comfort her in her sorrow. The woman's consciousness was elsewhere, however, and it was one of those occasions when physical gestures were totally inadequate. Slowly but inevitably, the woman responded to her daughter's embrace, and body and soul became reunited in a reluctant acceptance of her son's inescapable destiny.

Possibly the only positive outcome of such ignominious events affecting members of the lower classes was its unifying influence. This was of particular significance for Florence and Clem, each of whom was presently involved in comforting and trying to reassure their respective mothers. Although her own son had escaped with the lighter sentence, May Baxter was racked with guilt. She considered it her sole responsibility that the two youths had been foolhardy enough to get themselves into such awful trouble. Jimmy had been in her charge and she had failed to keep him from carrying out the deed which had resulted in such dire circumstances. She continued to admonish herself and plead for forgiveness from Mrs Gallagher as they made their way out of the court-room and into the entrance foyer.

In response, Mrs Gallagher insisted that no fault lay with her friend and that the boys had brought the situation upon themselves. Significantly, no member of the group opted to blame the system for the outcome of the incident. No one seemed to have noticed the fact that if the assault had been perpetrated against a lesser mortal than Lord Hase-Lore, then the punishment would probably have been far less severe. Only Clem intervened in their defence, suggesting that the sentences were far too severe for such minor infringements of the law, yet he too failed to acknowledge the reason for this.

To complete the act of unification, Florence completely forgot about her own troubles and supported Clem in his assessment. The five people left the courtroom alone. The officials had either made a hasty retreat or lingered on, awaiting the introduction of the next case dependent upon their duties. If the group were to discover the remaining processes of the law, they would have to investigate them for themselves. Clem enquired of the usher as to location and time of administering of the birching and was simply told that they would be informed in due course, as they would be informed of the name and location of the Reformatory to which the lads were to be despatched. The usher informed them of the procedure and they resolved to make their visits to the two unfortunates as frequently as was physically possible.

Florence had relinquished any animosity which she had previously felt towards Clem. The unrelenting power of the system, which had brought them to this juncture in their lives, had degraded, to the level of obscurity, any negative feelings which Florence had harboured towards him. The five people left the seat of justice and returned to the tenement home of Mrs Gallagher. Clem and Florence remained until they were reassured that the women had come to terms with the situation and then took their leave. It was incumbent upon members of the lower classes to limit the extent of their grief in response to tragic events to as brief a period as possible. The pressures and hardship imposed in trying to maintain an adequate level of existence took overriding priority, as always.

Clem had expended all of his limited financial resources through covering sundry expenses and taking extra time off work. He needed to return to the village and put in extra shifts in order to replenish his finances. There would be the extra cost of travelling to the Reformatory and taking extra food to supplement the meagre rations which the boys would have to suffer. There would be the need to bribe members of staff to keep the lads safe from the bullying and possible abuses which they had been led to believe might take place within the confines of such institutions. Since the staff tended to turn a blind eye to certain unsavoury acts and were often reluctant to intervene, in many cases to preserve their own safety, they needed financial incentives.

These matters were seldom spoken of but most members of the lower classes were aware of abuses within the penal and corrective institutions of the time. Unlike other members of society who preferred either not to delve too deeply into the more sinister depths of the penal system or to simply ignore that which they knew to be true. There was also the distinct possibility that Clem would have to contribute to the keep of the two lads. Although the cost was normally met by the Exchequer, it was not uncommon for the manager of such institutions to request that the parent or guardian be made to pay towards the keep of their children.

Clem and Florence took their leave of the three women and embarked on their homeward journey. The initial part of the journey was undertaken in silence, once again the two fellow travellers being preoccupied with their own mental deliberations. Clem was debating with himself whether or not the present time was appropriate for his second proposal to Florence. After all, she had told him that she would give him an answer after the trial. He was well aware, of course, that the outcome of the trial was far worse than expected but had also considered that the announcement of their engagement might stimulate a happier atmosphere. On the other hand, Florence's own melancholy state of being might prompt her to reject Clem's proposal which would only add to his own depression. Try as he might, he was not yet able to come to a decision regarding his present dilemma.

Florence also was deep in thought. It was now five weeks since her union with Harry Cropton and there had been no sign of her period starting. She was almost two weeks late and although she had not experienced any actual sickness, she had felt quite nauseous at times. Her thoughts had inevitably returned to the dilemma of her present plight, thereby ensuring that Clem's recent proposal was the furthest thing from her mind.

About the only positive effect derived from her isolation was that she had ample opportunity to consider her predicament. Contrary to her instructions, she had resolved not to inform Mrs Winston immediately of any tell-tale signs that she might be pregnant. She had in fact informed Mrs Winston only a week earlier that her period had started and that the possibility of her being pregnant had passed. This deceit had been engineered for two reasons – the first being that she had no wish to be swept along by the selfish decisions of others; secondly, that she had continued to hope that Harry would make contact with her and offer some positive solution to their shared problem. If it came to the worst and there was to be no communication from Harry, she would leave the manor and take her chances in the village or with her mother in Rotherham.

Whilst Florence continued to weigh up her options, Clem had come to a decision. His statement which broke the silence was like a bridge spanning a torrent of swirling foaming water.

"Florence," he waited for her to acknowledge his communication before continuing. She turned her face towards his and the tortured expression revealed on it almost caused him to alter his resolve. The words which were steadily flowing from his mind to the back of his throat in a neat orderly procession suddenly came to an abrupt halt. Those at the rear, unaware of the wavering up ahead, stumbled haphazardly into those in front. He paused and coughed tamely in an effort to reform an orderly structure to his sentence. "I know this is not the best of times to mention it, but I wondered if you'd given any thought to what I asked you before, Flori." She had absolutely no idea what he was talking about. His previous proposal had been buried deep in her mind by the weight of her present dilemma.

"Sorry Clem, I'm not with you. What do you mean?" Her expression changed to one of puzzlement whilst Clem's changed to one of dismay. The statement, supported as it was by the look on her face, confirmed immediately, to him, that she had forgotten all about his offer of marriage. He sighed.

He wanted to say, it didn't matter and wait for a more opportune time but his love for her wouldn't let him. His emotions carried him onwards.

"I mean, you and me. You know, getting married, and that." He had no idea what 'and that' was supposed to mean – it just squeezed out of his mouth and followed after the rest of the statement. Florence smiled fleetingly, she didn't know what the two words meant either but found their presence somewhat amusing. Then the real impact of his remark took effect.

She found herself almost in a state of panic unable to construct an adequate mental response, she simply blurted out the same reply as before.

"I can't marry you, Clem, I told you."

This time, instead of feeling confused, Clem became annoyed with her. "That's what you said before. Well, this time it's not good enough Flori, and don't you tell me it's owt to do wi' your Jimmy, 'cause I know it i'nt. So what is it Flori?" His annoyance gave way to reassurance. "Whatever it is, we can sort it out, I know we can." As he spoke, Clem stopped walking, whilst Florence continued as though she was trying to avoid the deluge which surged into her mind. There was no escape. She came to an abrupt halt and turned towards Clem. Tears had already filled her eyes and were tracing a glistening trail down her soft white cheeks.

She gripped her skirt at her thighs and lowered her head.

"Oh Clem! I'm so sorry. I've been so stupid." Her self-admonishment, together with the sight of her weeping, prompted Clem to rush forward and take her in his arms.

"Flori, Flori love, what is it? I love you, Flori. Whatever it is, I'll take care of it. I will." His resolve strengthened his reassurances. He felt certain that, whatever the problem was, he would be able to sort it out. The notion of the possibility that she might be pregnant had, naturally enough, not been entered into the catalogue of his most remotest thoughts. For Florence, there was no turning back now. She had set in motion a discourse which could not be diverted and she had to tell Clem everything. In fact she had reached the point where she felt that she wanted to tell him everything. She felt an overwhelming need to unburden herself and was not even about to consider the consequences of doing so.

Clem thrust his hand into his pocket and pulled out a handkerchief, feeling a sudden amazement at finding one inside it. He reached up and lifted her chin with a finger whilst wiping her anguished face with the hanky. She looked into his eyes and, beyond them, she could see deep inside his soul that he really did love her. Without further hesitation she placed all her trust in that love.

"I'm pregnant Clem, I'm so sorry." As she uttered her revelation, her weeping became more and more convulsive. Whether or not Clem had actually heard or totally understood the meaning of her statement was unclear. He may have understood it but simply refused to allow himself to accept it. In either event, his expression gave nothing away, the look on his face hadn't altered at all. Florence continued to stare through the haze of her tear-soaked eyes waiting tremulously for some verbal or visual response. As she braced herself for the reaction, Clem responded.

"What, love? I can't hear what you're saying." His intonation was flat and totally devoid of any emotion. She cringed inwardly. The effort and energy expended in building up to her initial announcement, combined with the emotional draining which accompanied its release, had left her utterly exhausted. She could not envisage any way in which she could summon up the energy to repeat her confession.

She had no need to bother. Clem's consciousness was slowly assimilating the contents of the statement which he had in fact heard quite plainly. Still, he refused to allow himself to acknowledge its significance. He was undergoing a mental struggle with himself. He tried desperately to distort or rearrange the structure and meaning of the statement but it had implanted itself indelibly in his mind.

Clem's only hope was that the statement he had heard was not the one which had actually been uttered. Somehow, on its short journey from Florence's lips to his ears, it had been altered, perhaps by the force of the wind or the busy conversations of the birds in the trees. He grasped vainly at this delusion.

"I thought for a minute there that you said you were pregnant." It was a futile gesture. His artificial look of bewilderment was immediately displaced by Florence's reply.

"I did, Clem. I did." In its place there developed an expression of total and utter disbelief. It was an expression which had actually been waiting for the past few minutes to emerge and it was the only communication he could offer for the time being.

Eventually, he released himself from his embrace with Florence and stood back. "Pregnant! Pregnant!" He repeated the word several more times in his head as though the meaning of it had evaded him. It hadn't, he was fully aware of what it signified and as he began to accept its meaning, he began to formulate his response. "You're having a baby!" His acknowledgement was complete, the statement was not a question but an affirmation of the fact. He diverted his gaze to the ground in a gesture of shame and betrayal. Suddenly, his anger surged to the back of his throat and wrapped itself around a plethora of questions and statements all jostling for position in the queue to emerge. They were thrust forth in a distorted, disorganised, rambling rage, the fine line between love and hate having been completely eradicated.

"So whose the father?"
"You've been raped haven't you?"
"How far gone are you?"
"I'll kill the bastard!"
"How could you do this to me?"
"You're a bloody slag, that's what you are!"
"You're a bloody whore!"
"How could it happen?"

Florence clasped her hands to her ears and screamed, in an effort to shut out his verbal assault.

"Stop it Clem! Stop it! You're driving me mad!" Her intervention caused him to look straight at her, and the instant that they made eye contact, his anger and distress dissolved. He passed back over the line that he had just crossed and felt his anger gush back into his being. At same time he began to weep, his initial reaction overwhelmed by his emotions. He still loved her, and, despite the gravity of the situation, his love hadn't been eradicated. He reached out his arms once again and she received his embrace with a warm enthusiasm. The trauma of the preceding minute had completely drained the two of them.

Clem looked around until he caught sight of a fallen tree trunk. He gestured to Florence.

"Come on love, let's sit down and talk about it." Florence proceeded to explain the circumstances surrounding her liaison with Harry Cropton. She omitted the details of their lovemaking and Clem was determined to interpret the episode as one of seduction by the dishonourable Harry of his vulnerable and naive Flori, so, without any contribution by herself to his interpretation of events, he had done just that. By the time she had finished relating the episode, his tears had subsided and, as far as Clem was concerned, Florence had been the victim of what he felt sure was a virtual rape. As if to substantiate his own interpretation of events, he needed confirmation of just one assurance from Florence.

"Tell me just one thing Flori. Do you love him?" She looked straight into Clem's eyes and opened her mouth to speak.

Her statement of confirmation was already composed. As though, once again, she had assumed the role of a character in a novel. If the narrative was to succeed, then she would have to be in love with Harry. After all, he was going to return to her and overcome the prejudice and hostility of his father. Somehow though, the words wouldn't materialise. She knew that she should be in love with Harry, she had felt that she was in love with him, but she had never actually told him. Even during their lovemaking, she hadn't told Harry that which she supposed to be true. Now, confronted as she was with the reality of actual affirmation, of actually saying the words, she was being held back by something which wasn't in the text.

The lapse in time that accompanied these deliberations was only short and all the while Clem stared into her deep blue eyes. She didn't know what to say – without the text being written for her, she was helpless.

"Oh Clem! I really don't know, I really don't." The confusion and distress intermingled with the words, which, for Clem, signified his greatest hope. He took hold of Florence's hands and squeezed them in a gesture of compassion and reassurance.

"Marry me Florence. Please marry me? I know you don't love me, but I'm sure you don't love him either, and in time I know I can make you grow to love me. I'll bring up the child as my own. I'll make you happy, I know I will." Florence was in no doubt that Clem's love for her was real; she couldn't find it in her heart to ask him to wait any longer for her reply.

He had offered to bring up another man's child as his own and although it meant that her dreams of escape were shattered, she found herself accepting his proposal.

"If you're really sure that you still want me after all that's happened Clem, then yes, I will marry you and I'll be a loving wife and mother." He released her hands and placed his own on her shoulders before gently pulling her towards him and kissing her on her soft, still quivering lips. She returned his kiss and wrapped her arms around his neck. For the first time in weeks, she felt safe and wanted by another human being.

Even as their lips parted, Clem was already plotting and scheming to secure their future.

"We'll tell everybody it's mine." The steady release of tension from her body was suddenly halted and she gave Clem a suspicious look.

"What do you mean Clem? The cautious tone in her voice did not deter him, he was already assuming the role of protector of his family.

"We'll tell everybody that the baby's mine, but that we love each other and were getting married, and we would have done anyway. Some people'll be a bit put out and there'll be some gossip, but it's not the first time couples have got themselves into a spot like this."

His confidence was increasing steadily, spurred on by the excitement he was experiencing as a result of Florence's acceptance.

"From what you've told me, love, nobody knows that you're actually pregnant except you and me. So you can tell them at the manor that you're not pregnant and leave like they want you to. We'll tell our mams that you're having my baby and that we want to get married as soon as possible." He paused and considered the possibility of the news of her pregnancy reaching the Cropton household. "When they find out at t' manor it'll be too late and they won't know for sure that the baby's not mine. In any case, I shouldn't think that old Cropton'll want to make a fuss and claim it as his grandchild. From what you've told me about that Harry fella, he's not coming back anyway." The sound of Harry's name caused Florence's heart to beat rapidly for a few seconds but Clem carried her onward with his outrageous plans. "The only other two people who know what's happened are Stevens and Mrs Winston and if their master keeps quiet about it, you can be sure that they will."

"That's it then, no one will ever know that the baby's not mine and, in time, even we'll believe it is mine, I promise you Flori. I don't plan on staying a miner for the rest of my life anyway – we'll be away from the village before long, you mark my words." Florence was flabbergasted – in less than half an hour of being given the devastating news, Clem had managed to work out a solution and plan the whole of the rest of their lives together.

"Clem...! You're mad, no, insane and brilliant." Suddenly she wanted to establish a degree of normality to the proceedings. "But are you sure that's what you want? It's a big decision Clem." Clem noted the seriousness in her voice and reciprocated with an answer of equal sincerity.

"I know I want you. I have since the day you laughed at my nose outside the chapel, and if you come with a child, then that's the way it's got to be."

The two of them stood up and embraced one last time.

"Now you go and tell that Mrs Winston that you're packing your bags and leaving. I'll meet you at the bottom of the drive on the track at six o'clock. You can come and stay at our house." They continued their walk back to the pathway to the manor, all the while going over their plan and making sure that they had covered all possibilities. Before they parted, they kissed and reaffirmed their meeting time.

Chapter Thirteen

Florence placed the note on the wash-table in her room. She had made up her mind, as she walked up the drive to the manor, that she wasn't going to approach Mrs Winston directly. She wanted to avoid any risk of confrontation and any ensuing awkward questions which she may not have been able to answer satisfactorily. The note simply informed Mrs Winston that she had begun her period, that she wasn't pregnant and she had no desire to remain in the house any longer. She made a point of thanking Mrs Winston for her consideration and apologised for her abrupt departure.

The room was growing dark and cooler by the time she was ready to leave. Located as it was on the east side of the building, it had long since relinquished any brightness afforded by the late summer sunlight. The greyness of the air seemed far removed from that fateful night when the warm glow of the candle-light encouraged the passionate embrace which promised so much and resulted in such acrimony. The urgency of her flight suddenly diminished as her thoughts returned, once again, to that night when she had entered into the new and bewildering world of physical love. Her imagination relayed mental images to her mind in an effort to relive that moment in her life when she had experienced the transition from girlhood to womanhood.

There were no regrets – for a time, the fear, anger and confusion, which had pervaded her emotions, during the past five weeks, had subsided and she was recollecting with fondness the rapture of their union. She indulged herself for several moments in recognition that, once she departed the room, such reminiscences would never be the same. Finally she surfaced from the depths of her conscience and slowly continued to prepare for her departure. When she searched the drawer of the table for any forgotten items, her hand made contact with a solitary object.

She was aware immediately that it was the book which she had been reading that same evening. The same book which she had so unceremoniously hurled to the floor when beset by her acute despair. Her first instinct was to place it on the wash-table and leave it behind, along with the memories which she had discarded. However, for some inexplicable reason, she decided to place it carefully on top of her belongings in the bag which she had packed. It had, after all, been given to her as a present by her lover, and if it had been missed, its return would surely have been demanded before now.

Her final gesture before leaving the room was to touch her fingers to her lips before stroking them gently over the white linen pillow which lay at the head of the bed. She felt the kind of sadness which one might feel towards the death of a close friend. Sorrow due to the loss, but happiness at the thought of having known that person. As she pulled the door shut behind her, she inhaled deeply in silent preparation for the encounter which she was about to make with the new life, that lay ahead of her. The secrecy of her departure was not difficult to maintain as the household was busy preparing for the evening meal and, since it was her statutory day off, her absence was expected.

It was about twenty past six when she reached the end of the drive. Clem was just beginning to worry for her safety. As she emerged, he rushed forward, grabbed her bag with one hand and her own hand with his other. They kissed fleetingly, turned and headed towards the village, leaving the manor behind to diminish rapidly both in stature and influence. Clem explained to Florence that he had already informed his mother of her pregnancy and their intention to marry. His mother was shocked, but already being wearied by the court proceedings, she accepted the situation with some resignation. Her suggestion that they would have married anyway was endorsed by Clem and she had wished them both well for the future.

By the time they reached the house, Florence's spirits had been lifted by Clem's own enthusiasm and positive attitude. Once again he revelled in his new perceived role as provider and protector, and had already worked out the living arrangements for them all in the restrictions of the two bedroomed terraced house. After the wedding, he and Florence would use the parlour as a bedroom, and, until that time, he would remain upstairs, leaving the parlour for Florence's own use. The question of finances had now to be addressed with some urgency for Florence's regular contribution to her mother's income had now been terminated. Meagre as it was, it had become a major donation to the income of the Gallagher family.

Clem would have to work more shifts and increase his output at the face. May Baxter resolved to try to get work on the pit-top in the coal-screening sheds. This was now possible since the two lads were incarcerated, and even when Tom was released, Florence would be at home to look after him and the house. With enough shifts, May would be able to earn more money than Florence ever could as a domestic. If May was not able to find work on the pit-top, a last resort would be for Florence's mother and her three other children to come and live with the Baxters after the wedding. Clem and Florence could share the parlour with the baby while their mothers shared the main bedroom. The children would all sleep in the second bedroom.

The absence of the two lads would not lighten the financial burden since money would have to be found to support their squalid existence in the Reformatory. These necessary practicalities and sacrifices were a far cry from the dreams and aspirations which Florence had imposed upon herself in recent times. The real world was now beginning to take charge of her life, and her leather bound promises were packed neatly away in the back of a dresser drawer in the parlour. The wedding took place two weeks after the announcement, by which time the whole village was aware of the circumstances surrounding the haste of the arrangements. After the initial, inevitable gossip and sly innuendoes, the community came to terms with the situation and apart from one or two determined agitators, the interest soon subsided.

It was not uncommon for young girls, some as young as fourteen, to become pregnant outside wedlock within the community. When confronted with economic deprivation and domestic overcrowding that permeated throughout the community, pregnancy followed by marriage to a wage-earning collier became an attractive prospect. However, there were more disturbing influences which resulted in the pregnancy of young women. In some households, where the mother had died at an early age and where there was a daughter who had reached puberty, the prognosis became very sinister indeed. The girl would be expected to assume the role of the mother in keeping the house and looking after any siblings. In some extreme cases, she would also be expected to assume the role of the mother in the bedroom.

As a result of this, occasional birth certificates would be issued where the baby's father's name would be the same as that of the young mother's father. The repercussions of this incestuous abuse were various. Quite often the secret would remain undiscovered and the father's name would be recorded as unknown on the birth certificates. Where the prospect of a prison sentence became apparent for the offending father, who may have been the only source of income for several children, the girl might have declined to name the father as her abuser. The prospect of children being placed in the care of the parish was, for most people, a course of action to be rigorously avoided. So there was always a small number of young women who refused to name the father of their child. Although in small communities such as pit-villages where secrets were difficult to keep, there was often the perception that neighbours were aware of the true nature of the situation.

The only effective course of action then was to ostracise the suspected abuser or possibly contrive a situation in which he might be set upon by a gang of 'drunken' men who had 'picked' on him for no apparent reason. There would be no prosecution of the assailants since the man would be made fully aware of the repercussions of reporting the incident to the authorities. It was this self-styled system of justice which kept the incidents of abuse down to a minimum in the smaller communities. Unfortunately, in larger towns and cities, the same deterrent was not as effective and sexual abuse, by fathers of their children went largely unpunished.

By the time the wedding day had arrived, both the Baxter family and the Gallagher family had resigned themselves to the enforced absence of the two lads. Frequent visits to the institutions were arranged between the members of the two families and they managed to keep themselves well informed as to their well-being. Clem had managed to make contact with one of the warders and was bribing him on a regular basis to maintain the welfare of the two boys.

There was suddenly a higher demand for coal from the local iron and steel industries which coincided with various rumours that war might break out in Europe. Clem ignored the rumours – Europe was on another planet as far as he and other members of the lower classes were concerned. He only knew that the increase in demand for coal meant more shifts and higher earnings. May had secured a job in the sorting sheds, also as a direct result of the increased demand, and they were managing to cope with the extra financial burden imposed upon them so the wedding was, not withstanding the absence of the two lads, a happy affair. Florence had made the occasional clandestine attempt to find out if Harry had tried to contact her. The response she received from her sources indicated that he had taken a commission in the army and that he was to join an expedition force to be sent to France. Other than that, there was no evidence that he was inclined to want to make contact with Florence.

There had been no unpleasant repercussions resulting from her abrupt departure from the Cropton household. When Mrs Winston discovered the letter that Florence had left, she had not been entirely convinced by the contents. For reasons known only to herself, however, she did not convey her suspicions to the Brigadier. On the contrary, she assured him of the authenticity of Florence's claim that she wasn't pregnant, and suggested that the matter be forgotten. Even when word got back to Mrs Winston that she was pregnant, there was no enquiry as to the accuracy of the report that the baby was Clem's. It would have been difficult, even for the Brigadier, to have posed any questions regarding paternity. He would have had to expose his interest and that was not an option which he felt disposed to exercise.

The ceremony took place in the chapel on a cool autumnal, October day. The heat of the summer had long since capitulated to the cooling of the air brought about by the onset of shortening days and lengthening night. Florence was almost two months into her pregnancy, but displayed as yet no physical signs of it, not at least, when fully clothed, even within the context of her slight figure. Her wedding-dress had been rescued from the confines of the blanket chest of a neighbour and hastily altered to achieve some semblance of a tailored garment. Clem had insisted on buying her a new one but Florence was adamant that money spent on such an item would be ill-used.

Her flirtation with the romantic influences of her life was rapidly receding into the distant past of her memories. The money would be better utilised in the service of her mother and two brothers. Clem was happy to acquiesce and could detect no threat to his authority as head of the family manifesting itself in the decision. At the chapel there were in attendance only members of the family and close friends. Three members of the colliery brass band had offered their services to perform selected musical compositions to accompany the ceremony. Transportation for the bride to the chapel and for the married couple back to the village was supplied courtesy of Marshal and Sons, coal hauliers.

The smaller wagon, normally used for steeper hill climbs, due to its lighter weight, had been modified with the installation of a bench-seat set into the cargo area of the cart. The whole thing had been scrubbed and cleaned to the best standard possible and the seats covered with a sundry mixture of coloured sheets and cloths. The horse had been draped and dressed with cloth cut into ribbons and whatever wild flowers were currently available at the time. The harness and brasses were cleaned and polished and someone had discovered a pair of small bells in the smithy's which were precariously hung onto a small wire scaffold which had been erected on top of the horse's head. Since friends and family had carried out the refurbishment of the cart Mr Marshal negotiated only a nominal charge for its provision. This was to consist simply of as much beer as he could drink at the reception after the wedding.

The bridal carriage arrived at the chapel a few minutes later than scheduled. Florence was accompanied by her uncle from Rotherham, who was to 'give her away' in the absence of her father. The bridesmaids, her two sisters, completed the entourage and they proceeded into the chapel in the prescribed order and manner. At the front of the chapel, Clem was waiting patiently, accompanied by Josh, the best man, and the ceremony commenced when Florence eventually joined him. After the ceremony, the bride and groom emerged to a crescendo of jubilation, accompanied by the customary showering of rice and flower petals. The pair of newlyweds climbed aboard the cart to be transported down the hill to the Queens. They were followed by their guests who were lead by the brass trio, insistent on trumpeting and tromboning their approval of the whole affair.

Weddings, as with celebrations of any sort such as births and christenings, were enthusiastically embraced in Connington Village. The consensus was that joyous occasions were of such rarity that when one came along, they had to be acknowledged by a spate of total indulgence and appreciation. It was to facilitate this that the reception was arranged to be held in the Queens. There had been no formal invitations to attend, the celebrations were to be held on a purely 'open house' basis. When Clem and Florence arrived, ahead of the chapel guests, the pub was already buzzing with well-wishers, happy to convey their congratulations.

The couple weaved their way through the tangle of handshakes kisses and cuddles and made for the relative, temporary tranquillity of the Snug.

The landlord had designated the Snug out of bounds for all his customers other than those who had attended the wedding ceremony. This was a customary procedure which would endure for approximately one hour before all and sundry would intermingle throughout the premises, regardless of allocated status and designated areas of occupation. Clem and Florence sat in the corner of the room, thrusting the noise of the celebrations into the background, at least for a few precious moments.

"Right Mrs Baxter, time you gave this married man a real kiss now." Florence smiled at Clem, a genuine smile of happiness not stimulated by any influences other than the contentment she felt at that moment. She was becoming more and more convinced that she was falling in love with Clem but not the notion of love which she had previously embraced. She was no longer directed by mental images generated by others, images which fell short of the reality of real life as she knew it. These images might have worked for those who had conveyed them, but not for Florence, not any more.

She still sometimes thought of Harry with fondness and was glad that she had known him and didn't regret their lovemaking, even though she had been totally unprepared for the outcome. She had also come to realise that, for all his privileges and apparent power, even Harry had not been in control of his own destiny. Before she could convey her deepening feeling to Clem, they were interrupted by the abrupt entrance of the landlord. He was carrying a tray with a bottle and two glasses on it.

"Nothing like a nice drop o' sherry to start married life. Expensive stuff this is, you know. Anyway, compliments o' me and the missus, and all the best for the future to the two, sorry three, o' you." Florence was not at all impressed by the facetious remark expressed by the landlord. She responded immediately suppressing any embarrassment which she might have felt. "Well, then Mr Thomas, you'd better hang on to that bottle for the christening, hadn't you now?"

Her remark was received with some relief by the landlord who had thought momentarily that he might have caused offence. The three of them burst into spontaneous and harmonised laughter.

"Rate lass you're on then. Just don't expect one for every christening you have thought."

"We'll be rate for t' first dozen though, eh Lenny?" Having been used to bar-room banter in the presence of male company, Clem forgot that Florence was sat next to him. As he spoke, he raised his elbow and jabbed it into the ribs of his companion who immediately let out a loud shriek.

"Oy you! You're not with your mates now, you know. Keep your elbows to yourself."

The laughter continued as the guests from the chapel began to arrive. The newly married couple were flanked by their respective mothers and the gathering throng rapidly settled down to an afternoon of drinking. The brass trio, due mainly to its outsized proportions, gave way to an accordion and a mouth-organ. Several plates of sandwiches were passed around and the trials and tribulations of existence were sent floating off on a river of booze. After the food had been consumed, tables and chairs were cleared from the centre of the room, under the dubious direction and supervision of Sam Jackson. This manoeuvre created a makeshift dance area, into which were thrust the luckless newlyweds.

Clem, by this time, solidly under the influence of numerous congratulatory offerings, stumbled and staggered his way around the confined area. Florence was more disposed to dance after him, rather than with him, but the whole affair was good-humoured with sundry verbal contributions being made by the onlookers.

"Never thought I'd see you run away from a pretty lass, Clem!" Soon they were joined by various other guests who introduced their own variations on more established dance routines and steps. Sam Jackson had requested May Baxter to join him on the dance floor and after having her polite refusal totally ignored, she found herself being lifted, somewhat indelicately, from her seat.

When they reached the dance area, Sam offered his own interpretation of the statement 'take your partner by the hand' which he transformed into something more like, 'drag your partner around the room'. His massive frame was barely enclosed in his dark blue suit, for which he was obviously several sizes too big. His neck tie and starched collar had long since been ejected from around his throat. Meanwhile the jacket buttons and the holes into which they were squeezed clung precariously and frantically onto each other under the enormous strain of his steadily expanding stomach. May Baxter was experiencing a whole new meaning to the phrase 'being swept off your feet' as Sam bludgeoned his way around the dance area. Within a few seconds, he had totally cleared the dance area and he and May had become the sole occupants. Eventually some bright person took the initiative and realised that the only way to save May, was to persuade the musicians to stop playing.

May expressed her thanks to Sam and tottered her way back to her seat. Undaunted by this rejection, Sam then turned his attention to Mrs Gallagher. She froze in her seat as he approached her, looking to May in a visual plea for some kind of diversion. Fortunately, Josh had noticed Sam's intention and the look of foreboding on Mrs Gallagher's face. He grabbed a glass of beer from a nearby table and thrust it in the path of Sam's huge torso.

"'Ere y'are Sam. You look like you need a drink after all that dazzling footwork." The distraction was total, Sam stopped abruptly in his tracks and took the offering from Josh's grasp.

"Cheers lad. That's rate friendly o' thee, that is. Don't mind if I do." He placed his arm around Josh's shoulders and the two of them turned away and retired to the Public Bar. Josh glanced in Mrs Gallagher's direction and gave her a reassuring wink as they left. Mrs Gallagher felt the nervous tension drain from her body as she realised that her rescue had been effected. In a gesture of relief, she reached for her own glass and took a large gulp of stout from the contents. The contrast of colour in the faces of the two women was extreme. May's complexion was still flushed, as a result of her excursion onto the dance floor and glowed a deep red. On the other hand Mrs Gallagher's had been completely drained of any colour whatsoever and she, in turn, glowed a pearly white.

All in all the celebrations continued in a boisterous but convivial manner. The two bridesmaids were going through a Jekyll and Hyde phase, revelling as they did in the freedom which such occasions presented. At times, they would project the impression of angelic innocence as they stood to be admired by different guests and would listen attentively to the words of admiration bestowed upon them and their bridesmaids attire. Then they would be off, scurrying around under the tables, rummaging for squashed beetles and spiders, which they collected up to perform their mischief.

They would reach up from underneath to the glasses on the tables, during the bouts of dancing, and discretely drop the corpses of these dead creatures into the drink. They then retired to a safe distance and waited for the return of the unsuspecting adults. There were generally two responses to the discovery of the intruders. One was simply to insert a finger or two into the liquid and deftly remove the offending insect and continue drinking, this course of action generally being preferred by the men. The other, and infinitely more entertaining, reaction was where the contents of the glass would be metaphorically flung to the four winds and finish up drenching some poor innocent bystander. This spontaneity was usually accompanied by a scream of surprise and indignation followed promptly by a deluge of apologies directed to those in the vicinity. Then there were those who hadn't detected the foreign body at all and continued drinking in sublime ignorance of the contents. This scenario was by far the most entertaining, since it introduced an element of suspense. The two girls experienced a sublime sensation of expectation as their victim put the glass to his or her lips and drank the contents. Sometimes the foreign body would reappear in the liquid after the act, which would produce a subdued fit of giggles from the children. Eventually, there would come a time when the glass would be replaced on the table, minus the intruder. The humour would lie, not in the disappearance of the insect, but in the expression of total oblivion on the face of the unsuspecting victim. This form of humour continued for a short time until Florence detected the perpetrators of the misdemeanour during one of their sorties.

Unlike the majority of the gathering, she had remained relatively sober. Apart from the initial glass of sherry, the taste of which, incidentally, left her totally unmoved, she had only partaken of a half of stout. The only observation that she could make regarding the taste of the second drink was that she preferred the sherry. Since this was her first experience of alcohol and she was not enamoured by its taste or its somewhat embarrassing influence, she had decided to avoid further consumption. She was therefore quite alert and had observed the two youngsters in the act. At first, she too found it amusing and couldn't help herself reacting with a carefully repressed giggle or two. She did however consider it prudent to put an end to the pranks and thereby avoid any tears which might result from detection and the consequences watch would accompany it. She caught up with the two girls and explained to them the benefits of ceasing their covert activities before they were discovered by a victim who might not have seen the funny side of things.

As the afternoon wore on, Clem was falling deeper and deeper under the influence of drink. Josh, who was no more sober than he, had detected Clem's obvious decline but was in sufficient control to offer a suggestion, hopefully before it was too late. He seized his opportunity to have a quiet word with him during one of Clem's excursions to the bar.

"Eh up, lad. Need to have a word in your ear Clem." His request was hazily acknowledged by Clem.

"Eh up Josh. 'Ow's it goin then. You having a good time then, kid? 'Ere let me get you a drink, I'm just off to t'bar for another missen." Josh's own state of inebriation seemed to smooth out the distorting slur of Clem's voice and he managed to decipher the request with surprising case.

"No, Clem. 'Ere I need to 'ave a word. Over there look." He gestured towards the end of the bar where a small space appeared available to afford them some privacy.

"Aye, well meck it quick lad, you're wasting good suppin time tha knows." Clem flung his arm across Josh's shoulder and the two friends staggered and fumbled their way to the end of the bar. For some inexplicable reason, they embarked on a zigzag detour which took them almost right around the room.

When they eventually reached their destination, they each placed their elbows on the bar and leant in a semi-propped posture. Josh took a deep breath in an effort to achieve some clarity in what he was about to say.

"Tha's not forgot what tha's 'ere for, have you lad?" Clem was totally bemused, he looked at Josh's face. His puzzled, almost gormless expression indicated to Josh that he had no idea what he was talking about.

"You what, Josh? What's up wi' you, lad?" Josh was becoming agitated, he took another deep breath.

"There's nowt up wi' me lad and there'll be nowt up wi' thee later on tonight if you keep knockin' 'em back like you are doing." Clem's expression didn't alter, he hadn't noticed the tone of emphasis that

Josh had placed on the word 'up', and apart from appearing marginally more stupid than before he was still totally confused.

"You're pissed, you are lad. You want to get yoursen sobered up a bit, You're talkin' a load o' rubbish Josh."

"Aye well, it's not my wedding night is it, you pillock." And if you drink much more it won't be your's either.

Josh raised his hand up to Clem's eye-level, directly in front of his face. When he was sure Clem was paying attention, he stuck out his little finger in a downward direction and wiggled it about. There followed a long, protracted and uncomfortable silence. Clem stared at the wiggling finger and, slowly but surely, signs of acknowledgement began to appear on his face. After a few seconds of stupefied deliberation and growing understanding of the signifier which Josh had continued to demonstrate, he reacted. He diverted his gaze away from Josh's finger, downwards towards his crotch. As he did so, his lower jaw dropped and his eves widened. The recognition of that which Josh had so urgently being trying to signify had finally dawned on him.

He returned his gaze back to Josh's finger, maintaining the dumbstruck expression which he had just adopted, and raised his own hand, wiggling his little finger in an effort to emulate Josh's gesture. He wanted desperately to say something but, try as he might, he couldn't persuade his gaping mouth to close to allow him to form any statement. Josh spoke for him.

"Penny's finally dropped then, 'as it." Clem just nodded as his mouth remained disconnected from his control, and he was still unable to effect a verbal response. Josh reached out his hand, placed his index finger under Clem's chin and gently pushed his lower jaw up to close his mouth. The spell had been broken, but his verbal expletive was totally inappropriate.

"Oh bollocks!" The metonym, as Josh pointed out, was slightly wide of the mark.

"Not quite, you want to be a touch higher up lad, and you've hit it on the head." Josh smiled and marvelled at his own quick, humorous reaction to Clem's verbal inadequacy. Suddenly Clem felt a good deal more sober, he peered along the other side of the bar.

"Pint o' bitter and a glass o' water when you're ready Lenny lad. I've waited a long time for this and I'm not goin' to spoil it now. Cheers Josh you're a real mate."

Clem spent the rest of the afternoon and into the evening concocting suitable responses to the steady flow of enquiries and innuendoes, regarding his sudden apparent aversion to alcohol. Not all of his answers were totally convincing and there were the inevitable sly comments regarding his ability to perform. The insinuations and innuendoes became more obvious when the time came for the newlyweds to take their leave of their guests, Clem had rented a room in the pub for the night in order to ensure their privacy, and he managed to consummate his marriage, without any embarrassing mishaps.

Chapter Fourteen

It was the twenty first of April, 1914 when Florence thrust Michael Clement Baxter into the world. He dived headlong into his new environment and marked his arrival, after some persuasion, with a high-pitched squeal of relief. The last physical bond to his mother was duly snipped and tied off. His father, having gone through the most terrible ordeal in the backroom of the house, was ushered in, panting with sheer exhaustion.

Clem leaned forward and gently kissed his wife on her forehead before he spoke.

"Well done lass, he's a smashing little lad." He hadn't actually seen the little fellow just yet but, like most new fathers, he just made the assumption that his child was beautiful. In reality of course, his child looked like a crimson-faced, baby gorilla. All wrinkles and no skin. He moved the cloth which was covering his son's face and confirmed his statement, regardless. Then he reached out and plucked the now silent bundle of cloth from the embrace of his mother. Again, he was totally irrational – even the brightest baby could not possibly have learned the complexities of the alphabet and English vocabulary in the space of eight minutes, yet Clem insisted on holding a conversation with the bundle of cloth which he held in his hands.

"Na then little un. It's nice to see you at last, you've been giving your Mam a bit o' bother tha knows. So I think you should say sorry, don't you." He turned the opening in the bundle towards Florence as if he expected it to produce some apologetic rhetoric.

He must have realised his mistake because he finally said it for the baby, but in a peculiar infantile tone of voice.

"Sorry to be such a bother, Mam." Even the dog, which had padded into the room behind Clem, appeared bemused and looked up at its master with its head tilted to one side. There was a distinct expression of disdain on its face. Florence smiled at the antics of her husband and reached out her arms.

"Don't be so silly Clem. You'll make him as daft as you are." Could it be that Florence too was slipping into the same psychological zone of irrationality as Clem?

Young Michael's arrival came at a time of some turmoil in the wider world and it was only four months after his birth that Europe embarked upon a war with itself. Little was known in the community about the reasons for the war or even its precise whereabouts. Shortly after the declaration, there was some talk of volunteers being sought after but none of the men in the village were too concerned about enlisting. The newspapers were insistent that it would only be a short skirmish and that the Germans would be defeated within the space of a few months. In any case, the increase in demand for coal meant that earnings were up and the men were not inclined to give up their increased income for the dubious rewards of joining the British Army.

It wasn't until after Christmas and into the New Year of 1915 that the war machine's propaganda began to stir a feeling of patriotism and duty within the community. It seemed so sudden, but in reality the surge of nationalistic jingoism had been building up since the onset of hostilities. Posters began to appear in public places urging young men to volunteer and the notions of honour and glory were being bandied around in local pubs and community halls and churches.

Even Lord Hase-Lore was getting in on the act. He made it known that the families of anyone who volunteered to fight for the King could retain their tenancies, even if there was no one in the family with a pit job. The proviso was included that the payment of rent must, however, be maintained. By the beginning of February 1915, the first volunteers were emerging from amongst the young men in the village. Clem was dismayed to find that Josh along with a dozen other colliers was determined to enlist. He was given the news in the Queens one Saturday evening.

He was enjoying a pint with his mate when he suddenly dropped it out.

"By the way, I'm joining up Clem." There must have been a vast number of young men throughout Europe who uttered similar words in different languages with absolutely no concept of the consequences. Clem tried to dissuade his friend from enlisting but not from the perspective of any danger which might befall him.

"You must be mad, you're earning more money now than you ever did. What about Alice as well – she'll be a bit peeved, won't she? I thought you were looking to get wed and get your own house."

"Well, I've spoke to her about it and she's all for it. She reckons I'm her hero, honour and glory and all that rubbish. Anyway, I thought you were the one who wanted to get out of the pit and make a fresh start. Well, now's your chance. Come on Clem, get thisen down to t' recruitment with us and sign up. It'll be great, all t' lads together." Josh paused to allow a broad smile to form on his face. "Anyhow, me and Alice'll get wed afore I go and his Lordship'll give us a nice pit-house, for me to come home to." Clem thought for a moment – he couldn't understand how his own efforts of dissuasion could so easily be turned into his friend's attempt at persuasion.

He repeated to himself the prospect of getting out of the pit, especially at this time of the year when the winter had set in. It was the time that he most hated, a time when he was most susceptible to persuasion.

"Come on Clem, just do it. It'll only be for a few months. We'll soon boot the Hun out o' France." Josh paused again, this time his expression changed to a more serious one and his voice took on a tone of authority. "Especially wi' our new secret weapon." Clem raised his eyebrows. Was this some new technical innovation which would win the war for the allies? He'd heard of a new machine which they were calling a tank, a lorry clad with armour that could cross fields and rivers and crush the enemy, but he couldn't confirm his supposition and he didn't want to seem foolish, by suggesting it, in case he was wrong.

"What's that then, Josh?" He waited impatiently for the reply, expecting to hear some tale of a massive thunder buster which would blast the enemy to kingdom-come and back. Josh sensed his friend's interest and was determined to keep Clem on tenterhooks.

"Don't know if I should be giving away top secret stuff to a civilian." Clem was on the verge of voicing his intention to enlist, if only to get Josh to divulge the secret.

Before be could speak Josh continued.

"Well, I'll tell you what, I'll tell you the code name, all rate. That way you can't go blabbin to anybody else."

"Well, get on with it, then."

"Rate come here then." The two men shuffled closer together and Josh directed his face towards Clem's ear. He whispered,

"It's Sam Jackson." As soon as the name had left his mouth he lunged forward and planted a big wet kiss on Clem's ear.

"Ger off, you pillock." Clem drew back in friendly aversion. "Tell thee what, we've no chance if you sign up mate."

"So what do you think then?" If there had been an instant during their interaction when Clem thought he might have succumbed to Josh's persuasion, it had evaporated in the humour of the moment.

"Don't think so, lad. Got the family to think about and then there's young Jimmy still locked up. Anyway, like you said it'll be over by t' end o' the year." It was by no means certain that Clem would have been of a similar opinion if he had foreseen the events of the following few months.

After the first wave of volunteers had left the village, things began to change within the community. Replacement miners were being recruited to replace those who had volunteered, but not from within the village. With houses being occupied by the families of those who had enlisted, miners were travelling in from outlying towns and villages. This anomaly introduced a new dimension to the community. It became less insular and more aware of the wider world. There was a stronger feeling of solidarity amongst the workforce. News was reaching the miners of growing union influence within the industry and new interest in politics and an Organisation known as the Labour Party was emerging.

In February 1915, the most significant event to affect the Baxter family occurred. With the growing recruitment of miners into the army, and the constantly increasing production requirements of the pits, a manpower shortage was beginning to occur. To combat this, the authorities began to look towards the prisons. Those prisoners who might be capable of contributing to industrial output were having their sentences commuted and being released early. James Gallagher had reached the age when he could start work and was considered suitable for early release. He had served less than two and a half years of his three year sentence and since he was now fourteen years of age and old enough to work at the pit, he had been released from his detention in the Reformatory.

This was a cause of great celebration within the Baxter household. The news was given to them during a visit to the institution when they were informed that Jimmy would be released the following week. Tom was already working underground and the addition of Jimmy's potential income gave Clem the opportunity to consider his own family situation. After the jubilation generated by the release of Jimmy, Clem and Florence set about planning their future. Clem was keen to move away from Connington completely and find a house in one of the towns. Rotherham, Barnsley, Doncaster or even Sheffield were all considered. He would then do what the new miners were doing and travel to his work at the pit.

Florence was opposed to moving out of the village – her mother wanted desperately to move back to Connington and reunite her family. Her own family had lived in Connington from the time that the shaft was sunk, she had made many friends and wanted to return to the community in which she had lived most of her life. Eventually, the more compassionate proposition was accepted and Clem and Florence resolved to maintain the *status quo* until they could find their own house in the village. By the Spring of 1915, a house had become available and the living arrangements of the Gallaghers and the Baxters were altered accordingly. Clem, Florence and Michael moved into the house, along with Florence's mother and her two sisters. Jimmy continued to live with Mrs Baxter and Tom where their combined incomes made the household just manageable.

Clem, however, couldn't reconcile himself to the domestic arrangements. He simply went along with them because he loved his wife, but by the end of the autumn he had come to a decision. Volunteers were still being sought after by the authorities and there was a small but significant number of applicants from the village, most of whom were friends and acquaintances of Clem's. He was beginning to feel isolated. It's true that if he had moved away from the village, he would have been separated from his friends but it would have been on his terms. He would have accepted the scenario on the grounds that it was a sacrifice worth making. What finally made up his mind was the letter be received from Josh.

The fact that the letter came from another country held its own fascination, but the positive tone of the contents stirred an enthusiasm in his ailing spirits. Josh wrote of the camaraderie, the high jinks at the training camp, the escapades they got up to during recreation. The most astonishing thing was that he hadn't even been in the fighting yet and that was what he was most looking forward to. He had written the letter the day before they were due to move forward, to what had become commonly known as 'the trenches.' When Clem showed the letter to Florence, she was dismayed at his positive reaction to its contents. They sat in the backroom of their 'new' house and discussed his intentions.

"I feel like I've let all my mates down, Flori. They're all out there fighting for us and I'm sat back here doing nothing." There was a stoic determination in the tone of his voice. Florence detected that he had already made up his mind and she felt obliged not to offer too much resistance. He had, after all, brought her family back together in the community.

She offered only token opposition to his decision to enlist.

"I'm just concerned that you might get hurt, love. They said it wouldn't last but it's been eighteen months now and for all the victories we read about they don't seem to be getting very far. I just think that you'll be gone for a long time and what if you get injured or something?" The last word in her sentence was not the one that she had composed inside her mind but somehow she couldn't bring herself to say it. Clem made light of her concern and made an effort to raise his wife's spirits.

"Aye lass. But if everybody thought like that, we wouldn't have an army, and anyway the more that volunteer, the quicker it'll be over and done with." He turned his attention to her family, as a form of distraction. "Anyway, you've got young Michael to look after you, and there's your Mam and the two lasses to keep you company. You won't even miss me."

"I know but you're my husband, you should be at home with your family."

She was rapidly running out of excuses for him not to go. When half the nation's husbands and sons had enlisted it was difficult to construct any convincing argument against joining them. She could see that he had made his mind up.

"So what's the next step then? How do you go about this enlisting?" Clem took her hands in his and commenced to explain the procedure for signing up. A week later, Clem was gone. Florence returned home from seeing him off at Doncaster station along with dozens of other wives, girlfriends and mothers. The presence of so many people going through the same ritual of farewells had seemed to trivialise any personal foreboding which she might have felt. Her individuality had been drowned in a sea of congruity.

She took solace in recalling their lovemaking the previous night in an attempt to reinstate her self-esteem and recover the significance of her personal relationship with her husband. Since their wedding night, they had come to experience more than merely the physical union of their two bodies culminating in the almost aggressive thrust of Clem's climax. They had discovered a sensuality which she had felt was always there but not quite attainable. It had needed the mutual co-operation and understanding of each for the other to realise the zenith of their lovemaking. A physical appreciation of one another, but borne on a tide of passion generated by their emotional interaction. Florence had elevated her own sexuality to a higher level and Clem had become aware of this. Now their lovemaking was geared to a mutual satisfaction and not simply one of self-gratification on the part of Clem.

Florence felt that this was the way it should have been but was also aware that her own experiences were not typical of her contemporaries amongst the other women in the community. Not that the sexual act was referred to specifically in general conversation. She had found, however, that other women would refer to it in detrimental terms when the subject was occasionally broached. It had become apparent to her that, for many other women, the sexual act was likely to be the finale to a night's drinking session by the men. The only apparent satisfaction derived by the women was that the act was so rapidly terminated. In many instances, in fact, it didn't even get started. Either way, the result was an extremely common one. The man would be spent, or not, and would simply fall away from, or be shoved off by his spouse without any further consideration, to fall, unceremoniously, into a deep drunken sleep.

She had thought, at first, that she had been privileged but later qualified that assessment to simply being lucky that she had a husband who recognised her own needs. There had also occurred to her the question of 'love'. Was what she was experiencing an expression of love? Had she fallen in love with Clem? If that was the case, then the pure, almost transcendental portrayals and interpretations that she had read about were far removed from her own reality.

Over the ensuing weeks, Florence and Clem exchanged letters regularly. Shortly before Christmas, she was able confirm to Clem that she was expecting another baby and expressed the hope that the war would be over by the time of its birth. In the new year of 1916 he informed her that his troop was being posted to France. After that, the letters became less frequent until she received one in July of that year.

> *My Dear Flori*
> *I can t spend long on this letter just to say that tomorrow we're going to fight a battle that ll definatly mean we'll have won the war by christmas The next letter i send will be from germany after weve occupied it. hows that for good news We re in some place near a river called the somm and the guns have been smashing hell out of the hun for days now. by the time we go over the top there'll be nothing left of them we ll walk straight through to Germany. Still haven't managed to find out were josh is i think he's in another part of france. pity he s not here we could win the war together anyway I'll have to go now love. all my love to Michael and every body. See you for Christmas then.*
> *I love you*
> *Clem*

The letter lifted her spirits for she had no reason to doubt the predictions therein. Why should she. It was true that the authorities were always saying how well the war was going and that there would soon be victory for the allies, even though the 'soon' seemed to come and go with worrying regularity. Now that Clem had told her that the war would soon be won, she received the news as confirmation of the news reports. She didn't even consider the accuracy or the source of Clem's information. She did, however, get annoyed with the spelling and grammatical structure of his letters.

She always felt like taking a pen to them and correcting the mistakes. The spelling was atrocious and the punctuation virtually non-existent, which had become a constant source of irritation to her. She still read herself, asking friends and neighbours to collect books for her, from the libraries in Rotherham or Doncaster. Now though, she was indulging herself in educational books, books that would expand her knowledge of the wider world. The book that she had so diligently placed at the back of the dresser drawer had remained untouched since she moved house. She had not bothered to read any further since that fateful day. Now, she concentrated on books that would give her the information she needed to help her children with their education. She had come to realise that, if they were to have a chance to better themselves and escape the grip of their destiny, the route would be through education.

About six months after the Baxter family had received notification of Clem's death, along with several other death notices in the village at that time, Florence received an unexpected letter from France. It read.

> *My Dearest Florence*
>
> *I beg of you, please do not discard or destroy this letter before at least having the good charity to read it first. I am aware of the recent, tragic loss of your good husband, and the anguish and grief which you must have suffered. Please accept my sincere and heartfelt, condolences. I had never met your husband, but feel certain that he was a good, brave man, who died for a cause in which he believed.*
>
> *As for my humble self, I have been fighting in this bloody, horrific war since it began almost three years ago; but I have also been fighting another battle. I have always cursed myself for my feeble-willed acquiescence to my father's demands and his efforts to part us. This terrible conflict has revealed many things about human nature of which I had previously been totally ignorant. I have realised, through my close proximity and confinement with ordinary men, many of whom I have had the unfortunate duty of leading to their deaths, that all men are the same. The divisions which separate us from one another are placed there by those who wield the power.*
>
> *My dearest Florence, please bear with me, I have made a resolve which I hope with all my being that you will embrace wholeheartedly. I have resolved, that when the war is over, I will return to you. My humble plea is that you will wait for me until then, and give me just the smallest chance to make amends for the*

disgraceful, abhorrent way in which I acted towards you. Though I would not presume to declare it publicly, my innermost feelings suggest to me that your first-born may in fact be the result of our expression of love, for one another, those three long years ago.

I will not be deterred by the threats of a man who has always been a stranger to me. If I lose my inheritance then so be it. I will not await a reply to this letter but I will make enquiries, after the war is over, as to your personal disposition. Should you be free to accept my proposal, then I intend to ask you to be my wife. Unworthy as I am, I pray to God that you will give me another chance.

I have always loved you
Harry

Florence didn't know what to make of the letter – she was certainly surprised, but that was the only reaction, to which she could apply a description. At least there was no immediate decision for her to make she could simply consider the implications during the passing of time. She leaned forward towards the fire grate with the intention of placing the letter in the flames but found that she couldn't bring herself to relinquish her hold on the pieces of paper. Instead, she sat back in her seat and proceeded to fold the paper.

First, she folded it neatly in half, pressing firmly along the fold as she did so. Then, after scrutinising her efforts for a moment, she stood up and walked slowly over to the dresser. The drawer slid open smoothly and she reached inside, right to the back until her hand rested upon the cold leather cover of a book. When her hand reappeared from within the drawer, it was holding the book. Without making a conscious effort to proceed, she slipped the letter under the leather-bound cover, stroked her fingers over the surface and placed it back at the rear of the drawer. There was no discernible expression of her face; it offered no indication of her thoughts at that particular moment in time.

Chapter Fifteen

When Florence reached the newly-laid lawned area, surrounded by the low wrought iron fencing, she paused. She had become accustomed, since its recent construction, to stand for a few minutes and consider the centre-point of the grassed area. The whole thing was constructed out of dressed Yorkshire stone. A pathway of cut flagstones led from a gateway in the fencing up to the front of the middle of the structure. At that point, it divided into two and branched off at right angles in opposite directions, to form a square frame around the centre-piece.

Inside the frame, there had been laid a stone plinth, raised by about eighteen inches above the surrounding area. On top of the plinth there had been erected a large four-sided stone slab the front of which faced forwards along the flagged pathway towards the gate, before which Florence presently stood. The stone looked clean and fresh. It had only been there a short while and the yellowish-tinged colouring appeared to glow in the failing light of the late July summer evening.

As she stood and pondered, Florence felt the hand of the person standing next to her slip gently into her own and she continued to stare straight ahead at the object of her attention. She surveyed again the chiselled inscriptions on the façade, her vision penetrated the channels until beyond each set she could see a face which she recognised. There were twenty-three names, not many compared to some villages' roll-call, but she had known every one of them and could recollect their physical features quite vividly. Amongst the orderly rows of precisely chiselled grooves, there were two in particular at which she paused for longer than the rest. Each one held for her different but lasting and endearing memories, which she had been careful to sift through, and retain only those which she cherished.

The first of the two names, upon which her gaze dwelt, carried the inscribed rank of private. The second, the rank of a Captain. Their location within the alphabetical listing resulted in their laying adjacent to one another and no other names separated the two of them. It was as though their closeness in death had affirmed their mutual vulnerability in life. Yet, in reality, they had experienced an infinite distance between their two lifestyles, cultures and environments. The only thing that the two of them had held in common was the love that they had each felt for the same person. Even then each one had been dragged away from their attachment, by events over which they found they had no control.

As she recalled each of them in turn, she maintained a gentle smile of fondness and affection. The tears of anguish had long since ceased to flow. Tears could not wash away the pain or sorrow but nor could they wash away the joy or happiness. At least they had each sprung there own traps, and had escaped the very thing which had in different ways, imprisoned them. The unanswerable questions had all been asked, and gradually discarded within the futility of things. She had long since dismissed the bitterness and anger which had been part of her initial grief and now all that remained was a fond recollection of happier moments.

She knew that her own life had not been engineered or manipulated, within the structure of a plot by a well-constructed text and narrative. Even the most skilful and dextrous of novelists could not have penned the conclusion to the story in any other way. She still read books written by those who she had once perceived to be more knowledgeable, more intelligent and more observant, than herself. She was, however, no longer influenced by the messages and promises which they imparted because she had come to realise, even at such a young age, that the only truth in life was death. As for herself there was one thing now of which she was sure, and that was not influenced by leather-bound promises.

The only certainty in her own life now, after bearing witness to the deaths of so many young men, was the certainty of the poverty and hardship, which lay before her. Neither of these impositions was new to her, she had experienced both for most of her life. Yet, if she was to continue experiencing this terrible existence, and there was no evidence, currently, to suggest otherwise, then why, she had asked herself, had so many men lost their lives in the war. A reason for which, even now after it had run its horrific course, was still not entirely clear? The only thing that was clear, yet again, was that those who benefited the least, had paid the highest price.

She had also come to realise amongst the trauma and despair which she had suffered, however, that she had eventually known the love of another person, what it felt like to love and be loved. It was not the impossible love in which she had once been led to believe, but a real intense, consuming and lasting love. A love which would endure long after the text had been enclosed within the bounds of its covers, long after the book had been read and placed back on the shelf patiently to await its next unsuspecting reader.

Then, without diverting her gaze, she gently squeezed the hand which had been so patiently and affectionately resting within her grasp. She looked across, and down at the face next to her and saw, within the affectionate smile that adorned it, her future. Precarious though it was, she felt that, at least for a little while, it would include the various and often confusing emotions which constituted the experience of real love.